CASTLE SKULL

JOHN DICKSON CARR

with an introduction by
MARTIN EDWARDS

This edition published 2020 by
The British Library
96 Euston Road
London NW1 2DB

Castle Skull was originally published in 1931 by Harper & Brothers
Publishers, New York and London. 'The Fourth Suspect'
was first published in *The Haverfordian* in January 1927.

Cataloguing in Publication Data
A catalogue record for this book is available from the British Library

ISBN 978 0 7123 5326 7
eISBN 978 0 7123 6736 3

Typeset by Tetragon, London
Printed in England by CPI Group (UK) Ltd, Croydon, CRO 4YY

CONTENTS

INTRODUCTION

"D'Aunay talked of murder, castles, and magic." The very first sentence of *Castle Skull* sets the tone of a highly atmospheric detective story, an early novel by John Dickson Carr, acknowledged master of the locked room mystery. It is the third in a sequence of four books written in rapid succession which feature the French *juge d'instruction* Henri Bencolin, a character firmly in the tradition of fiction's Great Detectives. Just as Sherlock Holmes had Dr Watson and Hercule Poirot had Captain Hastings, so Bencolin has an admiring friend, Jeff Marle, who recounts his investigations.

In this story, Bencolin is engaged by D'Aunay (a Belgian financier and "one of the dozen richest men in the world") to investigate the grotesque murder of an English actor called Myron Alison whose "blazing body was seen running about the battlements of Castle Skull". The castle on the Rhine had been inherited jointly by Alison and D'Aunay from a mutual friend called Maleger, a legendary magician who died in highly mysterious circumstance, and is now run by Alison's sister, "a veritable wild-woman, who smokes cigars, swears, and plays poker all night", and is known as the Duchess. Conveniently, the possible suspects are still present at the castle.

The brooding menace of Castle Skull is captured in vivid and indeed melodramatic fashion: "The name is not a fancy. Its central portion is so weirdly constructed that the entire façade resembles a giant death's head, with eyes, nose, and ragged jaw. But there are two towers, one on each side of the skull, which are rather like huge ears;

so that the devilish thing, while it smiles, seems also to be listening. It is set high on a crag, with its face thrust out of the black pines. Below it is a sheer drop to the waters of the river."

The interior is equally forbidding. In the room that makes up the crown of the skull, "noise buffeted the ear-drums, swirled you again into that half-sick tensity of waiting... The floor seemed to be of a black-and-gold mosaic in circular patterns of zodiac symbols, but I could not see what symbols because it was strewn with animal-skin rugs... and the animal-heads opened white-fanged jaws like an uncanny dead menagerie."

This is a young man's writing, brimming with energy, and occasionally over-the-top, but immensely appealing to any reader with a taste for detection and the macabre. In his admirable biography, *John Dickson Carr: The Man Who Explained Miracles*, Douglas G. Greene argues that although Edgar Allan Poe was a major influence at this stage of his career, Carr combined the genres of detection and horror "in a way that not even Poe had done before him, and few authors would do after him".

Bencolin accepts the challenge to solve the murder, and soon finds himself pitted against an old adversary, Herr Baron Sigmund von Arnheim, chief inspector of the Berlin police. (Carr must have liked the name; he'd used it in an early story he'd written as a student.) Von Arnheim is a typically colourful Carrian character: "very straight and wiry, with a mincing step and a cropped skull... The eyes were of a chill greenish hue, with blond brows forever raised... Around them ran the jags of sabre-cuts."

The battle of wits between the two detectives is one of the pleasures of the book. This sleuthing contest was a device that Carr would use again in his fiction, but it wasn't original to him: a notable example from 1923 is to be found in Agatha Christie's *The Murder on the Links*.

Almost until the end of the story, it is by no means clear whether Bencolin will triumph over von Arnheim.

Bizarre chapter titles ("We Hear of a Dancing Corpse", "The Torch That Was Alive") as well as the Gothic location contribute to the febrile mood: "The vast death's head lifted itself to stare with light… It watched, and it waited. For centuries it had looked down on the Rhine, but it was endowed… with a savage sense of humour. It appreciated in its old age the little people who were to walk inside it, literally like creatures in its brain… Ah, Baron von Arnheim, but you were a showman! Your French enemy should be humbled in a setting of which he himself would approve…"

The first edition was a "Harper Sealed Mystery", and the publishers placed the seal immediately after page 232. The seal was headed "A Sporting Offer", worded in suitably lurid terms:

"Surely never was there more fantastic, hideous gaiety than at this banquet. The guests of honor are Death and his henchman Murder. The fearful climax is approaching. Will Von Arnheim win? Will Bencolin? What fiend in human form will be revealed as the murderer. [Another sentence which would spoil some of the mystery to read it here.]

"If you can resist the desire to break this thin paper seal, to know the outcome of this gruesome tale, return the book to your bookseller with this seal intact, and your money will be refunded."

It would be interesting to know how many copies with seals unbroken exist today. If any survive, they must be worth a small fortune. Despite his youth, Carr contrives a very clever plot with a striking and unconventional solution that (as with a number of other novels written during "the Golden Age of Murder" between the wars) reflects an unorthodox but intriguing attitude towards the nature of justice.

Castle Skull was one of two Bencolin novels published by Carr in 1931; it appeared in the US on 1 October, with *The Lost Gallows* having come out on 4 March. Oddly, however, Hamish Hamilton, Carr's British publisher, declined to publish it. This may have been because he thought the book over-written and excessively sensational. As a result, the first British edition of the book did not appear until 1973. A small firm called Tom Stacey Ltd bought the rights, only to become insolvent; a few copies escaped into the wider world, and now command very high prices. Severn House bought the stock, and issued the book with a different dust wrapper in 1976. Even these copies are now uncommon, since most were destined for the public libraries. The present reissue also includes the Bencolin short story "The Fourth Suspect", from the pages of *The Haverfordian*, January 1927.

Carr (1906–77) drew on his own experience of travelling in the Rhineland for the background of this novel. In June 1930, not long after the sale of his first novel, *It Walks by Night*, he and a friend called O'Neil Kennedy had set off on a European tour together, visiting Brussels and Waterloo before heading for Mainz and Heidelberg. Doug Greene speculates that *Castle Skull* was based on the twin castles known as "the Hostile Brothers". Shortly afterwards, while voyaging back to the United States on the Red Star liner Pentland, Carr met Clarice Cleaves, a young woman who was to become his wife. Soon they would settle in England, and he would introduce his most renowned detectives, Dr Gideon Fell and Sir Henry Merrivale. The Bencolin series served as a marvellous apprenticeship, and the stories remain enjoyable in their own right.

MARTIN EDWARDS

www.martinedwardsbooks.com

CASTLE SKULL

To
Edward Coleman Delafield, Jr.
and
William O'Neil Kennedy

"For it's always fair weather…"

I

DEATH ON THE RHINE

D'AUNAY TALKED OF MURDER, CASTLES, AND MAGIC.
He talked of them at our table in an angle of the vine-grown wall, at the discreet restaurant called Laurent on the Champs Elysées. The pink-shaded lamps on the tables of Laurent were open to the stars, and to the thick trees hedging us in. It was late, so that there were not many diners. An orchestra, among palms, celebrated the grace of Lizette, the smile of Mignonette, and the cuteness of Suzette with that tune which all Paris was humming in the month of May.

Across the table sat Jérôme D'Aunay. He drank nothing but Vichy, and his fingers were always busy with the stem of his glass. His fingers were always busy in any case; he could not sit still; he must forever be toying with something, or writing imaginary notes on the table-cloth with a spoon. His restlessness disturbed the peace of the night. D'Aunay—one of the dozen richest men in the world—was a short, thick man, with cold blue eyes which kept on you a fixed and discon-certing stare. His thin dark hair was brushed flat across a great skull. The creases were deep around his thick nose, and round a mouth which seemed to have acquired a very startling flexibility from much talking.

D'Aunay said: "M. Bencolin, I am about to make you a proposi-tion which some men would consider singular. I have learnt enough about you to believe that you would consider it neither singular nor unwelcome."

Looking back over it, I am not sure what obscure impulse of bra-vado prompted D'Aunay to bring Bencolin into the case. Now that the thing is finished, I can recall him from that first polite arbitrary note telling me I was having dinner with him, to the final terrifying scene when I saw his patent-leather shoes motionless under a gaily coloured scarf; but still the Belgian financier remains a puzzle. Of course, he could not help breaking down when he saw that grinning figure looking at him beneath the candles of Castle Skull—still, it was his heart and not his bravado, which gave way. This is to anticipate events, but not (as you may suspect) to betray any of the sinister affair in which we became involved...

D'Aunay took a drink of Vichy water and continued his recital:

"I will come to the point at once. You are an official of Paris, M. Bencolin. Good. I want to hire your services."

Bencolin, studying his glass of Cointreau against the light, quirked an eyebrow thoughtfully. I have described this man in other records of his cases; and, if you know Paris, you know the celebrated *juge d'instruction* of the Seine. The black hair, parted in the middle and twirled up like horns. The long inscrutable eyes, with hooked brows drawn down. The high cheek-bones, the aquiline nose. The slow smile, stirring between small moustache and black pointed beard. All are as familiar to the street as they are to the caricaturists... He twirled his glass round, and the rings on his fingers glittered against the white shirt-front.

"To hire my services—" he repeated.

"I have investigated you," said D'Aunay, "as I investigate everybody. Good. You are the foremost police official in Europe. You are also a wealthy man, and your present position you bought—"

"Please!"

"Ah, but with justification!" said D'Aunay, waving his hand. "I do not blame you. You demonstrated your fitness for it, merely by making (with francs) your hobby a profession."

The smallest wrinkle had appeared between Bencolin's brows. As D'Aunay's gruff voice ticked off the statements, his eyes showed growing interest.

"You know much, my friend," he remarked. "Well?"

"For my purpose, I want the best in the business. With you, then, I will not insult a man who has followed your course by saying that you may name your own fee.

"At the present time, you are on a vacation. Good. I want you to take my case. I will not pay you one sou. But, when I have outlined it, I think you will work for me, because it will be the strangest affair you have ever handled."

D'Aunay was leaning forward, clicking out his words, staring at Bencolin from the fishlike eyes. You could feel the man's tremendous dominance. He rapped the edge of the table and said, "Well, monsieur!"

Bencolin was silent for a time. Then he chuckled.

"M. D'Aunay," he replied, "you have a form of oblique attack which I find fascinating. Damnation, yes!" His amused eyes ran over D'Aunay's tense face. "Very well, then; I answer just as bluntly. If your case intrigues me, I shall certainly take it.—But you have also invited Jeff here to your very good dinner. How do your arrangements include him?"

"Ah!" said D'Aunay. Turning, he regarded me steadily. "Mr. Marle is not a detective. Pray excuse me: I do not even think he is gifted with any particular intelligence. But you will need help, and I want no clumsy oaf of a Sûreté inspector mingling with the people to whom I shall introduce you. You find me undemocratic? So! Nevertheless, he has worked with you before. He will do as well; and he will not make himself obnoxious."

Staring at the little, stocky man, I felt inclined to point out to Jérôme D'Aunay a suitable jumping-off place. It was damned cheek.

And yet, I realized in a moment, he had no notion of being offensive. He saw what he wanted, and so he closed his big hands about it without comment or apology. So I did the better thing; I laughed. I said,

"I also congratulate you, M. D'Aunay. You hire one investigator by the solemn promise that you will not pay him anything, and the other by assuring him he is not overly bright."

The words seemed to trip D'Aunay, who brushed them aside impatiently.

"Well, but your answer, monsieur! Your answer?"

"The answer," I responded, "is yes. Yes—because of your infernal way of approaching it."

"Ah! Good. I have now only to show that it will interest you…"

Bencolin nodded approvingly at me as the financier sat back to gather the materials of his story into proper form. Suddenly D'Aunay shot out a question:

"You have heard, of course, of the magician Maleger?"

This was growing interesting. Maleger: of course. Everybody knew the name, even those of my generation, and the brilliant figure he had cut in the days before the war. The legends about him have been talked about by theatre-goers ever since he went to his death. Not even Bernhardt was a more picturesque personality. I stared into the shadows beyond D'Aunay…

One of my most vivid recollections as a child is the night my father took me to see Maleger perform during his American tour, at the old Polis Theatre in Washington. Afterwards I had the horrors all night. For Maleger was not one of your genial, smiling conjurors of later days. It was the man's personality, his trappings, the terrible and sinister force which carried you somewhat beyond the illusions of the theatre. At the snapping of his fingers, you might have believed, he roused black shapes from cracks in the earth, and commanded the powers of fire and thunder.

We had, I recall, front-row seats. He remained too long in my mind as an ogre for me to forget what he looked like then. I remember his uncanny penetrating look of dark eyes, and his great skull with its plumes of reddish hair. He stood in the middle of a stage hung in dead black, without any trappings at all. His loose-jointed powerful figure, his old-fashioned stock and queer clothes, his evil fingers outspread on a table. There was one point at which he gave a screech of eldritch laughter and flung up his arms; his head rose from his neck and floated out over the audience, smiling... It was a bit too much for a child of nine, and for many older people too.

Then I realized that D'Aunay was speaking:

"—and that is why I want to tell you something about him.

"I knew him well; perhaps better than anybody else. That surprises you? Well, it is true. I do not know whether he was a pure poseur or whether..."

D'Aunay was rolling bread crumbs in his fingers. "But he was a celebrity. Of what nationality was he? That I do not know. He spoke all languages; you could not tell which was his own. You knew, too, he was immensely rich?"

"I have heard so," Bencolin answered, nodding.

"Diamonds," said D'Aunay. "The man's age—damn it! That also I never could learn. I know he was in the Kimberley fields in '91, and he was not a young man. I met him later; I was working for the Belgian government then..."

"The stage was a hobby, then?"

"Like your own work, monsieur," D'Aunay said, spreading out his hands. "You should understand. Well, his public life began later. They could not neglect one so striking. You recall his weird clothes, his great black automobiles with drawn blinds always, his cigarettes dipped in opium, his collection of costly and nonsensical baubles—eh? Always his surroundings were exotic. The illusions he staged were hideous, and more. Three capitals went mad over him…

"I will come to the point. In 1912, or thereabouts, he wished to make himself a home. So he bought the famous *Schloss Schadel*, Castle Skull, on the Rhine a few miles from Coblenz. No place could have been more appropriate. And he perched above the rocks and pines, in the place where the Rhine is narrowest and swiftest… You have seen it?"

Bencolin shook his head.

"But you will," D'Aunay told him, "because we are going there. . He spent a year transforming that weird ruin into a place of the nightmare. I do not know many of its secrets, and I am glad. Not that I believe—monsieur sees! But every trick of his ingenuity was expended on devices to make the average man fear for his wits.

"You know, of course, that he had few friends. Myself, I am the remaining one. The other was Myron Alison, the English actor—you know *him*, naturally?"

The thin eyebrows tightened down over Bencolin's eyes, and his nostrils were a little dilated. He had forgotten his brandy; he was all attention now. In the background, our orchestra's waltz-tune swirled dimly…

"I know Myron Alison, of course," he said. "But why do you say 'was'?"

Nodding rather eagerly, our host said:

"That is the point; that is the case. Alison has been murdered. His blazing body was seen running about the battlements of Castle Skull."

"That," said Bencolin; "well, that sounds a little—"

"It is true. The man's vitality was apparently enormous. He had been shot three times in the breast, but he was alive when the murderer poured kerosene on him and ignited it. He actually got to his feet and staggered out in flames across the battlements before he fell."

There was a silence. Momentarily, D'Aunay had let his suppressed nervousness appear. Another drink of Vichy, and he continued:

"But I am getting ahead of my story. I was telling you that Alison and I were Maleger's friends. For many years Alison has had a summer home on the Rhine, across the river from Castle Skull. I myself—well, messieurs, I have become important since the days when I knew them first.

"You may recall when and how Maleger died. He was coming alone on the train from Mainz to Coblenz. No other passengers were in the first-class compartment he occupied. He did not leave the train at Coblenz, where his car was waiting to take him to the castle. Several days later, his body was fished out of the Rhine."

After a time of brooding, D'Aunay raised his head and opened wide eyes at the detective. He shrugged. "The tracks, of course, run for many miles almost on the river's brink. If a man tumbled out of the carriage, the momentum might carry him out, down over the slope, and into the water. It was night, and his fall would not be noticed or any cry heard. I do not think he could swim. But it was queer." D'Aunay drew a long breath.

"*Very* queer," he went on, thoughtfully. "It seems inconceivable that the man could not have saved himself. The space between the tracks and the edge of the river... the vegetation... unless it was suicide. And suicide in such a homely way, after his spectacular life? No, no, monsieur! I may add that there was no possibility of foul play. It was the last carriage on the train, and the guard swore that not another soul had entered it during the whole ride. The guard himself kept it under observation, because he knew who the famous Maleger was, and he was curious for further glimpses of him. I have a theory, of course. But let me go on.

"Maleger's heirs—this also will surprise you—were Alison and myself. He willed us, moreover, his Castle Skull, with the understanding that we should not sell it. He even provided a fund for the taxes and upkeep. There were other curious provisions, about the disposal of his effects, which we need not discuss now. In any event—"

"You are suggesting that this death of Maleger has a direct bearing on the murder of Alison?" Bencolin interrupted.

"I am forced to think so. But wait. You must hear.

"The doctor told me I had a nervous breakdown. *Bah!* I do not break down. But—these doctors—one is forced to believe. They know." Our host waved a deprecating hand. "I must rest, says he. Well, it might have been worse! The market is steady, and I can trust Dulac with my affairs for a few weeks. My friend Alison invites me to the Rhine.

"Rest—hah! What a house! It is managed by Alison's sister, the one they call the Duchess. This for no reason, since she bears no title. I assure you, a veritable wild-woman, who smokes cigars, swears, and plays poker all night. A fine influence, eh, for my wife? They keep no good hours, that crowd they have there. But it is pleasant, a great stone house with an enormous veranda overlooking the Rhine, where we sit at the rise of the moon. And right across the river, over the spiked tops of the pines, Castle Skull rises and stares at us.

"Monsieur, that is literally true. The name is not a fancy. Its central portion is so weirdly constructed that the entire façade resembles a great death's head, with eyes, nose, and ragged jaw. But there are two towers, one on each side of the skull, which are rather like huge ears; so that the devilish thing, while it smiles, seems also to be listening. It is set high on a crag, with its face thrust out of the black pines. Below it is a sheer drop to the waters of the river.

"It happened after dark. It was eight days ago that…"

"Wait!" said Bencolin.

D'Aunay was so engrossed in his recital that he was with difficulty dragged back to the calm of the Café Laurent. He blinked at the detective.

"I do not want to hear any more now," Bencolin told him. "Yes, yes, I will take the case!—But you would only confuse me. Do I understand that all these people are still at Alison's villa?"

"Why, yes. But assuredly, monsieur!"

"And my task, then, is to discover the murderer of Alison?"

"It is."

"I see. Well, then, I prefer to wait until I am on the scene before I hear any single bit of evidence. Otherwise I should only be prejudiced. Who is in charge?"

"The Coblenz police. There was some talk of sending to Berlin for a man; they may have done so by this time."

Bencolin leaned an elbow on the table, tapping his fingers against his temple. His pouched eyes were abstracted, staring into a glass, but the jaw had grown tight beneath his pointed beard. He did not speak…

"Then it's settled," D'Aunay said with decision. "I confess I do not understand why you don't want to hear—eh, that's none of my affair! I've hired you. Now, can you start for Alison's place in the morning?"

"Pardon?" asked Bencolin, rousing himself. "Oh… yes, certainly. Yes." He fell again into his obscure, frowning reverie.

"And you, Mr. Marle?"

I couldn't, unfortunately, and told him so. I was revising a book, and the thing had absolutely to be finished next day so that it could be sent off to London. D'Aunay was almost childishly irritated; but I promised to follow them without fail the day after, wiring the time of arrival.

It was only when we were preparing to leave that Bencolin spoke.

"There is something," he told D'Aunay, "I should like to know. Not about the murder of Alison, but about the death of Maleger…"

A curious interest and tensity flickered in the other's pale gaze.

"You saw the body when it was taken from the river?" the detective pursued. "You are sure it was really that of Maleger?"

Softly D'Aunay rubbed his hands together. He said:

"Ah! You verge towards my own theory, eh? Well!" He struck the table. "No, I am not. It was too badly decomposed by the water for recognition. I could not swear to it. They found on it his watch, keys, and a little amulet he always wore. Moreover, they found a certain peculiar ring which was something of a fetish with him; he never left it off, because he said it held his luck. But—"

"I see," murmured Bencolin…

We left the restaurant, the waltz tunes, and the shaded lights. The last glimpse I had of D'Aunay was when he shook hands with us with his foot on the running-board of his limousine; Bencolin had refused a lift. D'Aunay was hugely self-satisfied; he beamed complacently, and his queer square derby was tilted almost rakishly on his great head.

Bencolin stood looking after the car as its taillight moved into the whispering darkness of trees behind the Champs Elysées.

"I couldn't refuse this case, Jeff," he observed. "It's bad. That's the point: it's worse than anybody suspects. You heard what he said about the body of Maleger—does it mean anything to you?"

I said, "There's the obvious theory that Maleger's death was a fake, arranged by himself."

"Yes." Still he stood motionless, staring after the car. "I only wish it were as simple as that. No; I think it's worse than that, Jeff, and more devilish. More devilish…"

I I

U NDER A DULL AND SWOLLEN SKY, HEAVY WITH DARK CLOUDS, the steamer moved down the Rhine. I have always preferred to go by boat, even though it is slower than the train; besides, the current is so swift that these little steamers make remarkable speed.

There is a flavour, there is an old, dangerous, twilight charm, about the warrior Rhine when it leaves its lush wideness at Bingen. Thence it seems to grow darker. The green deepens almost to black, grey rock replaces vineyards, on the hills which close it in. Narrow and winding now, a frothy olive-green, it rushes through a world of ghosts.

I sat on the white deck, at a table beside the rail, and drank beer out of those enormous bottles they serve you. A wet breeze blew in my face. Over the hills ragged dark clouds crawled slowly. There were a few people on the deck: solid red-faced burghers, running chiefly to moustache, all of whom carried big hampers and ate sandwiches tirelessly. They were always jovial; frequently they sang. But it was so quiet that I could hear the ceaseless swish of water. The grey stateliness of Castle Rheinstein swept past on our left, far on its rocks above. Though they all must have seen it a hundred times before, the passengers crowded to the rail with craned necks, exclaiming…

Sitting back with that wet mysterious wind in my face, I dreamed. In Mainz I had bought a book at the railway station. It was in English, written by somebody named Brian Gallivan, and called, *Legends of the Rhine*. The jacket bore a picture of some Rhine maidens clinging to the side of a small boat in midstream and yearning up at its occupant, a startled wrestler in a winged helmet. In its pages lay the naïve charm, the love of mystery, like that of a child peering into the depths behind a Christmas tree, which is the spirit of those who love the old Rhine. I read of Drachenfels and the knight Roland, of the hostile brothers, the wisdom of Charlemagne, and the tale of Cologne's cathedral wherein (as always in these honest folk-tales) the devil is a gentleman…

"Like it?" inquired a voice, speaking English.

Looking up, I saw a lean man in a trench-coat, who had just pulled out a chair and sat down at my table. A disreputable hat was drawn half over one eye. From the corner of a wide, humorous mouth dangled an unlighted cigarette. His face was very long, with a bump of a chin and a high hooked nose which made him look like Punchinello. It should have been mournful, but his grey squinted eyes were grinning jovially.

"Sorry to barge in like this," he apologized, "but I felt like talking to somebody. D'ye mind?—Saw you reading that book. I wrote the damn' thing, d'ye see? It's pretty awful. My name's Gallivan—Brian Gallivan."

We shook hands, and I invited him to have a bottle of beer. He accepted with alacrity. I said, "American?"

"Uh-huh. But I'm with the *Evening Standard*. London, d'ye see?" He pushed back his hat, lighted the cigarette, and squinted through the smoke at the book I held. He said: "Blooey! That must be the first one they've sold this year. It's standard, though. Bunch of feature stuff I did once."

"Is that your line?"

"Uh-huh," he answered, somewhat shamefacedly; "it is usually. I've been sent to haunted castles all over Europe to get the story of the latest haunting. Funny racket, hey? My by-line always reads, 'Brian Gallivan, the Ghost Man.' But it gets you, I swear it does."

The bottles arrived then. He was silent for a time, squinting out at the swift-moving hills and the slow approach of twilight. He flicked his ashes over the rail, and the wind immediately blew them back into my beer. Still craning his neck, he remarked:

"Just been down looking into a cheerful little matter of a bloody arm in Frankfort. Business has been good, lately... Then the chief cables me to take up the trail again. Ever hear of Castle Skull?"

"Yes," I said, somewhat uneasily.

"Pretty funny business there. No ghosts, you understand, but a murder and a hell of a lot of legends for a Sunday spread. The boys have already covered the murder; this is just anything I can nose out. You know. But I doubt if I'll be able to get in, even. They say the place is being kept tight closed."

"Oh... It isn't haunted, then?"

We were nearing the bend in the river where rises the great Lorelei rock. Above the sweep of the bank, as the Rhine widened, the dull clouds were shot with low streaks of red. They lit the dark, jagged line of trees, they trembled in weird dapplings on the mysterious water. But they faded, to be engulfed in the grey massiveness of the Lorelei height. It loomed, as though our boat were to crash against it. Every passenger suddenly fell silent. We heard the wash of the water past our bows, and then the thin scream of a locomotive whistle. Out from the railroad tunnel which pierces the hill beyond the rock popped the engine of a fast train. It was a tiny toy there, hardly audible, rushing foolishly in a stream of white smoke. Then the height of the Lorelei hid the clicking toy...

Along the deck drifted a low, melodious humming. It gained in deep harmony, it swelled through the dusk; but for several seconds I did not realize that the passengers crowding the rail were singing, very softly, "Die Lorelei." The ghostly melody rose, sung ever more clearly. Lights winked on in the cabin. From above smote the clang of the steamer's bell. And, subtly, the Rhine was catching me in its magnetic waters...

"You hear that every time," I heard Gallivan saying, "and it never fails to get me. Listen to 'em sing!"

He had risen, leaning against the rail; but now he sat down and poured out a drink of beer.

"Hang it! You almost imagine... things up there. D'ye see? It's like that. Or d'you think I'm crazy? Anyway, what were you saying? About Castle Skull being haunted? Well, not by any really active ghost now, so far as I know. Just the usual tales... There's a story about it in there. Haven't you read it?"

I hadn't. It was not listed under the names of the castles, but by towns, and so I had missed it.

"Oh, save it, then," Gallivan advised. "It was built by a man who was burnt as a sorcerer in the fifteenth century, you'll see. But it's the Maleger affair which gives it the glamour now. That was the reason why the chief sent me. You've heard of Maleger, haven't you? You know—the magician?"

"Oh yes. Did you know him?"

Gallivan snorted into his beer. "Know him? I was the old boy's press agent the last couple of years he lived. Sure. Not that he needed one. And what I didn't know about *that* fellow—say! That's why I won't need to fake a story if I can't get inside his place. Yeah, sure. And I knew Myron Alison, too; that's the chap who got killed, you know. He was a pretty good sort, too," the reporter added, reflectively, wiping his mouth.

For a long time, while he shifted to other topics, I considered. There was small possibility of a mistake; this chance meeting could help us.

"Look here," I said, finally, "you may as well know this, and, if you like, you can probably be of assistance. I am going to Alison's home to help—to help the police investigate his murder."

Then I pointed out how little I knew. I couldn't, I said, give him permission to come with me, because I knew nobody at the Alison place. But if he intended stopping over at Coblenz, I could take his address and telephone as soon as I spoke with the authorities. I intimated that *somebody* was not altogether satisfied with something connected with Maleger's death. He had been staring at me, muttering, "What a break!" But when I spoke of Maleger's death, he almost jumped to his feet in excitement.

"I knew it!" he cried. "By God! Mr. Marle, that's what I've said all along. That old boy couldn't have fallen out of a window like that; and if he did, he didn't roll across a patch of gravel and trees, and then tumble down to drown. It's too crazy. But what could I do?"

"Suicide?"

Gallivan gestured impatiently. "Murder," he said.

"The train-guard," I insisted, "swore there was absolutely nobody else in the carriage, as I understand it. Moreover, he said nobody came near Maleger the whole time."

"I know. And the funny part of it," my companion said, gloomily, "is that the man was telling the truth. Fact. I heard his testimony, and we looked him up from A to Z. Listen! He was so excited over seeing Maleger on his train that he collected everybody's tickets before he got Maleger's, so that he could hang around and maybe talk to the old boy. Well, he couldn't. So he stationed himself in the corridor, after he'd taken Maleger's ticket. And he didn't have the door to the compartment out of his sight during the whole ride. As the train was pulling into Coblenz he went inside to ask if there were anything further he could do, and—bingo! Maleger was gone. I believe him."

"Well? That seems like—"

"It was murder, I tell you," Gallivan persisted, fumbling excitedly in all his pockets after cigarettes. I offered him one, and he lighted it with shaky fingers. In the dusk his face looked pale. "Don't ask me how, Mr. Marle. It's just as though some hand you couldn't see had picked him up out of that compartment and thrown him—"

"Nonsense!"

"You wait. Did you hear the story of the shadow they saw standing on top of the battlements when Alison ran around all on fire? You didn't? My God! what a detective! Don't you know the facts of your case?"

I was beginning to get a bit uneasy, and more bewildered. I said:

"Steady on! I'm only an assistant, and a poor one at that. I haven't read the papers; I'm merely acting under my chief's orders."

Gallivan suddenly put his hands flat on the table and leaned forward, staring beyond me down the Rhine. He said, softly: "There she is, Mr. Marle. There's Castle Skull."

It was still far away, but our steamer seemed to sweep with incredible speed now. At first it was a domed blot with two thin towers, swimming in spectral dusk, disembodied high above the pines on the right. Now the river lay dead black. There were white streaks in the grey sky behind the towers, but the dark fleece of thunderheads crawled to blot them out. From the left bank, a few lights ruffled the inky water. It had grown very warm…

Then Castle Skull grew in size, though it seemed even farther above our heads. Massive walls, battlemented and fully a hundred feet high, were built into the hillside. I bent over the rail and craned my neck to look up. In the centre of the walls, built so that the middle of the battlements constituted the teeth of the death's head, reared the vast skull of stone. The light was too dim to make out details, but I saw the eyes. I saw the two towers on either side, horribly like ears; I saw the whole thin, rain-blacked, monstrous pile move slowly above our heads.

Neither Gallivan nor I spoke until the river widened so that we could see the lights of Coblenz, built up the left-hand hill at the junction of the Rhine and the Moselle, and the unsteady lamps on the Bridge of Boats. Then we went inside to round up our luggage. He gave me a card.

"Here," he said, scribbling the address: "Hotel Traube, Rheinstrasse. Not very far from the landing-stage. Don't forget me, will you, Mr. Marle? I'll lie doggo until I hear from you."

There was a bustle as our steamer scraped in beside the little dock: a clang of bells, a thumping of luggage, a craning of faces under the pale lamps of the quay. At the foot of the gangplank I saw a young man in serge, white flannels, and yachting cap, who was scanning the descending passengers. He stepped up to me.

"Mr. Marle, sir?" he asked in excellent English. "Miss Alison sent the boat down to get you, sir. Will you come this way?"

He fired a few rapid sentences at the porter who was carrying my valises, and led the way along the platform. Behind me, hands dug in his pockets, hat skewered over one eye, I saw Gallivan's lean figure leaning against an advertising poster in the light of a street lamp. He gave me a Punchinello grin as we moved away. There were illuminated windows in the white houses lining the Rheinstrasse; a subdued murmur floated from the dusky crowds on the promenade, and on the terrace of a restaurant an orchestra was playing. Not far from the main landing-stage, a flight of stairs descended to the water. A motor-boat, long and dashing, swayed at their foot.

The cough of the engine deepened to a roar. We swept out in a half-circle, and I sank back into the cushions in the stern. That feeling of power and speed, with the wind in one's face! Water and lamps mingled in a shimmer within empty, rushing space. The beam of a searchlight in our bows fled far ahead. When we had left behind the last string of lights along the Rhine promenade, the hot night closed but for the single white eye in the tearing bow. Over the engine-throb I heard thunder. The top of the pilot's pale cap showed as he glanced up.

Retracing the way I had come, I saw before many minutes another pair of lighted steps on the right. The Alison place was built high among trees, with a thin stone staircase curving up interminably to its veranda. I climbed, my guide following with the luggage. The immense porch, which was paved in red tiles and open to the sky, ran across the entire façade. It was illuminated—a thing which seemed to me, somehow, grotesque—by Chinese lanterns strung on wires. A subdued glow through shades fell across the porch from high windows. You sensed the gigantic trees, rustling, which shadowed it.

In a wicker chair, her legs over the chair-arm, sat a girl. She had black bobbed hair, cut very square, and a puckered homely face which was vivid with make-up. A long cigarette holder was waggling in her mouth. She took it out and regarded me curiously.

"What *ho!*" said the girl. She added, with resignation: "My hat, another detective! The place is infested with detectives. You ought to get up a musical comedy, you know; male chorus singing 'The Sleuth Stomp' or 'My Derby and Me.'"

She took a few puffs at the empty cigarette-holder, and we exchanged grins. I admitted the charge, and asked where I should go—previous to interment, of course. She said:

"You're late for dinner... I say, don't be a surly brute. I know you. You're Jeffrey Marle, and I read a book of yours once. I hope you're cheerful." The glow in her elfin face faded. She nursed her knees, not quite easy. "This place has been rather awful. The Duchess won't let us go. And with My dead over there... I suppose you'd better go inside and see them. My name's Sally Reine, by the way. I paint. *And* I didn't kill My, I assure you."

I turned sharply. "They think somebody here—"

"Oh, rather! Who was the mysterious villain who drove My across the river in the motor-boat and came back alone? You'll see. I can't run one of the dashed things, anyway."

Then I realized that this assured young lady was on the verge of tears. They would streak queerly in the mascara on her black eyelashes. Her snub nose was wrinkled, and she turned away. In the pines above the house, wind had begun to stir with a seething noise. A leaf came whirling and fluttering down across the orange-yellow glow of the Chinese lanterns. I left her on the breezy veranda, staring out into the river-gulf.

My guide of the motor-boat was conferring in the doorway with a hairless, cherubic factotum in black, who addressed me in strongly accented English and asked me to follow him. But he added:

"If it will not inconvenience you, sir, M. Bencolin would like to see you immediately in Miss Alison's sitting-room. I will show you."

A hush was in the dim hallway. An opulent hall, furnished carelessly with a sort of savage and barbaric taste. There were thick tiger and bear skins on the floor, and the glow of two perforated lanterns shone on a height of gilded tapestry. But at the rear I caught a glimpse of a portrait. For the first time, death reached out and took me by the hand in the wind and silence above the Rhine. It was a full-length painting of Myron Alison in the part of Hamlet. As by some desire for self-torture, somebody had left burning the light over it, and as a living presence it looked down into the dusky hall…

A swaggering Hamlet, certainly, with hand on his sword and head bent forward. Thin in his black clothes, with the fine grey eyes, the flawless profile, and the sweep of dark hair. But a brooding, terrible

Hamlet, staring down, and an edge of madness twisting his lip. And yet Myron Alison must have been fifty-five years old when that picture was painted. The eyes looked speculatively after me as I was led upstairs.

Behind the door of a room at the front of the house I heard voices. Rather I heard a voice, tones resonant, positive, and decisive. The voice belonged to a woman, as I discovered when my guide opened the door.

She sat behind a card-table in a deep chair near the open window. A massive woman, a Matterhorn in white lace, glaring down over the icy slopes of herself. She shifted about in the chair, peering over nose-glasses on a black ribbon. Her hair was elaborately coiffeured, a smoky grey, and—I swear it—she was smoking a black cigar with relish. But for all her glares and blowings, it was not an unpleasant face. There were crinkles of laughter round her eyes. Despite her flabbiness, the resemblance to Myron Alison was marked.

"Hullo!" she broke off, as I entered. "Come in! Come in! Welcome!" She gave me a most ferocious stare, and then smiled. She waved the cigar. "I'm Agatha Alison, but call me Duchess. Everybody does. Have a chair."

Leaning against the ledge of the window I saw Bencolin, who waved a greeting.

"Hello, Jeff!" he said. "You should have been glad you didn't come with D'Aunay and me. The car was smashed up twenty miles from nowhere. We're a day late... No, nobody was hurt. Pray continue, Miss Alison."

Miss Alison's nose-glasses fell off. She said, "God damn!" and replaced them, puffing. After a few pleasurable pulls at the cigar, she went on:

"Yes, just arrived this afternoon, Mr.—your name is Marle, isn't it? Jérôme D'Aunay hasn't recovered yet. From the awfulness of smashing his car, I mean. Gave his chauffeur the sack directly... H'm.

"As I was telling you, it happened two days after the crowd arrived. We had D'Aunay and his wife, Levasseur—that's the violinist, you know—and Sally Reine. Young Dunstan got in from London the same day, and we insisted on his staying. H'm.

"Myron," she continued, calmly, "was making quite a play for Sally Reine. The old fool. Anyhow, it was after dinner. Myron had said something about taking Sally across in the motor-boat to look at Castle Skull by moonlight—that was like him, you know—but I'm almost certain she didn't go. Besides, it's a stiffish climb up there in the dark. I'd made him promise to come in here later and play poker with me and my maid. He *was* rather a marvellous poker-player, you know," she admitted, reflectively. "And so is my maid…"

She picked up a deck of cards lying on the table before her, contemplated them, and put them down. Her grey wrinkled eyes were those of one who has merely failed to draw a pair of jacks. A wind was playing with the blue chintz curtains. A long rattle of thunder drew nearer across the hills.

"I remember hearing a motor-boat on the river, as they'll tell you, but I don't recall what time it was. The night was very warm, and there was a moon. Frieda—that's my maid—and I were sitting here by the window, trying to play a two-handed game. Impossible. I don't know where the rest of them were. Oh yes; except Levasseur. I remember hearing his damned violin playing downstairs all the time. He practises half the day. I think Jérôme was lying down in his room, and the rest of them were right close around the house." She glanced out of the window. "It's too dark now, but with a moon you have rather a good view of the castle from here."

The trees whipped and seethed, but nobody made a move to close the window. Glancing out, I could see down on the red-tiled porch, and see the hairless butler hurrying to detach the Chinese lanterns from the posts.

Agatha Alison resumed: "I remember the time, because I was watching the clock and damning Myron for not coming. It was about ten minutes past ten. Frieda and I were making a mess of our game. And all the time we could hear Levasseur playing the violin. Just then he was playing a minuet or something called 'Amaryllis.'..."

She whistled a few bars of the tinkling tune.

"Some of them said afterwards they heard shots. I didn't hear any shots, and neither did Frieda. But I heard the most appalling scream from across—there. I looked out of the window. You could see the big skull. The moon was high and behind it, but it shone on the top of the head and the windows that look like eyes, and a part of the nose.

"All of a sudden something all in flames ran out of the place where the teeth should be. It was very tiny at that distance, but it looked like a man on fire, and it was screaming. You could hear the screams over the water. It started to run along the battlements in the jaws of the skull, wildly; and, damn it! I'll never forget that it almost seemed to be dancing in time to that 'Amaryllis,' that tune. Then it tumbled across one of the battlements and lay there, burning. H'm."

The woman's eyes had turned cold. She tried to puff away the horrible remembrance; she aimlessly picked up and put down the cards. Her cigar had gone out, and she suddenly looked very old. But she even achieved a sort of terrifying joviality when she said:

"I didn't know it, of course. But the man was Myron."

III

TORCHES AND MOONLIGHT

B ENCOLIN HAD TAKEN A CHAIR DURING THIS RECITAL; NOW HE sat with his hand shading his eyes, watching the toe of his shoe draw patterns on the carpet. He said:

"And then?"

"I hurried out in the hall and sent Frieda after Hoffmann—that's the butler—and Fritz, my chauffeur, who runs the motor-boat. I told them to nip across and see what had happened at the castle…"

The detective sat back. The harsh light in the room made shadows under his pouched eyes, and the hooked brows were drawn down.

"One moment," he interrupted. "Do I understand that the castle is not kept locked? M. D'Aunay informed me that it has been kept in repair, as it was when the former owner died."

"Brpf!" snorted our hostess, goggling round for matches. "Man, it wouldn't be possible to keep a huge place like that in the condition it was! No. The *rooms* are kept locked. There was a caretaker, but, my God! man, he couldn't muck about dusting Heaven knows how many rooms, could he?"

"Another 'was,' Miss Alison?"

"He disappeared," our hostess said, relighting her cigar.

Bencolin made a wry face…

"Well, you're supposed to be the best in the business, aren't you?" she demanded. "Back out now, if you like. I'll tell you this, though. Myron wasn't much good. But he was my brother." She struck the table with a large fat palm. "And somebody's going to swing for doing him in, do you hear?"

"Some one shall, as you put it, swing," the detective replied, politely, and his eyelids drooped with quizzical interest. "Please go on."

"Well! I was telling you I sent Hoffmann and Fritz to find out what had happened. When they got to the landing, they found that the motor-boat was missing. So they took a rowboat, and had a long pull. Moored to the other side they found the motor-boat—empty. They started up towards the castle, as I've told you, a stiffish climb. Halfway up, they heard the engine of the motor-boat. Somebody was coming back…"

Bencolin sat upright.

"… but nobody saw who it was. You see, somebody's always going about in that boat, and even when we heard the motor on this side nobody went to the landing-stage to see who was running it. Why should we? We didn't know anything had happened to Myron. Somebody brought that boat back and came up here without being noticed. H'm. Yes… But I was telling you about Hoffmann and Fritz. When they got to the other side—"

"Wait," said Bencolin. "I will question them. At the present I want most of all to see the scene of the crime. That's it—the scene of the crime. I—"

Never have I seen Bencolin so bewildered, so out of himself, and I could not understand the reason. The impersonal eye would never have noticed it; but I knew. He was, outwardly, the suave and the unruffled. A polite smile was in his pointed beard, and his abstracted eyes sought corners of the room. But I felt that, quite suddenly, he had lost his sure grip. No probing questions searched Miss Alison's recital. The daylight would not enter…

"Who is in charge of the investigation?"

"Bah!" said Agatha Alison. "Magistrate Konrad, from Coblenz. Messing about, that's all. *But* I have him in hand. I said he was going to make everybody stop right here until we cleared this thing up. He said it was against the law. I said I'd jolly well make it within the law... until Jérôme got his back up and insisted on going after the best detective he could find. I let him. Incidentally, I think Konrad is furious; told me this morning that they'd sent to Berlin for some ace. Highly irregular proceedings, and all that..."

Bencolin reached over and closed the window. "Yes," he muttered, "yes. By the way, Jeff"—he turned suddenly to me—"have you had anything to eat?"

A shout came from our hostess. Her flabby face showed the utmost contrition, and she slapped her knee. She cried, "My Lord! man, excuse me! I've been so tied up in this affair that—Nothing to eat? And neither have you, M. Bencolin!" To me she explained: "We dined early. As a matter of fact, your friend arrived here only a couple of hours before you did!"

"The accident?" I said.

"Yes. Then Jérôme took pills and went to bed—*bah!*" snapped our hostess. "But just you wait; I'll fix it. *Hoffmann!*"

Her voice bellowed out with such suddenness that I jumped. Almost immediately the big smooth face of the butler appeared in the doorway. A cold buffet, Bencolin said, would do us nicely; and Miss Alison mentioned beer with affection. We made our excuses...

Out in the hallway Bencolin stood motionless until the butler had descended the stairs. Only one lamp burned here, and the carpet muffled every footfall. He said, quietly:

"Jeff, that wreck was no accident. D'Aunay tried to kill us both."

Again that sense of an approaching evil, which was not only formless, but topsy-turvy and mad! It was enclosing the house slowly, like the hot storm. Into my mind jumped the cold blue eyes of D'Aunay, and his quick hands. I stammered, "But the chauffeur—"

"D'Aunay was driving. He left the chauffeur behind. That was why I thought it was queer from the beginning, because, you see, he was driving the limousine… There was a gully, with an eighty-foot drop on stones. I caught sight of his eyes in the mirror over the windshield. I give you my word—they weren't sane. He crouched, yanked the wheel over, and at the same time started to open the door on his left. Perhaps he thought of jumping…" The detective shrugged. "We plunged for that embankment. I jerked the wheel from him, and nearly broke his arms. We skidded; I confess I had a bad moment when I heard our front wheel whirring on the edge. And then we smashed into the bank on the other side…"

Bencolin was opening and closing the fingers of his right hand, staring blankly at it. Then the wrinkles of mirth crept round his eyes…

"Eh, most amusing! Presently he was sitting at a farmhouse drinking hot milk. He begged me not to mention the fact that he had been driving. He is subject to nervous attacks, he says—the reason the doctor advised a rest. He sometimes loses control of his muscles and is not supposed ever to drive a car. If his wife heard of it, he told me—"

"Bosh!"

"Ah, but he carried it off, Jeff! There's an insidious persuasion about him. Or perhaps he really is subject to these attacks… Anyhow, we agreed to blame it on the chauffeur…"

"But surely," I protested, "he must know that you suspect what happened?"

Bencolin shrugged. "Conceit, Jeff, is more than half of the solid, unbreakable force which has made him what he is. Once he loses that, his universe splits. His eyes become the eyes I saw in the mirror. And

I think that momentarily he did lose that belief in his invincibility, because—"

"Because?"

The deep lines tightened down past small moustache and pointed beard. Bencolin loomed gigantic in the dim hallway, squaring his shoulders.

"While we were talking there at Laurent's, something he said conveyed to me a question. And then, quite suddenly, a door opened in my mind." He made a slight gesture. "It was based on no reason. But I saw illuminated the features of a complex and deadly thing. I thought that I saw the truth about Maleger's death. It was only, if you will, a vision, and yet it may be that he saw what was in my mind."

"Riddles," I said. I was thinking of a Rhine steamer, and of Brian Gallivan speaking in the twilight of an invisible hand which hurled Maleger to his death. But I did not speak of Gallivan just then. As we turned towards the staircase, an enormous peal of thunder split across the house and rolled in tumbling echoes down the sky. Every window-pane rattled.

There was nobody in that barbaric lower hall, where the lighted picture followed us with its eyes. We found the dining-room at the back, in which Hoffmann had just finished laying out a cold meal. And, progressively, we seemed to walk into rooms whose atmosphere carried us ever backward into realms where invisible hands were possible. The dining-room was dark and heavily draped, furnished with a massiveness of Florentine oak. Now its carvings were subdued into shadow by the light of seven tall candles in a silver candelabrum, standing among the dishes on the refectory table. It was an immense repast, containing everything from caviare to roast beef; Hoffmann had added beer, port, and a bottle of champagne in an iced cooler.

"Just a moment, Hoffmann," Bencolin said, attacking the sandwiches. He had spoken in German; but, my own knowledge of the language being of the most elementary variety, he shifted into English. "Just a moment, Hoffmann. There are a few questions…"

The butler said, "Yes, sir." He stood with a naïvely guilty air, his stout body poised and hairless head cocked a little on one side. With his pale eyebrows under a bulging forehead, his round blue eyes, snub nose, and drooping mouth, he looked rather like a middle-aged kewpie doll. Out of the kewpie boomed a deep bass voice. He blinked. "Yes, sir. Shall I open the champagne?"

"By all means. Have you been long in Mr. Alison's service, Hoffmann?"

"Three years I have been in it, sir. Since he retired from the stage," the butler explained, busying himself with the champagne cooler.

"H'm, yes. But I understand he owned this house long before that?"

"Yes, I believe so. Many years he owned it." Hoffmann was rolling the bottle in expert fingers, and watching us furtively.

"A good master?"

"Ah! Very—very generous, sir."

"Easy to get on with, I suppose?"

"Ah!" Hoffmann repeated, pursing dubious lips. A plop, a faint creaming fizz, and he poured the pale wine with nicety into two tulip glasses. "So, meinherren! Was an artist, my master, and he had the temperament in no small degree, sir. You can understand. Sometimes he was in a rage. He did not like it because he did not receive so many letters from admirers as before. His hair, it—" Hoffmann made gestures round his own bald skull, and hesitated. "And he grew stout, sir, though he exercise."

Hamlet in the painting…

"Did he go often to the castle over there?"

"*Ach* yes, sir! Liked to walk the walls upon at night, and recite verses. But he did not like others to go inside the castle; he would not let them. From the outside only he showed it to them, you understand?"

Bencolin paused with the glass halfway to his lips, frowned, and set it down deliberately. After a time he asked, "There was a caretaker in charge of the castle, I believe?"

"Yes, sir. Poor Bauer!" muttered the butler, blinking. "Bauer was a little touched in the head, but harmless. He lived inside and kept the gate. He rarely left. You would see his lantern going along the walls to make the rounds every night, sir. Every night but *that* one."

"I see… Would you mind telling us just what happened when you made your unfortunate discovery that night?"

Hoffmann had opened his mouth to speak, when he looked over our shoulders and stopped. Into the dining-room had come a small woman who was regarding Bencolin as though she expected to see him bear some frightful wound. She was pretty, and with more colour she would have been almost beautiful. Her eyes were a deep brown, and her cloudy hair, caught loosely round her head, was of that indeterminate shade of futile washed yellow. But her lips were nearly as pale as her face, and shadows brought out the bewilderment of the brown eyes. She wore a blue frock—the only vivid thing about her. As she moved towards us, you realized that even the frock was wrong. In the flutter of this woman you thought of only one thing. You thought of the word starvation.

"I beg your pardon," she said in a thin voice, very markedly English; "you are the detective from Paris? You speak English?"

"A little, madame," said Bencolin. He smiled, and her eyes lighted somewhat. "I have not had the pleasure of making madame's acquaintance."

"Thank you. I am Isobel D'Aunay."

She was twisting her wedding ring, moving it up and down her third finger. This woman! D'Aunay's wife—I had imagined some strapping, common-sense Belgian, who would have an eye to market-baskets even with D'Aunay's millions behind her. And I thought: Madame Isobel, you are having a bad time of it. She continued:

"I was most frightfully sorry to hear of your accident. I—I do hope you suffered no ill effects?"

"None whatever, madame, thank you." Bencolin presented me, and after the introductions she hesitated.

"Poor Jérôme is quite overcome by it. He's lying down now. I really can't understand how such a thing could occur; Charles is usually such a careful driver." Her words were commonplace, spoken almost in a monotone, but her steady brown eyes asked questions. She asked, casually, "I presume you sent Charles back to town?"

"The chauffeur? Oh yes. We made the remainder of the journey by rail."

The questions remained unanswered. Bencolin's mildly surprised expression conveyed that he considered the matter of the chauffeur of no more importance than the sandwich in his hand.

"Of course." She smiled. She tried to speak lightly, with a lift of her voice. "Well, I—I do hope you clear up this horrible business directly. It's been rather a trying time for all of us. I fancy you want to question all of us again?"

Into her manner she had tried to put more of that light suavity, almost of coquettishness, but it went badly with the pale lips and the strained brown eyes. A nod of her head; but she would not look you in the face.

"I am afraid it will be necessary, Madame D'Aunay."

"Oh, we're quite accustomed to it! That awful man from Coblenz has made us letter-perfect in our parts," she murmured, smiling again. "Miss Reine and Sir Marshall Dunstan and I will be in the library, in case you want us…"

The throaty voice flickered away. I thought of the paper-and-tinsel dancer who stood before the doll's house in the story, and was whisked up by a draught to be carried into the stove. Bencolin turned back to Hoffmann when she had gone.

"Now, then! The events on the night of the murder?"

"About that, sir, I do not know much, except about myself," the other responded. "The coffee and liqueurs I serve in the library. After that I went to oversee the clearing away, and after that I went to my pantry. I did not leave. I looked over some accounts; I sat and listened to M. Levasseur play his violin. Is an artist, too! Yes. Famous."

"Where was M. Levasseur?"

"In the music-room, sir. Is at the other side of the house, but I could hear most well. Sometimes he played magnificent things; sometimes he just himself amused by light pieces. Like that 'Amaryllis,' which he was playing when I heard Miss Alison call from above, and Frieda ran down to find me. They told me to get Fritz and go… Fritz was in the kitchen."

"And when you reached the landing-stage you found the motor-boat gone?"

Hoffmann swallowed hard. He was growing more excited, and the kewpie face grew red. "Yes, sir. We took the—the skiff…"

"Wait! How many boats are there?"

"Just two, sir. The motor and the skiff. Well, Fritz and I, I said, 'Row like the very hell, Fritz!' For we could see a thing lying on the walls, over one of those parapet, burning. *Donnerwetter!* How we shot across that river in the moonlight! And when we arrived, it was strange—"

"Well?" demanded Bencolin, as the other frowned.

"That I did not notice at the time, sir; but I remembered afterwards. The motor-boat was tied at the little dock, yes. But—you see?—the current of the river is very swift. We always tie up the boat on the right, at the side of the landing-stage. This is so the current will keep it against the piles of the pier, and there will not be danger of it to break loose and be carried down. But now it is tied up in front of the landing-stage, and it tugs at the rope. No matter!

"We rushed the dock across and started up. It was steep. I am always afraid of that path. It is not well—what do you say?—kept up, buttressed? Some day the Rhine will rise and wash out the base, and—

"But I was telling you, sir." Hoffmann threw out his hands. "Half up I was panting; I almost fell. I seize a bush, and then I look up. High! High over me I see that big wall go, till I grow dizzy looking at it over the trees. Below it is dark, but the moon shines on the top through trees. It is pale; you see the rough stones and the battlements. I saw a man's hand in flames stick out over one parapet, and nearly I am sick.

"But something else! Beside that I see something else, for just one moment. A huge thing, like a shadow. Like a shadow on the white sky. The shape of a man, with a burning torch in his hand, looks down from the battlements. And then, while I watch, it is gone."

IV

A FTER A PAUSE THE BUTLER CONTINUED:
"A long time it took us to go up the path. It gave him time to come out and to—to sneak past us in the trees. For before we reached the top we hear the engine of the boat."

"And then?" prompted Bencolin, as Hoffmann essayed a sickly smile and stopped.

"The gates of wood across the causeway, they are closed, but not locked. We open them. I wonder where to find old Bauer, who does not answer our call. Beyond is a very long passage of stone, running through the wall many feet. On the floor in the middle is lying the burning torch, left behind. We hurry on through to the courtyard, up stairs to battlements, through arches to the teeth of the skull, and we find—

"Fritz takes off his coat, and—" Hoffmann shuddered. "His hands he got burned, but mostly the fire is put out. Fritz is brave. Of course, it is no use. But at least the head of the man is not badly hurt, and when we lay him down, softly, we see the master.

"And I feel like a pudding, and Fritz, who is so brave, he sits down on a parapet and he shakes, and I see by the moon that he is crying."

Hamlet, lying on his back on the windy battlements, his clothes still smouldering; two shaking servants crouched beside him, the moon above and the Rhine flowing below, overshadowed by the great stone skull... Back into view drifted the room of the seven candles, and Hoffmann's trembling jowls.

"Yes," Bencolin said, softly. "I see. Did you investigate?"

"No. No, sir. We could not. We did not even look to see what had come to the old watchman. We take up the master, carefully, and carry him down. We lay him in the middle of the boat. Fritz insists on rowing, even with his burned hands, and I sit in the stern and look..."

"But the police! What did they discover?"

"Sir, I do not know. Magistrate Konrad will not tell. He says, 'Detectives never tell.' You must ask him."

"Oh, fools!" Bencolin smote the edge of the table. "If he persists in this attitude, we shall get nowhere! Do you know whether they found the weapon? I am told that Mr. Alison was shot."

"I don't know, sir. I think not, though. *But,*" Hoffmann lowered his voice confidentially, "the servants tell me that he is not to remain long in charge. Do you know? Berlin is sending, they say, one who will know. They are sending the great von Arnheim!" Smugly he regarded Bencolin, and for the first time he could not keep a patronizing note out of his voice.

Bencolin snapped his fingers. His eyes opened in pleased surprise...

"You hear, Jeff?" he asked.

I had heard. I knew of Herr Baron Sigmund von Arnheim, Chief Inspector of the police of Berlin. For I had heard tales of the time, years before, when he and Bencolin had played the tangled game of "I spy" across half Europe, and moved pieces on a deadly board behind the guns.

"That will do, Hoffmann," the detective said. "Now you may go. There will be questions later..."

When Hoffmann had left us, I saw that the old Bencolin was himself again. He lifted his glass with a flourish. His moustached lip was raised in a smile, showing teeth in the pointed beard. The candlelight accentuated his high cheek-bones and the hollows beneath them. It brought out the gaiety of his moody eyes. He cried:

"So von Arnheim is to be here! Drink up, Jeff. This is better than I had hoped for. It is the spur to me; I shall not be a dolt for the first time in my life, with that incentive! Eat, man. We have work to do."

But I could not get a word out of him. We finished a hasty meal and drank the champagne; then we went out into the hall. As we did so, door and windows blazed white with lightning. The frothing roar in the trees was drowned by a crash of thunder so close that it brought one's heart jumping; and then with a sudden rush the storm tore down. It drove against the windows like buckshot. It hissed and spurted on the tiles of the porch. It rose to a drumming uproar, whispering from every part of the house.

From beyond a door at the front a heated voice cried:

"I say, Sally, that's rotten! Shut the thing off, won't you?"

Bencolin pushed open the folding-doors. We were in a long library with a beamed ceiling. Wall-lamps were reflected on a dark rich-gleaming floor, on the backs of rich-gleaming books, and in the glass of lighted portraits opulent with colour. Portraits, all of Myron Alison. Alison as Macbeth, Alison as Cyrano, Alison as Tartuffe. It went beyond bad taste and became a kind of mad shrine. In the midst of a scattering of deep chairs, Sally Reine stood by a table on which a portable gramophone was scratchily playing "The Love Parade."

Open folding-doors at the end of the library showed a billiard-room beyond. A young man was striding out of them with a billiard cue in his hand. His fair hair was tousled and his eyes were dark with anger.

"*Will* you shut the silly thing off?" he demanded. "Please be a good fellow, Sally. You know it isn't right to—"

She hooked a defensive arm about the wildly shrilling gramophone. Her black bobbed hair was flung back, and her elfin face screwed up.

"I won't," she cried, "have this place like a morgue any longer! Anyway, you don't care about it. You—"

"You are my ide-e-al, my love parade—" squawked the machine. The gusts of rain swept in waves across the windows. File-raspings sawed at the nerves of everyone; hysteria was growing… "Oh, I say!" muttered the young man, catching sight of us as we entered. He handled his cue awkwardly. Sally Reine shut off the gramophone, and the sudden cessation of noise left an aftermath of trembling. Now we could hear only the dim tumult of the storm. The young man said:

"I—er—Good evening…" Again he regarded the cue, as though he wished he could make it disappear.

"Hullo!" the girl greeted us casually. In a flash she seemed to be enjoying the situation. She put a cigarette between her red, very full lips; the black eyes squinted mockingly. "Come in and add your respective sunshiny tempers to the occasion. M. Bencolin, Mr. Marle—Sir Marshall Dunstan."

Dunstan bowed. The light hair fell in disorder on his high forehead. It was a sensitive face; lean about the jaws, with a long nose, a dissatisfied mouth, and restless eyes. Already there were furrows between his eyebrows. For some reason he was very much embarrassed.

"Howd'youdo?" he acknowledged. He added, dubiously: "Won't you—?"

We took two of the chairs he indicated in his gesture. Then, subtly, Bencolin took command. The man could be genial when he chose; leaning back with a cigar in his fingers, he spoke lightly and with frankness of the whole affair. He mentioned the incongruity of French detectives and German crimes. He discussed the amusing possibilities of an encounter between himself and Baron von Arnheim, and sketched one of the more intriguing tales of spies in war-time.

"… so, you see," he said, amusedly regarding the tip of his cigar, "I shall most certainly need help. We allies must stand together."

Dunstan had been listening to the spy story with absorbed interest, leaning forward in his chair, a wrinkle between his brows. Occasionally he muttered, "Fancy that!" Sally Reine, her outlandish batik dress curled up in a divan, blew smoke-rings approvingly. She winked, and applauded behind Dunstan's back with silent glee.

Said Miss Reine: "*Vive la France! A bas le boche!* That's a sporting proposition, Duns. I begin to feel a bit less guilty already."

"You're a queer sort of policeman!" observed Dunstan, ruffling his hair. "You see"—he frowned, groping for words—"the worst of being cooped up in this confounded place is the realization, the awful realization—"

"Don't get dramatic, Duns, please," urged Sally Reine.

He turned on her hotly, pink mounting to his face. "I'm not getting dramatic! You know I'm not. Hang it! I'm just trying to explain. Maybe I'm no good at explaining. What I mean is, some-body here, now, under this roof, is the one who killed Myron. Somebody we're eating with, and drinking with, and talking to… And every time somebody is alone with you, you suddenly wonder whether they'll go crazy and jump for your throat. You're always suspicious; you look behind you, and… it's all the more horrible because they're all people you've known for years! D'you remem-ber how Myron looked, with his body burnt away, and half his face rot—"

"Draw it mild! Quit that, Duns! Do you hear?" snapped the girl. She hurled her cigarette into the empty fireplace.

"You understand what I mean, don't you?" the young man appealed to Bencolin, his pinched face very earnest. "And then there's something worse even than that…"

"Oh, undoubtedly," said Sally Reine. But I thought that, for the second time this evening, she was very close to tears. There was a queer breathlessness in the look of a half-hysterical pity she directed at him.

"Look here. I've got to get this off my chest," he pleaded, his nervous fingers playing with his jaw. "You see, it's wondering whether maybe—this is the worst—whether I might have done it. Oh, I know I didn't! I know that; but just the same you get the thought, just the same, what if maybe I really *did* do it? It's the same as when you've been drinking, and for a while there are blind spots you can't recall. You wonder whether you did some ghastly thing then. You know you didn't, but all the same…

"And then," he whispered, "you go through seven different varieties of hell until time makes you forget. Or maybe you don't… I wasn't drunk last night. I'd had only a few, but when I try to recall *everything*, I can't…" He drew a deep breath.

Sally Reine said, "You're being silly, Duns."

He nodded, staring at the carpet. "Oh, I know. Lord knows I've good reason to realize I couldn't have…"

A pause. Fear flickered in Dunstan's eyes as he checked himself. He had said too much, we all sensed, but I for one did not understand. The gusts of the storm smashed on our windows, slithering and whirling over the sides of the house, as with the rise and crash of waves. Dimly, the frames on the portraits of the dead man rattled. Bencolin, inscrutable, watched the smoke of his cigar curl upwards.

"Suppose, Miss Reine," he suggested, "you try to tell us what really happened that night."

She answered, wanly: "I'd better, hadn't I?… Well, I've told it half a dozen times to that walrus of a Konrad, and I've tried to recall other things… What do you want me to tell?"

"Everything, if you please. Begin with dinner. Did Mr. Alison seem—upset?"

"Upset? Oh no! He was in excellent spirits. And jolly handsome, too, even if I did happen to know he wore corsets to keep his athletic figure. He joked all through dinner. There was just one thing—"

"Well?"

She scowled, chewing at her upper lip. "Well, I'll tell *you*. I didn't tell Old Sleuth, because what would have been the good? I think My was afraid of ghosts."

"Ghosts?"

"Yes. We had come in here for coffee. Levasseur—have you met him?—he's a little wasp-waisted Frenchman, all teeth and bows, but a magnificent violinist—Levasseur was talking about Castle Skull. He said something like: 'You know, monsieur, you've never shown us through your castle. One hears that there are strange rooms...' Myron was standing over there under that picture of himself as Romeo—he liked to pose under the pictures—with a coffee-cup in his hand. His hair was as dark as mine, mind you! He smiled, and said something about its being locked and in ruins; not fit for inspection. Levasseur said, 'Ah, but all the better! I have it. Why not take the entire party and spend the night over there? I feel sure it's haunted. I feel sure we should see a werewolf.'"

Sally Reine's puckish face was thoughtful, and she leaned her chin in her hands.

"Well, we all began to yell at him to second the idea. The Duchess slapped her knee and said it was the God-damndest best idea of the century. But; Good Lord! I was watching My. He was frightened. His cup skittered on the saucer, and all of a sudden you saw how old he was. Then Duns here"—she nodded at the young man, who gestured fiercely—"Duns pulled a floater. He'd had a goodish bit of wine with dinner. He laughed, and said, 'I say, sir, you're not afraid of dead people, are you?'

"It was just as though somebody had blurted out an obscene word. We were so quiet, dead quiet, that we heard Hoffmann put down the tray of liqueurs on the table. My was—white. Then Jérôme D'Aunay piped up in that queer English of his, and said, 'What about a game of billiards?' But the undersigned," said the girl, bowing, "saved the situation. Enter our heroine, gaily. I said: 'Be quiet, all of you! He's promised to show *me* the castle, alone, by moonlight. Haven't you, My?' Then I gave everybody a knowing look. I could see he was grateful, and he said, 'Rather!' And laughed... Got a cigarette, Duns?"

The young man passed her his case. She looked at it with wryly humorous meditation, but did not light it. A loose shutter banged somewhere upstairs, under the eternal lashing of the storm.

"He excused himself later, and I walked out to the hall with him. He made a feeble effort to suggest, 'Shall we?' but I just told him, 'No, Myron; you haven't eaten your oysters tonight. Off you go.' He was going upstairs to work on his book. He has been writing his memoirs, and he spent a lot of time locked in his room.

"He stood with one foot on the stairs, looking out the front door. Then he went on up. That was the last I saw of him..."

"One moment," interposed Bencolin. "At what time was this?"

"I'm not sure. A bit past nine, I should say."

"At that particular time, then, he had no intention of going to the castle?"

"I think not... Anyhow, I wandered out to the veranda, and sat on the balustrade, and just *thought*. It was a lovely night, you know. I saw a couple of lighted boats go past on the river down there, and there was a sort of scented breeze..." She drew a deep breath; her mouth was wrinkled almost in a sneer. "Mooning, like a silly ass! I don't know. When I came in…"

"After how long?"

"Haven't the foggiest notion," she answered, crisply, and lighted the cigarette with a decisive gesture. "When I came inside, the group had broken up. D'Aunay and the Duchess were going upstairs. He was telling her all about the healthful values of hot milk at night, and she was doing a post-mortem on poker hands. This is not an orthodox house, you know; you do just as you damn well please… I heard somebody clinking bottles in the dining-room…"

"I was the one," vouchsafed Sir Marshall Dunstan.

"H'm, yes. You would be," snapped Miss Reine. "I also heard Levasseur plunking a few notes on his fiddle out back."

"And Madame D'Aunay?"

"Don't know. She was somewhere about, I dare say. I went into the library, not feeling very fit. I pulled up a chair over in that corner by the billiard-room, and got down a book. The only light was the one by my chair; and, what with listening to the wind in the trees and everything, I got drowsy. Levasseur began to play his violin, softly, and that lulled me, too. I was just dozing off to sleep when I heard footsteps in the hall…" She hesitated. "They were going towards the front door, walking rather fast. Of course I paid no attention to it at the time."

"The footsteps of a man or a woman?"

"I don't know. There appeared to be two people, and they were talking in low voices. It was impossible to tell. Of course it must have been Myron and—"

"The murderer," supplied Dunstan.

"If you insist, the murderer. That's all I know, really. I must have gone to sleep. The next thing I remember is being conscious of dreadful screams, somewhere far away, and of hearing the Duchess bellowing something from the upper hall. I got up, still rather foggy, and wondering what it was all about. By that time Hoffmann and Fritz had already started down to the landing-stage... You know how it is when you've just awakened. I tried to find out what it was all about, but Levasseur was still playing his violin—I suppose he hadn't heard—and I didn't want to disturb him at practice. I went up and asked the Duchess. She was worried, but she said it was all tosh—a scare—forget about it, you see. So I came down and stood on the porch. Over on the battlements of the castle I could see figures milling about—Hoffmann and Fritz. That's all."

"You were on the porch when the motor-boat was heard returning?"

Her answer was quick. "I must have been. But I'm afraid I didn't pay great attention to it. There are always noises like that on the river."

"And you saw nobody come up from the landing-stage?"

"Nobody. But then a person wouldn't have to come by the water-stairs. There's a path up the hill on down a bit. A person could have come up that path to the side of the house without being seen."

Her look was engagingly candid, and she had dropped entirely her bantering manner. Overdrawing it, she became almost girlish. Bencolin, leaning back in the chair with his head inclined against his fingers, seemed interested chiefly in the whipping tumult of the storm. His eyelids drooped. The fingers tapped slowly on his temple.

"I am very much afraid you are not telling the truth, Miss Reine," he said.

V

A VIOLIN AT NIGHT

SALLY REINE DID NOT REPLY. SHE REMAINED STARING AT THE detective, steadily, but nodding her head as though a fear had been confirmed. Yet she herself was not afraid, you knew...

Then we became conscious of another figure in the room. How long the man had been there I cannot say, because all of us had been watching the girl. He was leaning against the door to the billiard-room, easy and negligent. A little man, with polished black hair and a swarthy face. A cigarette smouldered in his fingers, and under one arm he carried a violin-case.

"I beg your pardon," he said. His English was good, though he spoke with a guttural accent which was queer in a Frenchman. "I could not help hearing Miss Reine's—testimony."

He advanced towards us, putting the violin-case carefully on the table. All his gestures had a curious fluent smoothness, like that of an orchestra leader. His dark face was knife-sharp, his dark eyes whimsical. An emerald stud shone in his shirt-front. He said, "Permit me. I am Emile Levasseur. A terrible affair, is it not?"

With those quick, light steps of his he had moved between Sally Reine and the accusation directed against her. He sat down, carefully drew up the legs of his trousers, and put his finger tips together.

"I have the pleasure," he told us, cocking his head on one side, "of confirming all the early part of Miss Reine's testimony."

"And the latter part?" asked Bencolin. He had not moved. Even his glance did not go to the newcomer.

"I regret! No, I can tell you nothing. Once I had shut the door of the music-room, after the group had broken up in here, I went into another world. Music is more a barrier than sound-proof walls." His white teeth flashed. "I knew nothing until they knocked on the door to tell me…"

Sir Marshall Dunstan put in:

"That's right. That was the worst part of it. When they were carrying the body in, the violin was still going. Somebody said, 'Isn't he ever going to stop that damned sawing?' and went and knocked on the door."

Levasseur said, thoughtfully, "A term, my friend, which I think highly erroneous…"

"I say, no offence!"

"… but highly pardonable, also, under the circumstances," interposed the other, smiling again. For some reason he reminded me of a monkey on a stick. With his brown face, nervous movements, and fine hands upheld with finger tips together, I almost expected to see him shoot up towards the ceiling.

"A strange tableau to see, I assure you," Levasseur informed us, "when I went out into the hall. A picture some one might transfer to a fine ghoulish thing in music. My good friend Sir Marshall Dunstan leaning on the wall, repeating, 'My God! My God!' Madame D'Aunay standing on the stairs, very white. Hoffmann saying to Miss Alison, for no reason at all, 'I am sorry—' and bobbing his head. And the charred body lying on a couch under the body's portrait as Hamlet, for the last time.

"Was it not fine? Ha! In music it would be—" He checked himself, running over something in his mind.

"Yes," murmured Bencolin, looking at Dunstan. "You were in the hall, my friend? You had just come in?"

"Just. That's what I wanted to tell you. *I* can't supply any story. I had been wandering about in the woods above the house here for almost an hour. I heard some kind of commotion, but the trees are very thick, and—"

"And so you can tell us nothing at all?"

"Nothing!" the young man said, earnestly. "I know that sounds suspicious, but, hang it! that's the mortal truth! Just messing about."

There was a silence. Nobody seemed inclined to question Dunstan's statements, as apparently he expected, and he sat looking from Bencolin to me with relief lightening the worried expression of his brooding face. Levasseur, absorbed, flicked imaginary dust from his trousers. He said:

"I wonder, M. Bencolin, if it is possible for me to have a few words with you and your colleague in private?"

"It isn't," Sally Reine broke in. She started a nervous laugh. "I'm about to be had up for lying. You interrupted it."

Bencolin raised his hand gently. His look was one of mild surprise.

"On the contrary, Miss Reine! You are not going to be 'had up.' I merely informed you of the fact; I shall not question you any further. But I felt called on to point it out to you"—he smiled obscurely—"as a friendly warning to an ally. Let me advise you earnestly that, should we be favoured by a visit from Herr von Arnheim, you do not attempt to perpetrate such a tale on him. I have too great a respect for the good baron's intelligence. It might be embarrassing for—several people... Do we understand each other?"

That old, wise, tired scrutiny! She remained returning his gaze with unwinking black eyes which had turned rather glassy, her cigarette held motionless.

"I'm beginning to be afraid of you," she said in a slow voice, and almost in a whisper. Then she said: "Come on, Duns. Let's get out of here. I feel the need of a drink. A large drink. Of appropriate strength."

She shook him by the shoulder, and the lean young man got hesitantly to his feet. He directed an inquiring glance at Bencolin, who shook his head. She was trying to talk gaily when she led him from the room, but the effort was not a conspicuous success...

"Youth," said Levasseur, looking after them. "I offer my thanks to the good God that I am not young. It is a hideous time. Youth can do nothing, not the smallest and most harmless action, without a sense of guilt. The only thing we learn with age is that our actions are not so reprehensible or fraught with consequences as we thought, and that is why we are content." He sighed very theatrically; he was enjoying himself.

"As though one of those two could have shot and burnt M. Alison!" he exclaimed, after a pause. "Ridiculous!"

"You wished, I think," said Bencolin, "a word in private?"

"Yes. It is about a matter which I have not mentioned to that blundering camel of a Konrad." Levasseur examined his hands—another trick he had when he appeared to be meditating. "Do you know who urged that you be sent for? It was I. Yes. D'Aunay did not wish to go; I made him, because I thought the pressure of a great—money-power would be of more influence in persuading you to come than, for instance, myself."

"Ah," murmured Bencolin.

"Correct, was I not?" smiled Levasseur. "No, he did not wish to go. 'You have,' said I, very politely, 'something to hide?' He drew himself up, he looked fanatical, and, *voilà!* he went to Paris. But there is a bit of information...

"As I told you, I was playing my violin. And always I play in the dark. The goblins are summoned, the giants and the genii from *that*"—he indicated the violin—"with a more potent lure. Always I am lost. But on one occasion, when I finished the canzonetta from Tchaikovsky's concerto, I looked up. There was bright moonlight in the room. The windows stretch to the floor in there, and beyond them there is a stone staircase which goes to a balcony on one of the rooms upstairs. In the moonlight, when the influence of music receded, I suddenly became conscious that there was a figure standing on the staircase outside. I could see the silhouette. The next instant it ran upstairs. For a long time I debated whether it was an illusion, sprung from dreams, or whether I had really seen it. And I decided." He lifted his dapper shoulders. "It was no illusion."

"H'm. The figure of a man or a woman?"

"That I do not know. I saw it as an image across the tail of the eye; a fragment, an impression such as one receives on waking from sleep. But I am convinced that it was real. Had I told this to our good magistrate, he would have shouted, 'Man or woman? man or woman?' until his face purpled, and would have been convinced that I lied when I assured him I could not be sure. If I were superstitious—ah, but I am not. I wish to the good God I were—I should have a better emotional time. Conceive, my friend, the witchery of a world full of spectres and—"

"And at what time did you see it?"

"Monsieur," cried Levasseur with some testiness, "how should I place time? By great moments in life, yes. But not by clocks. Since everyone assures me I was playing 'Amaryllis' at the time of the murder, that is more definite. A foolish tune. But good exercise for the fingers. I played the canzonetta next. It is long…"

"At any rate, you saw this figure some time after the murder?"

"So far as I am able to ascertain, yes."

"And to the balcony of what room do these stairs lead?"

Levasseur sat back. His swarthy face wore a deprecating expression.

"To the room occupied by Monsieur and Madame D'Aunay," he replied.

Bencolin rose without a word, went to the door, and pulled the bellcord. When Hoffmann appeared, he addressed to him a rapid order in German. Levasseur was again examining his hands, turning them over and over. Not a word was spoken until Hoffmann returned to the room some five minutes later with Jérôme D'Aunay and his wife. In the meantime, Levasseur had been listening to the storm, his eyes roving as though he were thinking of it in music...

"Is there to be no sleep for me?" D'Aunay complained. His eyes were red and drowsy, and the thin hair ruffled across his big head. He wore a Turkey-red dressing-gown. "Good evening, Mr. Marle. I am delighted to see you here."

He had spoken in French, and by tacit consent we carried on the talk in that language. I returned his greeting, wondering what high explosives were being juggled now. Isobel D'Aunay was conscious of the tension. Her light hair had come a little loose; for a pretty woman, she looked almost dowdy. She had apparently been lying down, for her blue dress was wrinkled, and her expression harassed. D'Aunay strode to the centre of the room, giving Levasseur a curt nod.

"Well?" he demanded.

"Repeat your story, monsieur," Bencolin said, quietly.

Levasseur told it, looking somewhat bored, his gaze wandering past the Belgian. The latter stood with neck thrust out, stocky and inscrutable; but you could see the deadly rage gathering behind cold eyes, and the slow pulling down of his mouth, as each soft word fell. It was as though those words were being dropped into a sizzling pot on the fire, and slowly stirred until suddenly the mess boiled. The red dressing-gown jumped forward.

"Monsieur," D'Aunay said, distinctly, "you are a damned liar."

Monkey-on-the-stick leaped, even as I had imagined in that weird fancy. His emerald stud winked. He smashed his fist into D'Aunay's mouth, and then the whole thing became a turmoil. Isobel D'Aunay screamed. I seized Levasseur's shoulder and flung him back against his chair, so that he stumbled over its arm and almost fell. Over thick panting breath from D'Aunay, I heard Bencolin's cold voice.

"M. D'Aunay," he said, calmly, "once today I was on the point of breaking your arm. Do not force me to do it again. Now stand back. You can adjust this affair to your own satisfaction when we have settled more important business. In the meantime, be quiet."

He released D'Aunay, who stood quivering and staring, his hands aimlessly grabbling up and down the sides of his dressing-gown. On his lip were small beads of blood. The titanic dammed wrath of the man sent shivers through me—all thick wrinkles and hot-smashing eyes. Under the storm we heard his harsh breathing again.

"If the pig has damaged my hand," said Levasseur, examining his knuckles in a matter-of-fact way, "I think I will kill him." He flashed on me a gleaming smile, and bowed. "My sincerest thanks, monsieur. You saved me from damaging my hand."

Little cock-sparrow! With the exception of Bencolin, he was the coolest person in the room. His polished hair remained unruffled.

Isobel D'Aunay cried, "Please!"—in that futile and uncertain way of hers. She had a futile bit of a handkerchief, with which she tried to wipe her husband's lip, but he thrust her aside.

"The affair *will* be settled to mutual satisfaction," D'Aunay observed, thickly.

"Ah," said Levasseur, with resignation. "By monsieur's lawyer, I dare say."

"But before anything whatever is done, I am going to answer your implication." With an effort D'Aunay put his hands in the pockets of the red dressing-gown. "I am going to answer it, and then I will deal with you. Whether or not you know it, I am subject to nervous attacks…"

Levasseur sighed. I confess that bringing this point up at the time did sound a little foolish and prim. It was bad judgment. D'Aunay went on:

"I cannot sleep. I am given veronal, which my wife prepares each night. It is sufficient to insure sleep without waking for eight hours. On the night—the night of the death, I was given the dose as usual, shortly after nine o'clock. Miss Alison's maid was in the room at the time, and will testify to this. I went to bed immediately. Any doctor will tell you that I could not possibly have left my room. They could not wake me even when they tried to do so after the discovery of the body… Is that correct, my dear?" he suddenly demanded of his wife.

"Why, of course!" she told us. She smiled deprecatingly. "Of course it's true. I gave him his veronal, and he went to sleep."

"And you, madame?" asked Levasseur, gently.

"I?" Oh no; she was not quick-witted. It took a long time for even that. Her brown eyes widened and grew darker; the pale lips drooped apart, then tightened back in a horrible fear. "Oh!" she muttered, still staring fixedly at Levasseur. "I see. No. It wasn't I. But there would be that. It's just about the last…

"I was in bed. Jérôme always insists that I go to bed when he does, to—to preserve my health." Very pale and straight she faced us. Far away, she looked at an approaching catastrophe; sudden contempt hardened the weak countenance. In a low, detached voice she said, "A lot—of—good—that—does."

The breathless words were spoken by another person. Behind her gaze you saw an opening of doors and a sudden realization. I thought, illogically, of the sun in English lanes; and I thought of the shuttered mausoleum at Brussels, which had once been pointed out to me as the home of Jérôme D'Aunay.

"You were asleep?" Bencolin inquired, casually.

"I was asleep until I was roused by the commotion, and then I got up and put on a wrap and went downstairs to see them bringing in the body," she told us, firmly. The gaze was level now. "I trust monsieur is answered?"

"Completely, madame," said Levasseur, with a slight bow. "I spoke to your husband only."

D'Aunay turned to regard his wife. "*I* was asleep," he asserted, "and *I* can prove it. But you…" His anger flared. "By God! Myself, I begin to wonder whether I dare let you give me veronal at night."

Smiling at the ceiling, Levasseur said, pleasantly: "Monsieur is a liar, a coward, and, I must insist, the illegitimate offspring of a she-dog."

"That's enough!" snapped Bencolin. "M. D'Aunay, none of that!— Stay where you are! Friend Levasseur, will you have the goodness to reserve these compliments for another time?"

"Ah! I admit," said Levasseur, "that, in the heat of pardonable irritation, I may have been a trifle more complimentary than I intended. But I was ever generous. So I will go." He rose and picked up his violin-case. "I shall always be in the house, within reach, monsieur…"

It took some time to smooth down D'Aunay's rage. Bencolin was still suave, though personally I felt inclined to shake hands with Levasseur. The woman said nothing more; she stood with her pale lips tight, studying D'Aunay as though she had never seen him before.

"May I point out," Bencolin interposed, "that a person going up those stairs might not necessarily be either of you? You did not keep your doors or windows locked?"

"No," growled D'Aunay. "In case of fire, we—"

"Precisely. And somebody who wished to gain entrance to the house without being seen, knowing you two were in bed, might readily have passed through the room."

Presently D'Aunay went stumping out, mentioning his health and also the probable state of Levasseur's health when he had finished. It was windy, but it did not quite carry conviction. He growled an order to his wife, and the red dressing-gown lumbered through the folding-doors. Isobel D'Aunay stood a moment in the doorway, regarding us with a smile. She had become flushed and almost gay, and as she tossed her head in farewell there was a suggestion of a sparkle in her eyes. Dimly from beyond the billiard-room floated the weird notes of a violin…

Bencolin whirled jubilantly to me when we were alone.

"Excellent, Jeff, excellent," he said, rubbing his hands. "The best yet! Levasseur has baited a trap, and it may tell me something I very much want to know… Ring the bell for Hoffmann, will you? There is another thing—"

"A trap? A trap for the guilty person?"

"A trap," said Bencolin, "for the innocent one… Ring the bell, man!"

VI

WHILE WE WERE WAITING FOR HOFFMANN, BENCOLIN STRODE up and down the room. He was imbued with that evil good-humour which struck him when he was directing, all unknown to them, the actions of those around him. He paused by a writing-table in the corner of the library, and looked speculatively at the blotting-pad. Then he sat down, drawing pen and paper towards him. I could see that he was printing something in large characters on the paper, but I did not question him. If you interfered with Bencolin's dramatic effects, it spoiled his pleasure; and, I had found from bitter experience, very often it almost spoiled the solution of the case. I followed the wandering, haunting air of the violin…

When Hoffmann entered, the detective put his sheet of paper into an envelope and sealed it up. He put it carefully in his inside pocket, and then looked at his wrist-watch.

"Eleven o'clock," he said. "At what time do you generally retire, Hoffmann?"

"With the things as they are now, sir," the butler answered, "I do not ever know. I make my rounds to lock up when they give me orders."

"Well, I shan't trouble you much longer. But I want to look at Mr. Alison's rooms… Tell me, did he keep a valet?"

"No, sir."

"Good. Now, the clothes and shoes he was wearing at the time you found him… were they entirely burnt?"

"Yes, sir. The clothes were. The shoes, only partly."

"Excellent!—You did not keep them, I suppose?"

"I believe they were put in his closet when—when the undertaker—"

"I see. Will you take us there, please?"

We went out into the hallway and upstairs again. From the door to the dining-room we heard a bottle clink, and the sound of Dunstan's voice:

"… and listen, Sally. I could damn well have designed those sets! That's what he wanted to see me about, you know. He was going to come back in 'Richard the Third.' Well, I—Knock this back, old girl! Good stuff."

The voice dimmed away. I could fancy Dunstan sitting at the table in there, leaning back with a glass in his hand, and displaying all his feelings in the manner of a shirt hung on a clothes-line. And I could fancy Sally Reine, her elbows on the table, elfin face in her fists, and unwinking black eyes upon him… Now we were in the dim upstairs hallway. Bencolin laid a finger on his lips for silence. He spoke in a whisper:

"Whose rooms are these, Hoffmann?"

The butler pointed to the two doors at the front on our left.

"Miss Alison's sitting-room and bedroom, sir. You were there. Next on the left, M. and Mme. D'Aunay's room—that's directly over the music-room—with a bath attached. The wings here in the rear…"

His nod then indicated the left wing of the house as you faced the front. The wing ran out on either side of the house to form the head of a T with the main body. "Mr. Alison's quarters—study, bedroom, and bath. The right-hand side and wing have corresponding rooms. Miss Reine is in the front one, corresponding to Miss Alison's sitting-room. The other two have been set aside for you gentlemen. In the right wing, Sir Marshall Dunstan and M. Levasseur occupy the two rooms, with a bath between."

"And the servants?"

"On the third floor, sir. We have a service staircase at the rear."

"I see. Is a light generally kept burning here in the hallway after the house has retired?"

"No, sir. All the rooms have private baths, and—"

"See that there is a light tonight. Not a bright one. The lamp burning now will do nicely. Now—Mr. Alison's quarters."

We went softly along the left wing, and from a large bunch of keys Hoffmann selected one and opened the door at the end. This was the side exposed to the drive of the storm-blasts; if anything, the night was growing worse, and I thought I could feel the entire house quiver to its shakings. For nearly an hour there had been no diminishing in that furious onslaught, in its dashes and spurts and swirlings. Through all its uproar the violin downstairs wove an eerie thread of melody...

Hoffmann snapped on the lights from a switch beside the entrance, and Bencolin closed the door. Even in nine days' desertion, the place smelt of decay. The lights had a harsh glare. It was an oak-panelled room, the windows hung with draperies of a sombre brown dully figured in gold. Framed photographs crowded the walls, a pageant of the stage in its finery, dating from those gaslit days of the 'nineties when Myron Alison had scored his first success. A typewriter stood on a side-table, with an easy chair pushed back from it and a smoking-jacket flung across the chair-arm. It was all lightly blurred in dust.

Bencolin's eyes moved restlessly round. An air of tensity and suppressed excitement had been on him since the door opened; but he did not seem to find what he was looking for. He looked at the door. Then he hurried over to the two windows, whirling round after a momentary scrutiny.

"Lock and bolt on his door. Heavy shutters on his windows..."

"Afraid of something?" I said.

"Be quiet, Jeff!" The restless gaze moved along the walls, floor, and ceiling. "Still, it doesn't matter. I want to see the bedroom. It must be in the bedroom…" He had been speaking to himself in a sort of obscure musing, but now he broke off. "Hello! You still here, Hoffmann? I've a commission for you. Every night, Hoffmann, Monsieur D'Aunay is in the habit of taking a dose of veronal to make sure that he sleeps well. I want you to find some pretext to get in their room and discover whether he is taking it tonight. Make any excuse. Say you want to change the towels in the bathroom—"

Hoffmann looked shocked. "But it's the *housemaid*, sir, who—"

"Well, then, anything! Knock and ask them if they want sandwiches and coffee. I don't care how you do it. Wait! Say Miss Alison heard he was very much upset, and wondered whether he might want a sleeping-powder. He's in a rage; he'll tell you—with comments. But do it."

Looking very dubious, Hoffmann left us. Bencolin was regarding a curtained alcove which apparently led to another room. He walked over and raised the curtain. The narrow alcove communicated with a bedroom, into which a little light fell. But the detective was staring at a small Persian rug in the alcove—a rug slightly disarranged.

"Lock the door, Jeff," he said, quietly.

When I returned he was kneeling by the rug. He had struck a match, and he was holding the tiny flame close against the floor.

"Mud," he continued; "caked mud. The rug almost covered it." Shaking the match out, he rose and hurried into the bedroom. I heard him fumbling about before he switched on the lights.

It was a big room, richly sombre, dominated by a Renaissance bed grim in dark oak carvings and red hangings. The grey-green tapestries, the cabinets of Japanese lacquer bearing vases of hammered gold, the panels of woven gargoyles—a contrast here to the simplicity of the study. This, you felt, was the man's real den. Above a Florentine chest of drawers hung a big mirror framed in gold leaf; on the chest of drawers were ranged toilet waters, astringents, face creams, and a vast array of hair-tonics. A Venetian lantern hanging from the carved ceiling threw pale grey light…

"The soul of neatness," said Bencolin. "You see how those articles are arranged? But I'm hunting for a wardrobe…"

He found it, in a corner by the bed. Throwing open the door, we saw that it was filled with suits neatly hung up. The hat-boxes were in careful order. On the floor, shoes with shoe-trees all stood precisely with toes pointing out. But, one sinister touch in the precision of the closet, a pair of thick walking-shoes had been thrown into a corner. Bencolin took them out and examined them. Their heavy leather was scorched and blackened, the laces burned away. Yet we could see that they had been thickly crusted with a greenish-black mud which still emitted a faint and nauseating odour.

"There they are," Bencolin muttered, turning them over in his hands. "The shoes he wore when he… H'm. He didn't wear those to dinner, obviously. Look for a pair of evening slippers, Jeff. Do you see any?"

After a thorough search we failed to find any. Bencolin said:

"This won't do. No evening slippers! An immaculate dandy with such a wardrobe as this, and no patent leathers. Damnation!… Ah, but wait! Here's another pair of walking-shoes. Dry, but so wet before that the leather is stiff to the point of cracking. And—mark it, Jeff—again this mud, almost to the ankles." He flung them out on the floor with a thump. "And this. This is out of place, too, in our immaculate gentleman's possession…"

He was holding up a very disreputable brown topcoat, stiff and mudstained, with smears across the elbows. Turning it round under the light, he put his hand into one pocket. Abruptly he stiffened…

"What's the matter?" I demanded.

For a moment Bencolin did not reply. He took a coat-hanger from the closet and hung the topcoat over it with meticulous attention.

"It is just as well, Jeff, that I have told you nothing," he breathed. "Twice, so far, I have been compelled to revise my estimate of this case. I wonder, now, whether I must not revise it again. No, no! Who else would have a motive—! But there must be! There must be a motive I've overlooked... You'd better go out, Jeff. I want to be alone; I want to think. Go and talk to somebody. I will prowl and prowl around."

I left him standing in the middle of that mediæval room, staring unseeingly at his own reflection in the mirror. Walking out to the door, I thought of those grim shoes plastered with mud. Myron Alison wore them on his night-prowls through Castle Skull. It was inconceivable that the path up to the castle was in such bad condition as to plunge a walker ankle-deep in that foul stuff. No, the mud suggested the *cellars* of the castle. It suggested deep vaults and winding stairs, with torches moving down them. Torches...

Unlocking the study door and closing it behind me, I came upon Hoffmann. He lowered his voice in the dusky hall.

"M. D'Aunay has taken the veronal, sir," he said. "He was taking it when I knocked. Is there anything else?"

"No; that's all, Hoffmann..."

I stood for a long time motionless after he had left. Suddenly I knew that some sound was missing, some noise to which I had been accustomed. It was not the flapping of the black wind and rain, but... the violin. The violin had stopped. Levasseur was probably going to bed. On an impulse I walked to the front of the house and knocked at the door of Miss Alison's sitting-room. The rousing voice bade me come in.

She sat behind her table in a flaring negligée, drinking Guinness' stout and glumly contemplating a chessboard.

"Come right in, young fella-me-lad!" she greeted. "Have a bottle of stout. Always drink three, myself, before I turn in… 'White to play and mate in three moves!' Ah, to hell with it! Nothing like poker. How's the detective business?"

"From my point of view," I admitted, sitting down, "distinctly bad."

She closed one eye behind her glasses. She assumed such a motherly air, with her broad humorous mouth and upturned nose, that I grinned.

"Well, well," she consoled, "you just tell the old Duchess all about it. Plague take me! When all your fancy detectives are stumped, *I'm* going to take a hand. Look here, you're not a detective, are you? A kid? What I mean, laddie, aren't you just the gifted amateur or something?"

"Writer," I said.

"H'm. Is that so? Damme!" she muttered, scrutinizing me with her cheeks puffed out. "You don't look it. I've seen lots of 'em up here. They have a far-away look, and long hair, and talk about their art. What they need is a swift one in the snout… H'm. Writer, b'Gad! Play rugger, don't you?"

"Baseball," I said. "I'm an American."

"You do? Well, hang me!—And look here, laddie, don't you think because I'm a bloody Britisher I don't know the outfield from home plate. Listen. I saw the whole World Series in '09, the year Wild Bill pitched against the Pirates. I was a young un, then," she added, reflectively, "and good-looking. Never think it, would you? Had 'em all running after me. Now I can't even get anybody to play poker… Have a bottle of stout?"

She fished one up from behind her chair, along with a second glass. She opened the bottle and poured out the creaming brown stout.

"Always good for young men," she explained, winking. "Hey? There's a lot of funny business going on in this place—love-making and the like." She grew philosophical. "But I like to see the young folks have a good time. Old, meself."

I murmured something about the charm of the prime of life. She bent on me ferocious scowling brows, and the glasses made her grey eyes terrifying in size. Then she wagged a portentous forefinger.

"Now you just be quiet, laddie," she said. "Don't talk like that man Levasseur. Tell the truth and shame the devil, and also drink that stout. H'm." Holding up her glass, she frowned at it. "Let me give you a piece of advice. Whatever else you learn, learn how to grow old. Look at me. I'm quite content playing poker and chess, and working those Goddamned cross-word puzzles in the *Times*. And that, mind you, in spite of the fact I was a beauty in my day. If you don't believe it, I'll show you photographs... But Myron never could learn how to grow old. That was his trouble. He went on imagining he was going to be Monsieur Beaucaire till he died. And so he wasn't fit to live with."

"I hope you won't think I'm being nosey," I said, "but—you didn't care much for him, did you?"

"O Lord, no! Why be a hypocrite, laddie? And listen. There's something I'm going to tell you. I've always suspected... You know about this man Maleger, who owned Castle Skull?"

"Yes."

"That was seventeen years ago," she said, "and I've never stopped having the idea—well, anyway, the half-idea—that Myron was mixed up in his death, somehow. Oh, it didn't matter. I could get on with Myron well enough... But he would never tell me how he met Maleger. It was out in the Kimberley diamond-fields, you know. Some trouble..."

"Your brother was in Africa?"

"Rather. Didn't you know? We come from Australia, though Myron never admitted it. He'd had no education; I admit he concealed *that* beautifully. And no money. He beat his way across most of the world before he got to London. Fell into acting quite by chance… But about Maleger. Maybe I'm just a bit cracked. No chance for anything except accident or suicide—that's the devilish part! Nobody else near the man."

The old puzzle! Everywhere we turned somebody mentioned it, and the smoke of ancient scandal curled out of boxes long laid away. Dead Maleger lived in every mind, an aggressive, haunting face, framed in plumes of red hair. We could talk to nobody but that a finger wrote a word in the dust, and the word was "murder."

At that moment, for some reason I found my hand shaking, and I had to put down my glass. It was as though a fist were hammering at some gate in my brain; it was as though, inexplicably, heavy doors were to swing open on a revelation. No—it was the damned violin. It rose in a wail, in a weird and human cry as of its own volition. I thought of a lighthouse and the rising sea, and the storm smashed on our windows once again. But amid the turmoil I knew that the chaos of impressions lay behind a sound downstairs. There had been a muffled bang—the front door flung open. Heavy footfalls ran upstairs. Agatha Alison stared at me curiously as I jumped up. I muttered an apology and hurried to the door…

A beefy man in a streaming raincoat stood at the head of the stairs. He was glaring from under his sodden hat-brim. And, as I watched, Bencolin walked from the main left-wing passage into the main hall. The newcomer pointed his finger and snapped out some quick sentences in German. Bencolin returned his gaze steadily, but he did not speak. I did not catch what the man in the raincoat was saying, yet I knew that this was Magistrate Konrad. He was motioning Bencolin downstairs with an imperious finger. From below sounded a querulous voice, "I say, what's the row?"

The newcomer's baleful gaze turned to me; his big moustache bristled. I heard, "Go downstairs, do you hear?" I remember thinking, as I followed Bencolin, that the open front door was causing a terrific draught in the hall. Dunstan's curious face was craned out of the dining-room…

Konrad strode into the library, where he whipped off his hat in a shower of raindrops and poked forward a red, truculent face. Bencolin followed leisurely. I saw Hoffmann hurrying to close the open door, and Dunstan coming at a run from the dining-room, a glass in his hand. The magistrate had not stopped talking. He beat his chest.

"From Paris… interfering… the law"—words flashed out of the tirade. Then with a triumphant look he leant across the table and snapped a single sentence into the detective's face.

Dunstan said, abruptly, "He—he's found the watchman's body."

"And I," said Bencolin, "have found the gun."

From his pocket he took a heavy Mauser pistol, which he threw on the table with a crash. That sound seemed almost to have an echo. The laugh of the distant violin followed its noise, the mirth of a thin Stradivarius holding its lean sides, and floated away into the roaring storm. Konrad reached slowly out to touch the pistol, as though he feared it. From the tail of my eye I saw Hoffmann slide through the folding-doors, and his kewpie face puffed, beaming with the knowledge of great tidings. He drew himself up. He announced in a loud, sudden voice:

"Herr Baron Sigmund von Arnheim!"

VII

I T WAS ONLY AFTERWARDS THAT I REALIZED HOW MY HEART HAD jumped at the crazy unstaged melodrama of that moment. It was Hoffmann's voice which did the trick. He was unaccustomed to announcing people in this free-and-easy house; but his eye had caught drama, German fashion, and he thundered. I stood staring at his flushed face, with the small button-nose held up ridiculously, and the triumphant upward gleam of his eyes…

"Thank you," said an amused voice.

Soft dark hat in his hand, the newcomer lounged in. He wore a shining black water-proof, which he threw back over his shoulder as he entered. A little man, Baron von Arnheim, very straight and wiry, with a mincing step and a cropped skull. His face was pale and impassive, and sharp lines from his nose made a triangle with his level mouth. The eyes were of a chill greenish hue, with blond brows forever raised; they moved quickly over all of us. Around them ran the jags of sabre-cuts. As he saw Bencolin, he smiled suddenly, bowed, and clicked his heels together.

"It is a pleasure to see you here, my old friend," he said in French. "Has that swine been making trouble for you?"

His nod indicated Konrad, and the greenish eyes became somewhat unnerving to watch. They struck the magistrate with the suddenness of rifle-shots. Into one of them he screwed a monocle. He took a few steps forward, with a stiff-legged grace which suggested the goose step. I noticed that across his high forehead ran just an edge of blond hair.

"Get out of here," he said, jerking his hand. "Wait in the hall. March."

As Konrad, who had said nothing, went past us towards the door, Bencolin made an almost imperceptible nod to Dunstan. The young man's lips framed, "Righto!" and he slid out discreetly.

Von Arnheim advanced to the Frenchman with hand outstretched.

"I deeply regret, old friend, the bad manners of my underlings," he said, deprecatingly. "Rest assured I will have him out of office. Pah! It is disgusting…"

"He suffers from too much energy," Bencolin answered. "But please leave him in his position. It is to Magistrate Konrad that I owe the honour of this meeting with you. Naturally I am grateful to him."

The whole strained business was so studiously and uncomfortably polite that I fidgeted. I preferred the roaring conversation of the Duchess. When Bencolin presented me, von Arnheim clicked his heels together again before we shook hands, and ducked his edge of hair with a mechanical precision which made me fancy I had put a penny in a slot.

"I am doubly glad to meet any associate of my friend Bencolin," he assured me. "And now shall we sit down? You have just arrived? Good. I shall be happy if you discuss the whole affair with me…"

He threw his water-proof over a chair, revealing a tight-waisted dinner jacket beneath. From his pocket he took a crested case.

"A cigarette?" he suggested. "They are German and, I am sorry to say, intolerably mild. Our tax on foreign tobaccos is prohibitive. They manage these things better in France."

I felt an impulse to say, "For God's sake get this over with!" But both of them were so obviously enjoying themselves that it seemed like breaking in on the whole-hearted game of some children. For the first time since I had known Bencolin, I felt towards him rather like a schoolmaster. Von Arnheim sat down luxuriously and smoked. Bencolin, inscrutable, took a chair just opposite. They blew rings. I wondered who was It.

Von Arnheim broke the pause. "I arrived in Coblenz this evening," he stated. "Konrad gave me an account of the case. I had decided to remain at my hotel, in consideration of the storm. But Konrad, I noticed, effaced himself. I think he was desperately trying to steal a march on me with a last look at the castle before I took charge. Lest he should indulge in more bungling, I came up here..."

"You had not, of course, heard of my arrival?" said Bencolin.

Von Arnheim waved his hand. "It was a delightful surprise," he answered, pleasantly. They smoked during another silence.

"Konrad informed us, just before your arrival, that he had discovered the body of the watchman," Bencolin asserted, with carelessness.

Von Arnheim's narrow eyes opened ever so slightly. He took the monocle out of his eye. "Ah! Is it possible? Yes, perhaps. But they searched before, he told me... We will bring him in."

Konrad was summoned. He stood just inside the door, shifting. His pale eye fixed itself on a corner of the chandelier.

"One moment," interposed Bencolin. "Does he speak English or French? My friend here..."

"He speaks very good French," the German assured us. "He learned it in—a prison-camp, I think. Good. We will continue." A cold eye fixed itself on Konrad. The corners of his mouth were pulled down, so that the triangle grew distorted. "Speak up, then. Tell us what you discovered. Be brief."

Von Arnheim's words crackled round the red ears of the magistrate. To be addressed in French, and to reply in that language, almost choked him. The good baron looked contemptuously at his cigarette.

"Yes—yes, monsieur the—the baron. Of course. Immediately," said Konrad. "There is not much to tell. I have the keys to the castle, as you know. This evening I thought I would go up for another look round—"

"You told me, I think, that you and your men had searched it thoroughly?"

"So we had, monsieur, of course. But it is such a big place—!"

"Ah!" Von Arnheim said, gently. "You overlooked it the first time?"

"But that's the trouble, monsieur; we didn't! I mean, the place where we found it had been searched before! That is what puzzles me. I remember distinctly going over that room. There was nothing in it. But tonight, when I flashed my light in, I saw the body of old Bauer hanging in chains on the wall. Somebody had put it there since…"

"By God!" the baron breathed, very softly. "You are not lying?"

"I swear it! Two policemen who searched it with me the first time will tell you, monsieur."

"How long had he been dead?"

"That I do not know, monsieur. I was coming over here to use the telephone for the police surgeon… Many days, I think. It is not pretty, that body."

"And how did he die?"

"Bullet wounds, I think, monsieur. In the head." From humility, Konrad was passing to eagerness. He kneaded his hat. The sweat stood out on his red face. "If this discovery will restore monsieur's favour…"

"Be quiet, you fool. Where is the room?"

"In one of the towers, monsieur; with monsieur's permission, I will show him. But I take my oath that when we first looked it was not—"

"Go and phone the police surgeon. Then come back here."

Von Arnheim glanced at his watch. "If that Konrad is merely covering up his own inefficiency by claiming he just now discovered the body—well, we shall see!" He smiled in his tight-lipped fashion.

"Would it incommode you, messieurs, to take a run over to Castle Skull? It is late, but that need not bother us. It did not bother us in the old days, eh, M. Bencolin?"

"Not in the least," murmured the Frenchman. "But wait. You have, I understand, the physician's report on the body of Alison?"

"Yes. He was shot three times: once in the groin and twice through the left lung. They were soft-nosed bullets, fired from a Mauser three-twenty-five."

Bencolin nodded, inspecting his finger tips.

"His wounds were, of course, fatal, without the fire?"

"They would shortly have been fatal, yes. Actually, it was the fire which killed him. He had inhaled the flames."

"Ah yes. And this kerosene which was poured over him—from where did it come?"

Von Arnheim drew a notebook from his pocket and riffled the pages.

"It is presumed to have come from a supply belonging to the watchman," he answered. "The watchman's rooms were lighted with kerosene lamps. But no container for it has been found."

Ever since that announcement of Konrad, they had dropped that grotesque politeness. Their voices were hard and professional. Bencolin was watching his adversary, and he leaned forward intently now.

"Tell me, my friend. You have already the foundation of a theory, have you not?"

Again von Arnheim smiled, in a way that bunched up his mouth. "I have a glimmering, I think," he answered, shrugging.

"Yes. And since you have evidently no desire to question members of this household, I fancy I can tell you what it is... Now, my dear fellow, go to the table and look at the pistol lying on it, and you will have your theory blown in a million pieces. It is the Mauser with which

Alison and the watchman Bauer were murdered. I found it upstairs in the pocket of an old coat hanging in Alison's wardrobe."

A pause. Von Arnheim's face was still impassive, and his greenish eyes did not wink as he stood motionless, the monocle in his hand. But the faintest tinge of colour had come into his cheek…

"You fancied," Bencolin went on, dreamily, "that the murderer was the magician Maleger. You believed that he was not really dead. You believed that he had arranged a fake 'death'; that he leapt unhurt from his train, and later threw into the river some medical-school corpse, or some body from a rifled grave, with his watch and rings attached.

"And at first glance it is a tenable hypothesis, which does credit to the well-known acumen of the Baron von Arnheim. Before I left Paris, I used the services of our files. Maleger, Alison, and D'Aunay were together in the Kimberley diamond-fields, where Maleger made his fortune. I lack details—with which I presume you are supplied—but shall we say that in some fashion Maleger defrauded them? Shall we say that years afterwards they obtained proof and were about to prosecute and wreck him? Then the trumped-up 'death,' in which Maleger disappears with vast quantities of cash still in his possession…" Drowsily Bencolin waved his hand. "Ah no. It won't do, I assure you. My friend the Baron von Arnheim will himself see that it is untenable, without objections from me."

Von Arnheim crushed out his cigarette in an ashtray.

"My theory," he said, thoughtfully, "has not yet taken definite form. We must not speculate now. This pistol—to whom does it belong?"

"To Alison himself. His initials are carved on the grip."

"You took care of fingerprints?"

"My dear baron!"

Von Arnheim threw back his head and uttered a queer chuckle of laughter, which seemed to consist of upheavals through his throat ending in a gurgle behind closed teeth. He beamed. He nipped the glass into his eye and said:

"My joke, my joke! Now let us see."

Picking up the pistol gingerly by muzzle and grip, he examined it through his eyeglass. "*Ach* yes. Newly cleaned and oiled—within the last two weeks. Unskilled job, though. Bits of tobacco adhering to the muzzle and trigger-guard; that would be the pocket of the coat. A deep pocket. What's this? The pistol hasn't been used in many months before the killings, I fancy. It lay in a drawer—eh?"

"In the drawer of Alison's bureau, Hoffmann tells me," nodded Bencolin. "It was never disturbed."

"Yes. The oil overlies much dust, and there is a distinct smell of camphor. My monocle," said von Arnheim, "is actually a strong lens. Well, whoever used it wore gloves. These smudges are apparent. With a stronger glass I could tell the type of gloves; fabrics, my friend, have marks as distinct as fingers." He drew out the clip. "Five shots fired; that tallies. Soft-nosed bullets; so does that."

With the clip out, he pulled the trigger several times. The mechanism appeared to be stiff. "So! Whoever fired that pistol was particularly strong in the fingers—"

"But was not a very tall person," mused Bencolin.

"*Ach*, you saw that? Yes. The glove-smudge on the trigger itself extends only halfway across. The person who fired it could reach no farther. Inference: a small hand, but terrific strength in the fingers. Try firing a stiff pistol with finger only halfway across the trigger. Who fits?"

"Too many people," said Bencolin, shrugging. "You know the characters in this little affair?"

Von Arnheim tapped his forehead. "Their testimony is here. I have not met them, no. Can we start for the castle at once?"

"If they will lend us the motor-boat. By the expression of your eyes, my dear baron, I perceive that they will... However, I suggest that first you go up and pay your respects to Miss Alison. The household is unusual, but—"

"My friend Bencolin's courtesy is never-failing. I will."

"And I might suggest the advisability of your asking Miss Alison's permission to spend the night here. There is, I am sure, one person you will want to keep an eye on..."

Von Arnheim's pale blond eyebrows rose in interrogation.

"Namely, myself," said the Frenchman. "In fact, my friend, I rather expected you here this evening. To such an extent did I credit this premonition that I asked Hoffmann to move my own luggage to the room formerly occupied by Alison, so that you might sleep in my room. I must insist on your being comfortable."

Again the dry chuckle convulsed von Arnheim. He rubbed his hands together. His shrewd, pale, ugly face wore a stiff mask of delight. He said: "I perceive that my friend's brain has lost none of its cunning. And I fancy there is something of singular interest in those rooms of the late Mr. Alison, eh?"

"You see that I am being fair. There is. You will find it, of course."

"Yes, you are fair," agreed the German, nodding slowly. "In the past, I recall, you did your best to mislead me; but you were fair. I shall remember it in this instance... Now for Miss Alison. Will you see to the motor-boat? We shall need lights, too, I imagine..."

With a short bow he left us, and we heard him talking with Hoffmann in the hall. Bencolin grinned; the air of laziness left him.

"A stimulating fellow, von Arnheim," he mused. "I have felt a positive affection for him ever since we exchanged revolver-shots during a little informal gunplay in Constantinople. I regret, of course, the instance on which cyanide was dropped in my brandy during dinner with one of his secret agents; but I feel sure the good baron had ordered nothing more than knockout drops. This error I pointed out to him, in a polite note, and he promised to censure his careless operative most severely. But this would be difficult, he explained, because—doubtless due to some similar oversight of mine—his agent was no longer on the payroll... You had better get your raincoat, Jeff. It will be a wet trip."

VIII

THE BODY IN THE TOWER

B RIGHT RAIN-NEEDLES FLEW IN GUSTS ACROSS THE BEAM OF THE searchlight. That white light rocked unsteadily on a foaming Rhine, a muddy torrent whose writhings made our launch stagger in midstream. Through the motor's roar you could hear the deep, sullen rushing, the crashes, the splashes, and plungings of the headlong river; and you could hear the hollow *whoom* of the wind tearing at the tarpaulin over our heads. That tarpaulin thrummed and rattled on its posts, and the sharp rain stung into my eyes from a blackness which was everywhere save in the path of the searchlight. Under my feet the deck was bobbing until I had to kneel and hold to the side of the boat. Dim figures were about me, sheathed in water-proofs. The flying launch seemed to skip, its prow clearing the water; then it heeled and plunged with an impact which flung a ghostly mane of water up past the reeling searchlight. My knees were trembling with the motion; I was gasping and half-blinded…

It took some manœuvring for Fritz to run the boat in beside the little pier below Castle Skull. After it had been secured by ropes and chains, it floundered wildly in the current while we scrambled out. Fritz was carrying a big bull's-eye lantern, which he moved about to see that we were all present, and the rest of us had flashlights. Fritz led the way, with Konrad following; von Arnheim was next; I was after him, and Bencolin brought up the rear. The ray of the bull's-eye, smeared with rain, swung across a wooden dock, and moved to a stone-flagged path ascending the slope among dwarfed shrubs. At first glance it seemed almost too steep to climb. The rain had already carried down deposits of gritty black soil and churned mud which made the path slippery underfoot; in a rattle of small stones, a bowlder came bouncing down the slope, struck the dock with a thud, and disappeared into the water. All above us shouted a wild creaking and straining of trees...

Our four hand-lamps drew weird designs of light. We plodded, catching at shrubs on the open height; it was hard going, and you could see only with difficulty against the rain. Now the gusts came screeching full at us, driving the breath from my lungs. Von Arnheim was nearly tumbled off his feet, so that I had a vision of us all knocked down the slope in a cataract of stones. I could hear Bencolin's panting breath behind his flashlight, and I could hear the rush of the Rhine far below. Up and up! So many times we turned and twisted that all sense of direction was lost. The shrubs merged into thick dark trees, where our ghost-lamps danced. A torn branch slithered past my head, and Bencolin's hand whirled it over his shoulder down the path.

Winded and none too steady, we emerged at the top. Fritz's light disclosed that we were at the stone parapet of a moat, from whose depths issued a hissing of water. A stone causeway led across to the tall gates. Throwing my own light upwards, I saw the dark walls soar into gloom.

"You have the keys?" von Arnheim was yelling.

We stood before gigantic wooden doors, bound with arabesques of rusty iron. Konrad, in the brightness of four lamps, was unlocking them. It took a heave of his big shoulder to push them inward. Once inside and the gates slammed shut, Konrad staggered against the wall.

We were in a wide passage of stone, cold and very damp. Here the noise outside was only a murmur. Wet of face but not at all ruffled, von Arnheim stood in the middle and directed his light about, peering from under the brim of his soft black hat. Bencolin was lighting a cigarette. He wore a shapeless tweed cap and a trench-coat; the flame of the match, as he raised his eyes, showed that he was studying the German. Fritz waited quietly at attention. There were iron link-brackets on the walls, and at our right a low door, which presumably led to the quarters occupied by the watchman. Above the gates was a shapeless, rusty apparatus, which resembled an enormous vat on wheels and pulleys.

"A quaint conceit of our ancestors," said von Arnheim, playing his light over it. His voice boomed back in startling echoes. "Thus you poured boiling lead on the heads of the impertinent. And this torch, which the butler and our guide found lying here in the passage after the murder…"

He exchanged words with Fritz, who indicated a spot about the middle of the passage. Then von Arnheim motioned Konrad to lead on. A whole rumbling train of echoes followed our footsteps; Konrad's distorted shadow rose in a vast blur and bent across the roof as he lumbered towards the back. Thirty feet farther the passage turned at right angles, and at the turn a flight of stone stairs led up to its continuation on a higher level. Von Arnheim's light indicated narrow slits at the base of the treads.

"Archers' slits," he explained. "They gave the enemy a whole belly-ful of arrows in those days. And the turn in the passage—admirable for defence. Admirable!"

Another thirty feet, and once more the passage turned back to its first course. On the last stretch it ran nearly twice the distance, so that our lights barely picked up the staircase at the end.

"Have you noticed the ceiling along the way?" von Arnheim asked me in English. "At four places they could drop a portcullis to cover retreat. The castle is as strongly fortified as any I ever saw. I wonder who needed such elaborate defences?"

"That," murmured Bencolin's voice out of the gloom, "may be our answer."

The German's head jerked back over his shoulder. Bencolin's cigarette-end winked. The thin, tall shadows, the voices in whispered echo...

We emerged at last into a courtyard paved with stone flags. It was impossible to see the surrounding walls, but Fritz led us with sure instinct to an outer staircase going up the front one near the centre. Again we fought the storm; along the battlements it was terrific, for they stood higher than any point in the countryside.

As I have indicated, the walls must have been nearly ninety feet thick. The skull of stone, as nearly as I could judge by our befogged lights, was built up entirely upon the front wall itself, in the fashion of a gigantic tower. It appeared to be rather larger than a good-sized house, and on closer inspection its resemblance to a death's head was lost. Just at the end of the beams we shot up over it. I could discern a huge triangular window which might have been mistaken for a nose, but the upper part was only a blackened dome lost in rain. The teeth resolved themselves into pointed stone arches shielding a gallery from the battlements. As we stood there huddled, clinging to the parapet and fighting for breath, the whole sky suddenly went white with lightning...

For one instant I had the terrifying sensation that I was being hurled from the battlements, and my wet skin grew hot with fear. We were balanced at an incredible height. Far below, the black pines tumbled outwards, down to a narrow river which leapt out boiling grey under the lightning. So vivid was the flash that we could see our tiny boat bobbing at the pier, and we could see on the other bank the chimneys of the Alison house, with its windows as pin-pricks of light. The sky went black. Thunder crashed in an appalling blow behind our heads. I found myself clinging to one of the arches, half sick at the stomach, and it seemed to me that all the arches quivered to the thunder-peal.

"I don't see any signs of blood," said von Arnheim's level, business-like voice. "A haemorrhage of the lung would bleed badly, too. But then the rain would wash them out."

He was standing within the arched gallery, throwing his light along the floor. He addressed Konrad, still in his exquisite French:

"Speak up! You were over the ground. Were there bloodstains? Where was Alison shot before he ran out here?"

The magistrate's teeth were chattering so much that he could hardly reply. He started to speak in German, but corrected himself after an abrupt, savage look from von Arnheim. He said:

"If you will all follow me, I will show you..."

Motioning Fritz to throw the bull's-eye ahead, he turned to the right. At the end of the gallery was a heavy wooden door, which Konrad opened with one of a big bunch of keys. Our probing lights found a high hall inside the curving head of the skull. Its walls were whitewashed, and far up in the curve was a pointed window of many-coloured glass. A staircase of rosewood, carpeted in black, followed the contour of the wall down to a black floor which reflected the lights in dazzling patches.

"Onyx," muttered von Arnheim. He made a gesture. "And well kept up. This is mad. Whitewashed walls and onyx floors! Damnation! Is the place lighted?"

"Only candles, Herr Baron," Konrad replied.

"Light them up, then!"

A sconce of carven ebony, standing as tall as a man and containing six tall candles, stood beside the newel-post. Konrad kindled the flames; their light made streams of unsteady shadow high up into the hall.

"You see, messieurs?" the magistrate said, eagerly, when he had finished. "Here at the foot of the stairs is a bloodstain. On the carpet three treads up is another—so. Now come up a little way. Here are some bloody finger-marks on the wall, where the victim tried to steady himself. Near the top of the flight there are more. We know he must have been shot about the top of the stairs, for there are no other stains. When the fire was applied, he broke from his captor and ran downstairs, staggering. I wrote it so in the notes I read you…"

Von Arnheim hurried up to look at the marks on the wall. He bent his monocle on them, a humped figure in his water-proof.

"He didn't run downstairs," said a quiet voice. "He was carried."

Bencolin was standing at my elbow, his hands thrust into the pockets of his trench-coat and a gleam of amusement in his eyes. The sodden cap contrasted weirdly with his Satanic face in the candlelight. Von Arnheim turned slowly from the wall. For a moment he looked with a blank gaze at the Frenchman; then he glared down at Konrad.

"Yes, you incredible fool," he said, crisply. "He didn't run. Did you take a glass to these marks? I thought not. They are the fingers of a right hand, and a man going down this stair would have to put his left against the wall. They point obliquely down, as you would know if you had ever looked at a fingerprint. There are scratches dug into the wall at their tips, with torn bits of finger nail in them. In short, Alison was carried over somebody's right shoulder, feet first, down the steps, and he was seizing at the wall to retard his captor's progress…"

He paused. His wiry body grew tense. The six candles on the newel-post sconce lighted the tightening muscles of his jaw and a big cold eye behind the monocle as he stared at Bencolin.

"But," he continued to the Frenchman, "how the devil did *you* know that? You haven't looked at these marks!"

Bencolin shrugged. "We came over here, I think," he said, "to see the body of the watchman. And you know the rules we have maintained, my friend. Until we are ready to divulge everything, we never tell."

"Lead on, Konrad," von Arnheim said, grimly. As we were going up the stairs after the magistrate, von Arnheim addressed him again. "Proving that he was not set afire until the murderer had reached the foot of the stairs. He would not, of course, have carried down a man in flames."

Bencolin had nodded. He paused to inspect the finger-marks on the wall, holding his flashlight close; and I looked over his shoulder. It seemed to me that they were piling it a bit thick on poor Konrad. To the naked eye (or to my naked eye, anyhow) the finger-marks were mere bloody smears, such as a man might reasonably make in balancing himself there. They were fairly high up, too; and that they were upside down would have been plain only to one who knew the loops and whorls of fingerprints. Bencolin glanced at me over his shoulder, smiling in a curious way.

"Remember that, Jeff," he said. "Keep a picture of those in your mind."

I hoped that, presently, Konrad would do something right. He was waiting at the head of the stairs, his moustache drooping, and I think he will remember this night to his dying day. We were in a long gallery with a fantastically carved balustrade of rosewood; the side stretching to our left was lost in shadows, but at the right—just at the stairhead—was another door. The big hall was very quiet. The stone sides and roof dimmed the storm to a mere whisper; we were not even halfway up the great height of the stone head.

"On the left, Herr Baron," Konrad said, very humbly, "the gallery goes to some rooms formerly occupied by Herr Maleger, and furnished. Another staircase goes up, for there are two floors above this one. The door on the right, however, is the one we want. It leads to one of the towers at the side of the skull, and there is the watchman's body. I—"

He broke off to look down at Bencolin, who was standing on the stair before the window of dark and coloured glass, staring at it curiously. But at von Arnheim's summons Bencolin joined us, and Konrad opened the right-hand door... Good God! Here were more stairs! I despaired ever of seeing an end to them.

This round tower was built out from the side of the head. It was about twenty feet in diameter, one very lofty room for this floor. Our lights gave us only a glimpse of the Savonnerie carpets, of the silver fire-screen, and of those *haut-lisse* Gobelins which were woven, one yard a year, to glorify Louis Quatorze. Walnut panelling had been superimposed on the stone, as I saw when we mounted the staircase... The floor above it was bare, with stone walls and archers' slits, in sharp contrast. On the third and last, Fritz, going ahead, let out a cry.

The top had been divided into two parts. We stood on a narrow landing. Before us was a stone wall, pierced by an arched doorway. The door had been thrown back, and, as the rays of Fritz's lamp fell inside, a cold sickness of horror crawled up to my throat... The watchman's body...

At first you saw the top of a man's head, lowered as though he were about to run forward like a bull, and you saw the dirty greyish hair hanging towards the floor. Then you realized that the man was suspended against the wall. Rusty chains had been wound about him, hooked under his armpits, and then fastened to iron staples in the wall on either side. His bony arms, with large-knuckled hands, hung far out of his coat-sleeves. To give details is not necessary, because they were not pretty. He must have been hanging there for nearly a week. There was an odour, too.

The ray of the bull's-eye wavered, because Fritz could not control the shaking of his hand. He blurted out some words as though his mouth were full of pebbles, and I saw his white face as he pushed past me, thrust the lantern into von Arnheim's free hand, and clattered down the stairs.

"Well?" rasped von Arnheim from behind me. "Don't block the landing. Go on in, man!"

I said: "Sorry. I hope I've got a strong stomach, but I can't look at the damned thing. I'll wait here."

Von Arnheim nodded curtly. He motioned to Bencolin, who stepped past me, and together they entered the tower room. I heard, distantly, the wild booming of the wind, and I gritted my teeth to hold the flashlight steady, so that I should not betray the knocking that pounded horribly in my chest. Von Arnheim was silhouetted momentarily on a white glow as he moved to close the door. When he had closed it, I saw beneath its crack the flashes of their moving lights. I heard the scrape of their quick footfalls—the creak of a chain—a thud—and the murmur of their low, impersonal voices.

IX

THE WINDOW OF THE MANY-COLOURED GLASS

ONE OF MY MOST VIVID RECOLLECTIONS IN THE WHOLE CASE is that time when I saw nothing at all; when I waited in the dank tower before a closed door. My heightened fancy could colour each detail. First there was a very long silence. Then I heard Bencolin's voice:

"Shot twice through the forehead. Dead—say eight days."

There was a grunt as of some one getting up from his knees.

"But clearly not here in this room. You see the marks of his heels here in the dust where he was dragged across the floor?" said von Arnheim. "Damnation! Look! These chains have manacles on them!—Manacles! And oiled, in perfect order. The murderer did his job up right. It was fortunate he left the key in the lock. Well…"

Another silence, and the noise of footsteps wandering about the room.

"No furniture," continued von Arnheim, "and no windows. I wonder what the room was ever used for?"

"They tell me it was Maleger's workroom. It was here he perfected his illusions, and he wanted no spying eyes even in his own house. Have you seen the door?"

Another pause. "Tut! A sliding panel in it. It resembles," muttered the German, "the door of what they call in America a—a speakeasy. He could see anybody who came up the staircase without opening the door an inch. Heavy lock on the door, too; but here's the key…"

"Oh yes. The murderer wanted us to find this."

"Workroom, eh?... Nothing here now. Wait! Turn your light over there!"

"What do you see?" Bencolin asked.

More quick footfalls, and a faint rustling; then the sound of some one slapping his knees as though to free them from dust.

"Newspapers," said von Arnheim; "a whole pile of old newspapers. In English. Here's the London *Times*, October 25, 1913, and... I'll take care of these. Well, I think that's all. We had better let the police surgeon fill out his record before we continue."

The door opened. Von Arnheim took the huge key and locked it on the outside. His misshapen shadow shot up over the roof as Bencolin held the light behind him. Under his arm he carried a dusty pile of yellowed and discoloured newspapers. His tight smile turned towards me.

"Evidently, M. Marle," he said, "you do not appreciate the beauties of—?" He waved a hand delicately. "Where is our good friend Konrad? Hello! I see lights downstairs."

When we had descended two flights to the room of walnut panels, we found it glittering with candles. Konrad had kindled every taper in the massive silver brackets around the walls, and the lights were doubled by their reflections in fragile mirrors behind them. Above them stretched the tapestries, blue-green scenes of the riding hunt. Konrad himself sat glumly in a chair beside the marble table, but he sprang to attention when von Arnheim entered. Von Arnheim put his newspapers on the table.

"What amazes me," he commented, screwing in his monocle, "is the singular industry of our dead watchman, Bauer. This room, the hall—every occupied part of the house, for all I know—everything is swept and garnished. Look!" He ran his finger along the table. "Not even any dust. The silver is kept polished. Why, the place is ready for a tenant at any time. What do you make of it?"

Bencolin was regarding a window high up in the outer side of the tower; that is to say, on the side opposite the door entering from the main hall.

"I am more interested," he told us, meditatively, "in the direction of the wind."

"The direction of the wind?"

"Yes. Hear how it beats and drives on that window! In the sound of the rain on windows, Baron, I find a tremendous suggestiveness."

Von Arnheim beat his knuckles thoughtfully against the pile of papers.

"I know you too well," he replied, "to think you are wasting words. Well?"

Bencolin turned. His narrowed eyes wandered slowly about the room. They paused on the door to the hall, which was, as I have indicated, at the corner of the room.

"You recall," he continued, "that when we were coming up that curved staircase in the hall, I stopped to examine that window of dark-coloured glass?"

"Yes. And why did it interest you?"

"Because," Bencolin said, gently, "though the window faced the storm, I heard against it no sound of rain."

Von Arnheim sucked in his breath. And with a sudden shock I remembered what I have mentioned before, and what struck me before as queer and sinister, though I could not explain it. I remembered the silence of that hallway, where one could hear only the whisper of the storm against stone. Slowly von Arnheim took off his hat. He ducked his edge of blond hair.

"First blood, monsieur," said von Arnheim, snapping out the

words. "I am a fool. O my God, but I am a fool! Of course our magician Maleger would have had the place honeycombed. A passage
between the walls…"

Bencolin went over to the wall which stood at right angles to the
door into the hall. He raised the tapestry hanging there, disclosing
the walnut panelling. He had only to push the nearest panel and it
swung open.

"It follows, you see, the curve of the skull downwards," said
Bencolin. "But it took the storm to tell us that. Get your lights, messieurs, and we will investigate."

"Remain here, Konrad," von Arnheim instructed. "The policemen
from Coblenz will arrive at any minute. Take them upstairs."

We took our flashlights and followed Bencolin through the opening in the wall. It was a narrow, enclosed stair curving down between
stone walls, damp and musty.

"The head of the skull is double along this side," said Bencolin,
"and of course it far antedates Maleger's time." He knocked against
the wall on the left. "This is the real outer wall. You see? There is a
corresponding window of opaque glass just opposite the dummy one
we saw on the staircase. Nobody could look through it."

"And of course it explains why we found no bloodstains past the
top of the stair," nodded the German. "Look sharp! There's one on
these steps—get your light on it. See? Alison must have been carried
up here before he was taken down the other one. And if we trace this
passage, we shall find where Alison was really shot…"

His voice was muffled and hollow as we descended the curve,
picking our path carefully to avoid treading on possible bloodstains.
You breathed with difficulty in the cramped place. I had a feeling that
this whole wild case was nothing but a nightmare of stairs. Dear God!
why should we jump all over Konrad? The place was a rabbit-warren.

A dozen men might hide out of sight of a searching-party. The body of the watchman might have lain here for days before some ghoulish whim of the murderer prompted him to carry it up and hang it in chains from the tower wall.

The stair ended at last, in a closed wooden door. Bencolin opened it, poking his light cautiously ahead. At first we could see only frowsy coats and a tangle of pails, brooms, and mops.

"It's the back of a closet," the detective explained. "The outer closet door is here, and it's locked. Wait."

He put the lamp in his pocket, poised himself, and crashed his shoulder against that locked door. Another lunge, and the lock splintered; the door flapped back against the wall with a crash, and rebounded. Tripping over pails, we emerged. There was a heavy smell of dirty rags and furniture polish. Something clanked under von Arnheim's foot; it rolled out before us, and Bencolin's questing light picked up a two-gallon can whose spout was splattering some white liquid on the floor.

"There's the kerosene-can," he observed. "These are the watch-man's quarters, I suppose. We are right back beside the entrance passage to the castle."

It was a grimy and ill-smelling room with a low ceiling. An iron bed was in the corner, covered by a patchwork quilt. As the beam swept about, I saw a wood-stove with a coffee-pot balanced on the edge, a stack of used dishes in a wash-tub, and a pair of overalls hung on a peg. On one sweating wall was pasted a photograph torn from a magazine—a big coloured picture of Myron Alison as Romeo. The face was begrimed.

"Somebody," said von Arnheim, "has recently scrubbed the floor."

Bencolin was opening the low door on our right. "Watchman's rooms, all right," he said. "Here is the passage by which we entered the castle." The Frenchman walked slowly back to the middle of the room, glancing at his watch. "Well, my friend!" he continued. "It seems to me that we have made enough discoveries for one evening. And even I grow tired. It is nearly one o'clock. Shall we let Konrad take charge now, and return? The thing is merely a matter of routine."

"Return *now*?" asked von Arnheim. "Why, we have only begun to explore! All of the rooms..." He broke off. Both of them had directed their lamps at the floor, so that I could see only two dim shapes. "I sometimes wish," he went on, musingly, "that my friend Bencolin would do something in this world without a reason behind it. I wish he would play a joke, for no reason except that it was a joke. I wish he would go to a theatre, for no reason except that he wanted to see the play. I wish he would have a whim behind which there was no devilish cause... And there is a reason behind this wish to return, I think."

Bencolin's soft chuckle echoed in the low room. "There is. I invite you to return, you know."

"We each have our theory," said von Arnheim. "I know they are different. And I will not use another man's brains... My investigations are here, and so I will stay. Go, by all means. But I tell you"—he swung his light up into the Frenchman's face—"I will beat you yet! Yes. You are taking the wrong course, and remember that I have warned you."

"It is like the old days!" cried Bencolin. "Come, your hand on it, Baron... Now, Jeff, if Fritz will drive us across, I have some matters to discuss with you on the way."

"But wait," said von Arnheim, laying a hand on his arm. "Let us see whether we are agreed on anything."

A kerosene lamp with a cracked glass shade stood on a deal table in the middle of the room. Von Arnheim lifted the shade and kindled the wick, so that a feeble yellow light illumined the room. He sat down in a wooden chair, opening his notebook and spreading out the pages.

"The course of events, then. I have notes of all the testimony you yourself have heard...

"We deal, then, with Monday, May 20, 1930. On this evening Myron Alison was last seen alive by Miss Sally Reine, when he went to his room about nine o'clock. Some time afterwards—let us say nine-thirty or nine forty-five—Miss Reine heard two people leaving the house. These two are Myron Alison and his murderer, since all the others (one of whom obviously lied) are occupied in other ways. These two take the motor-boat, whose noise is heard on the river at that time. About ten-fifteen, the body runs out on the battlements in flames." Very deliberately von Arnheim drew out his cigarette-case, extracted a cigarette, and lighted it. He went on:

"By the things we have seen here at the castle tonight, we can reconstruct what happened in this interval of from half an hour to forty-five minutes. We assume that in some manner the murderer prevailed upon Alison to accompany him to the castle. Since Alison had gone to his rooms previously, we also infer that the murderer visited him there. While there, one of them took the pistol in the drawer of Alison's bedroom. Which one is not important, since, if Alison had no suspicions of his companion, he might readily have let him carry it. The murderer might readily have expressed a fear of burglars in the castle at night, and so have obtained permission to take along the Mauser."

Von Arnheim smoked in silence for a moment. Bencolin was leaning against the wall, his arms folded and his eyes half shut.

"So," proceeded the German, "Alison drives the boat across. The two go up, and are admitted by the watchman. They come in here. Whether there was an argument, or whether it was deliberately planned, we do not know; but we may safely say that the murderer came here with the intention of killing Alison. He shot him here. To carry out his plan, the watchman also had to die.

"The watchman's body was flung into the secret staircase. Alison lay dying of wounds in the lung. Taking that can of kerosene from the closet, the murderer saturated Alison's clothes with kerosene. Then he took a mop or rag and carefully scrubbed the blood from the floor in here—lest, by finding the blood, the police search here too thoroughly and find the secret stair..."

"One moment," interrupted Bencolin. "Why should the murderer be so anxious to hide the secret stair?"

"Why should he have carried Alison upstairs?" countered the German, shrugging. "I do not know; it is a part of the motivation we cannot yet explain. But by those bloodstains we know he *did* carry Alison up. He took him out, and down the other stair in the main hall. He pushed him out on the gallery before the battlements and set fire to his clothes. I do not know why. Somewhere there is a powerful, devilish, warped mind, working for reasons we cannot yet fathom. Alison was no light burden. Yet the murderer carried him up a tremendously long flight of stairs, went to all these infinite pains, so that he might hurl a blazing corpse out before all heaven. Rest assured, it was no mere whim... As witness the fact that later in the week the murderer comes across here, removes the watchman's body, and hangs it in the tower room... But to return to the death of Alison:

"After setting fire to the man, the murderer lingers to see that his work is neatly done. He leaves only when he sees Hoffmann and Fritz on the path below. He darts back in, up and down the secret staircase to this room—thus avoiding the two as they enter by the passage."

"Softly, softly!" the Frenchman protested. "You are forgetting that the murderer had left here before Hoffmann and Fritz reached the gates. When they were almost here, they heard the motor-boat returning."

Von Arnheim looked slightly disconcerted, but only for a moment.

"*Ach* yes! But it doesn't matter. Well, then, he ran down the secret stair, out the door in this room, and went down the slope by another path, tossing his torch in the passage as he ran. *So!*"

The German shut up his notebook; he sat back and regarded Bencolin with the utmost complacence. Bencolin opened his lazy eyes.

"Tolerably good," he said, thoughtfully. "The only trouble is that you don't believe it."

"But—don't you?"

"I follow your own amiable technique," responded the detective, "in refraining to explain my own ideas... But, whatever hypothesis one uses, he has still to explain those stubborn and extraordinary facts: first, why the body was set afire in that spectacular show, and, second, why the watchman was hung in chains some days after his death."

"I think *I* can explain them," nodded von Arnheim, examining his nails in a reflective way. "Especially when I have had a good look at those newspapers from the tower."

"And I," said Bencolin, "will follow the evidence of a pair of muddy shoes, and of a note left under a door—"

Von Arnheim sat up straight, reaching for his notebook. "I have no record of that! What note? Who left a note under a door?"

"I did," said Bencolin. "Good night, Baron, and good luck."

We went out into the shadows and echoes of the passage. Von Arnheim still sat motionless by the table, with the yellow light illumining his pale face, his duelling-scars, and his monocle. The corners of his mouth were pulled down; his hands were stretching and crisping at his notebook, unconsciously, like the claws of a cat.

"Let me make you a prediction, Jeff," said Bencolin, when the door was closed. "Whatever else the good von Arnheim is doing, he is planning something to humble me. He is planning an act more sensational than any Alison ever staged during his greatest days; I know him. To show us drama, give me your phlegmatic Teuton above all people. And I—well, I enjoy a good show, but I really cannot let him indulge in—"

I mentioned something about the pot and the kettle. I also said, "What's this about a note you left under a door?"

"Ah yes. We go to see the effect of it now. Jeff, the murderer of Alison and Bauer is across the river in Alison's house now, peacefully sleeping. And the more peacefully he sleeps, the better for my plan... Let's go and find Fritz to take us over."

We left Castle Skull to the owls and the storm, leaving unexplored all those shadowy rooms where Maleger had prowled in the heyday of his magic. We left behind the reverberating corridors, the candle-flicker on decaying finery, the archers' slits, and all those cunning devices, creaky with rust and old blood, which craftsmen in chain-mail had once fashioned to make Castle Skull hideous with the screams of its enemies. For this sense of the past was not easily to be dispelled, even by revolver-shots. The halls still smelt of oiled bowstrings and harness leather, and behind them shadows stirred in a twinkle of steel caps. When we stood with our lights in the stone passage, we were anachronisms, and the halls did not like us. We had no torches in our hands. We did not walk stiff-kneed in iron and scarlet. Across the causeway we did not guide skittish horses with a mailed wrist. We were intruders.

The tempest still flapped about the battlements on the downward journey, where Fritz's lantern illuminated the way. Once, risking a bad fall, I glanced behind me. A yellow glow streamed from the door opening on the gallery beneath the teeth of the skull, far up there in darkness. It silhouetted the battlements. Momentarily I saw von Arnheim standing there, his arms folded, looking down after us. The light gleamed on his black water-proof. We descended towards the trees' vast tossing, and the sullen, tumultuous rushing of the Rhine.

X

CERTAIN ANTICS OF A LADY

"I WANT YOU TO LISTEN CAREFULLY," SAID BENCOLIN.

We stood in the lower hall of the Alison house. One of the perforated lamps had been left burning to guide our return; tiny sieve-spots of light made a weird pattern on the ceiling, and against them Bencolin's Mephistophelian profile was bent forward. My wet shoes pressed soggily against my ankles. I felt soaked and dispirited. There remained too vivid a memory of the Rhine making an eggshell of our boat. In a low voice the detective continued:

"My luggage has been moved to Alison's rooms. You are in the second front room on the right. Miss Reine is on one side of you, and von Arnheim on the other. There is a door from your room into that of Miss Reine. When we go upstairs, we bid each other good night in loud tones. Go to your room, and after about ten minutes knock on Miss Reine's door. Keep her silent; tell her it is most important that I see her immediately. Bring her to my room—and whatever you do, don't make any noise and don't let anybody see you. Is that clear?"

"Yes. But what's the idea?"

"You will see very soon. I may be wrong; if I am, I shall have started a hornets' nest, but it's worth the risk. A certain thing that girl can tell us, if she will, may be the pivot-point of the whole case... *Parbleu!* I commence to get qualms myself. This is a dangerous trap I am laying. Nevertheless..." He was peering about him into the shadows of the hall, with the glow moving dappled spots across his face. "Let's start it."

The whole house was quiet. We went upstairs noisily, and exchanged loud good-nights in the middle of the upper hall—with remarks on the extreme complexity of the case and the need for sleep. He went clumping away round the corner of the wing; I opened my door.

A night-light was burning beside the bed, whose covers had been turned down. The contents of my valises had been neatly put away; brushes on the chest of drawers, shaving-things in the bathroom adjoining, and a suit of pyjamas laid across the bed. I changed my wet shoes and put on a dressing-gown. Then I sat down in an easy-chair to smoke a cigarette. Watching fat raindrops splatter on the windows and go crawling in blind staggers down the pane, I gave in to gloom. A bronze clock on the mantel made a nervous effort to strike one-thirty; presently it coughed, and expired on the whir, after which it continued its ticking in an embarrassed way. The pattern of the wall-paper, evidently designed by a neurotic gardener, annoyed me. I was making a capital dunce of myself in this case. In that last affair in London, the Jack Ketch murders, I had contrived to show some intelligence. But here ideas would not come. Curses jostled in my mind; moreover, drowsiness was creeping in. I got up and knocked softly at the door communicating with Sally Reine's room.

She could not have been asleep. Immediately a voice said, "Who's there?" and I heard the creaking of a chair.

"Jeff Marle," I answered; "and open the door, will you? It's important."

A bolt was withdrawn, and the door opened on darkness. The homely, attractive face, with hair a little tousled, was poked through the aperture. Her black eyes were naïve and interested. One plucked eyebrow travelled higher than the other. She whistled, making a pout of her small red mouth.

"Unprofessional conduct of a detective," she greeted me. "I *say!*"

"Oh, dry up!" I said. "This is business. Will you come in, and keep your voice down? What I mean is, I'm not…"

"It's absolutely O.K. with me," said Sally Reine, making a gesture like a walking doll. She was wearing hideous scarlet-and-black pyjamas, and had red mules on her feet. "Only you might lock the door. Can't be too careful of my reputation."

She went over to the table, perched on the edge of it, and clasped her hands about one knee. Rocking, she looked at me moodily. "I was just sitting by the window, anyway. What's on your mind?"

I told her what Bencolin had said. She tried to remain mildly interested, but you could see defiant resolve hardening in the mutinous expression which crept into her eyes. She murmured:

"Your friend has a positive genius for melodrama. And why does he want to see me?"

"I don't know."

"Don't you? Well, *I* have a dashed good notion!—I'm to get a polite form of the third degree, that's what. And that grinning devil will know just how to do it. Information extracted painlessly. It's like having a tooth drawn with a local anæsthetic. You nearly faint for fear it'll hurt; then out she comes smoothly, and you leave the office relieved; so just when you're beginning to congratulate yourself on how well you came through, the anæsthetic wears off and it begins to pain like nobody's business. That's the way I feel after I've talked to him. That Bencolin," she said, becoming elaborate, "could have crucified a certain Man we've heard about, and taken only an artistic pride in the way he drove the nails. Suppose I don't go?"

I shrugged. "That's your privilege, of course. But, look here! Don't you want this thing cleared up?"

"No. No, I do not." She drew a long breath. "All the same, I'll go, because I want to find out what he knows. He does scare me, you know. When you talk to him, he just smiles and agrees, and you begin to believe everything you've said is a lie." She inspected me with a wry sort of smile. "I wish *you* were in charge of this case, old dear. If you got me in a tight corner, I should just turn on the tears, and you'd say, 'Er— sorry!' and change the subject. You're no good as a sleuth, you know."

That stung a little, but I had to say, "Yes, I suppose that's right."

"I say, that was rotten of me," she muttered, after a pause. "I'm a bit off my feed, or something; you mustn't mind it. But my nerves are all on edge. If somebody jumped out and said 'Boo!' to me, I'd scream. Can't stand much more of this." She was brooding, wriggling her feet in the red slippers.

I said, impulsively: "Look here. If there's anything I can do... I mean, damn the detective business... If you'd just tell me..."

She put up a hand and shook me by the shoulder. Again the wry smile, and a wrinkling of the snub nose, and a sort of queer thanks glimmering in the lights of her dark eyes.

"No good telling," she answered. "Ah, what's the good of anything? I'm ready for Torquemada now."

Extinguishing the lights, we went out softly. The dim night-lamp guided us as we moved on tiptoe down the hall and round the corner of the wing. I pushed open Bencolin's door. He had closed the shutters and drawn the draperies together in the study, so that no light could show from the outside. He was standing, fully dressed, by a lamp burning on the typewriter table. When we had come in, he rolled up a small rug and laid it across the crack at the bottom of the door.

Sally Reine tried to be very lazy and amused. "I came," she greeted him, "chaperoned. I thought it was wise. But, please, why all this sneaking about in the middle of the night?"

"In order to help mademoiselle," said Bencolin, pushing out a chair for her. "Is mademoiselle always a good chaperon herself?"

"I'm not good at subtleties…"

"Presently," he told her, "I think I can explain. I asked you to come here chiefly in order to set your mind at rest. Miss Reine, you are alarming yourself unnecessarily."

He was the picture of earnestness, his hands spread out, and an expression of sympathy on his face as he bent forward in his chair. But she did not trust him. She was trying to remain very calm, and yet her hands were far from steady. There was a long silence…

"I wished to demonstrate this to you," continued the detective, "through the evidence of your own eyes."

Another pause. We were all conscious of something behind his manner—the air of expectancy and tense waiting which not even he could conceal. It was as though a slow drum were beating. She was sitting on the arm of a chair, swinging her slipper against its side, and her eyes kept darting into corners of the room. Now the rain had become a mere steady droning on wooden shutters. The black bell of her hair fluttered as she shook her head. Against the chair the slipper was swinging faster, in soft little thumps. You could hear a clock, too…

"Well, get on with it!" she said, defiantly. "I can't wait here all night."

Was there another noise? I had heard nothing; but Bencolin was cocking his head on one side. His eyes were blank and slowly he rose from his chair. He took Sally Reine by the arm and, as she gave him a startled glance, he began to lead her towards the door. She started to say something, blurting it through stiff lips; but he silenced it with a tightening of fingers on her arm. He said, softly:

"Jeff, stand over there by the lamp. When I give the word, turn it out. Miss Reine, when I open the door, have the goodness to look out into the hall."

"Let—me—go!" she said in a terrified whisper. "You must be—"

But she checked herself. I felt my heart pounding as I stood with my finger on the button of the lamp; even across the room I could see the strained expression of her eyes as she looked up at him towering over her, a frightened girl in scarlet and black, her face contorted in an ugly way. I heard her quick, short breathing. Bencolin's fingers could tear a deck of cards in two...

"Now, Jeff!"

The tense whisper barely reached me. I pressed the button of the lamp, and there was a darkness unbroken by the faintest suggestion of light. It was a heavy darkness in which you had an impulse to duck your head, lest something were rushing at you. The noise of breathing seemed to grow louder. I did not hear the door opening, but by degrees I became aware of figures silhouetted on a dim glow. They were motionless. So long they stayed that I thought it was never to end. What was going on out there? What were they watching? The questions grew and pounded like the increasing noise of the downpour...

Very slowly the figures were blotted from my view. I heard the faintest of clicks from the closing door. All about was a hollowness, an echoing silence, in which you could feel the quiver of palpable waves. It was as though a new wound had been touched with a lancet; you could feel beside you the shock and stiffening, the stifling of a gasp, and the shuddering release of breath from the lungs. These things gathered and became overpowering. The clock went on in its measured ticking. Out of the gulf breathed a small voice, hardly more than a whisper.

"You devil!" it breathed. "Oh, you devil!..."

It was trancelike, it was incredulous, it was amazed and trembling on the edge of laughter. "Why," it rambled on, "you—you planned that... Of course."

"Put on the lights, Jeff," said Bencolin.

Blinking as they were switched on, I saw Sally Reine sitting in an easy-chair. She was very pale, so that lipstick and mascara were grotesque; but she was absolutely composed. She looked straight across at a window, and even her breathing had quieted. Bencolin kicked the rug across the door-sill, after which he turned sharply.

"Miss Reine," he said, "on the night of Mr. Alison's murder a certain thing occurred which you neglected to tell us. You said that you had fallen asleep in the library at some time before ten o'clock; that, being roused by the commotion of Hoffmann and Fritz starting across the river to investigate the blazing body, you went out on the porch. There, you said, you waited for some time, but saw nobody anywhere about. I insist that just after you had gone out on that porch you saw somebody come hurrying up the steps from the river in a fine state of agitation. He begged you to keep quiet about seeing him—which you did... Are you now prepared to admit that this person was Sir Marshall Dunstan?"

She looked at him with blind eyes. She answered in a hard, steady voice,

"I won't tell you a damned thing."

The clock ticked steadily...

"Furthermore," she went on in that abstract tone, "it was the rottenest trick I've ever seen played, anywhere. What do you think Duns is to me? Do I look like one of your jealous Latins? Do you think that, even if I had lied, I'd squeal on him now?"

It was like looking into eyes that were glass, unnerving in their fixity. Her voice never wavered from that impersonal fashioning of each clear syllable. She looked at me.

"Let me tell you what I saw out there. I saw Isobel D'Aunay going into the room of *Sir* Dunstan. Well," she blazed, "and why the devil shouldn't she, then?"

"You are a young fool," said Bencolin, calmly. "I am trying to demonstrate to you the innocence of Dunstan. You saw him come running up that path to the house after the murder. You thought he had been concerned in it, and he admitted it. Well, he lied. He lied, because where he actually had been was with Madame D'Aunay. And I wanted you to see her going into his room tonight to show you what actually happened on the night of the murder. He would rather have you think him a murderer than *that*."

Bencolin was speaking in a voice as level and impersonal as her own. He seemed to turn the thing over behind weary eyes.

"Miss Reine, do you understand now the figure which was seen going up the outer staircase to D'Aunay's room? His wife was returning from her assignation with Dunstan. She came up a side path, and he by the steps from the landing-stage. They were frightened out of their wits lest they be discovered, even with D'Aunay apparently in a drug-sleep from which he could not be roused... Rest assured, you will not fare so well at Baron von Arnheim's hands as at mine. Do you want to put a halter around your own neck as well as his?"

He flung the words at her contemptuously. His bitter gesture caused a little colour to come into her pale face. She opened her mouth several times, and brushed a vague hand across her eyes.

"That cat!" she said, with sudden low venom. "That rotten little cat! Yes. Oh yes! I thought of something like... And I don't blame Duns; I don't blame *him*. She faints and clings all over the place. That's what he likes."

Her words were jerky, and she kept blinking and blinking, with an expression of terrible determination on her face. She fumbled at her throat and undid the top button of the pyjamas. Under them a platinum engagement ring hung on a cord round her neck. Drawing it out, she let the ring swing free...

"You see, we were going to announce it—when—Duns broke it—gently to the family." Her forehead was wrinkled as she looked up, and her voice very far away. Quite suddenly a new light flashed into her eyes. "But *you*—are you human? How did you know all this?"

"How I knew of the affair between those two," Bencolin answered, "I must not tell you now, because it is vitally concerned with the solution of the case. But your own fondness for the young man—forgive me—was apparent in every look and word and gesture." He smiled faintly. "Isobel D'Aunay…"

"Little rotter!"

"Charity, Miss Reine, charity! A crushed woman, but at bottom, I think, a reckless and passionate woman… H'm." For a time he looked into space. "That startles you? I don't think so. She has just begun to discover that she dares to be reckless, and the knowledge is strong liquor to her. I shall not forget that unpleasant affair tonight when D'Aunay flared out with a charge that she might poison his veronal. It shocked her so deeply that her last scruple went down the wind. The look she gave us from the doorway as she left… if I had not already known the truth, I should have known it then. The look said, 'It is finished.' The look said, 'I have a lover, and I am going to him, and you people, I do not care particularly whether you know it.' Rest assured, Miss Reine, that I knew this. I knew that the lady is not—overly intelligent. On a letter I printed: 'My room. Two o'clock. Burn this.' When I had made certain her husband had taken his veronal and was asleep, I put it under her door. So she went to Dunstan. And I verified my theory."

Sally Reine was regarding him curiously, with an expression almost of horror. "Yes," she said, in a flat voice, "you verified your theory. You *are* a devil, you know—literally. You verified your theory! O my God! And what's to happen when she discovers he didn't write the note?"

Bencolin bowed. "Precisely what I desire to happen. When I bring the whole affair up for discussion with them, they cannot possibly deny it."

"You know," the girl said, after a reflective pause, "I shall really have to go back to the nursery. I thought *I* was hard. What a simpleton! O yes, you're right. Duns did come up the path that night. And he let me believe he was concerned in the murder…"

"Ah," said Bencolin, rubbing his hands together. "At last we know."

With a spasmodic motion the girl got to her feet. She said, desperately:

"Look here—d'you mind?—I've got to go. I've got to get back to my room. I—want to curl up somewhere and die. And I've got to think this thing out. Please! I—"

She was peering about her as though she had gone blind. The soft mouth drooped, and she beat her hands together. Mercifully, I turned off the light and I was cursing Bencolin with all the vigour the occasion demanded. I saw the line of dim light expand as he opened the door, and in the dark I found Sally Reine and gripped her hand hard. Again she stood on tiptoe to shake my shoulders, and she whispered, *"Stout fella!"* Then, in a whirl of scarlet and black, she was gone…

I stood there motionless, feeling rather sick, looking with dull eyes into the empty door. With a shock of surprise I realized that the door was not empty. The dull light shone on a shaven skull with a slight rim of blond hair; it found a monocle and a tight mouth.

"So," Bencolin was saying, very softly, "my good friend the baron decided to follow me, after all. I dare say you heard it?"

Von Arnheim stood very stiff, a silhouette with back-thrown shoulders in the doorway.

"Fortunately," he responded, "I avoided the—the somewhat congested traffic in these corridors. I heard. *Ach* yes!" He was breathing heavily. "We can discuss it in the morning."

A match rasped and flared. Bencolin was lighting a cigarette. The gleam lit his sardonic, evil, amused glance. Another long silence…

"Second blood, Monsieur Bencolin," the German said, gruffly.

"Second blood, Herr von Arnheim," replied the other, bowing.

Von Arnheim's hand hesitated on the door. Still farther back went his shoulders.

"Bon soir, Monsieur Bencolin. Dormez bien."

"Guten nacht, Herr von Arnheim. Schlafen sie wohl."

With a military bow and a precise click of his heels, von Arnheim turned and walked down the hall towards his room.

XI

BEER AND SORCERY

THERE WAS BLESSED SUNSHINE AGAIN. I BREATHED DEEPLY AS I walked downstairs. The front door was open; the sunlight gleamed on the red tiles of the porch, and lay in broad shafts across the hardwood floor. Through the hall stirred a warm moist breeze, very fragrant with the smell of the ground after rain. I walked out on the porch for a moment before going in to breakfast.

The house was still sleeping in the washed and polished clearness of morning. Behind the dark dome of Castle Skull across the river, motionless white clouds were piled in a sky of very pale blue. All along the deep-green crags, at whose foot the olive-green Rhine glimmered, the trees had been new-born; they were fresh trees, grown mysteriously overnight, and wind drove the sunlight over them in great rippling waves. Birds skirmished in the vines. Far down the curve of the river I heard the dim *put-put* of a motor-boat.

It was pure exhilaration, which cleansed away the fogs and headache. A grey squirrel bounced across the porch and sat up on his haunches to eat something. He ate it with quick short motions of his tiny paws, watching me the while with a furtive and wary eye like a nervous tourist. Finally he decided he could not trust me, and scurried away. But I felt a positive affection for that squirrel. There had come to me in the night a sudden idea about this case…

I went genially back to the dining-room, whose high windows were now flooded with sun. Von Arnheim sat alone at the table, eating his breakfast and reading a newspaper. Rising to bow formally as I entered, he wished me good morning. He wore blue serge of an excellent cut, and looked almost as gay as I felt. Hoffmann brought me coffee, rolls, and jelly. I said:

"Anything interesting in the news?"

Von Arnheim looked reflectively at the newspaper. "Nothing of consequence," he answered, in his careless and perfect English. "I see that a certain Archduke Ferdinand has been assassinated at Sarajevo, but the writer of the leading editorial here in the *Times* is convinced that it is of negligible importance. This is one of my papers from last night, Mr. Marle... Heigho! And it makes a man feel old on a bright morning like this."

For a moment he sat opening and shutting his hands, looking out of the window unseeingly. He continued:

"But there is something very interesting here on an inside page. A marked story, telling of the triumph of our distinguished actor, Myron Alison, in some distinguished play I never heard of. All of the newspapers contain such items—over a period of years. Do you find that suggestive?"

I shrugged.

"Tell me, Mr. Marle: you have wisely refrained from saying anything about this case so far. What are your opinions?"

"I said nothing," I replied, "because I was entirely stumped. Until—"

He nodded. "Ah! You have an idea, then? May I ask if it coincides with the theories of our friend Bencolin?"

"You never know what Bencolin is thinking about," I said, "particularly when he tells you."

A voice from the doorway said, "Not very flattering, Jeff." Bencolin came into the dining-room, rubbing his hands together and beaming. He wore a light-coloured suit, and had a flower in his buttonhole. "Ah, good morning, Baron! Good morning, good morning, good morning!

You slept well, I trust? Excellent. 'The castled crag of Drachenfels frowns o'er the wide and winding Rhine—'"

"Your own slumbers," said von Arnheim, "were undisturbed?"

"Now that I come to think of it," Bencolin mused, frowning in a reminiscent way, "it occurs to me that I neglected to go to bed at all. But coffee and a cold shower work wonders after a night of prowling about. In my younger days, Baron, I was told that I had rather a remarkable bass voice. On such a morning I could favour you with a song. Well do I recall the time when Detectives Flynn, O'Shaughnessy, and M'Googan of the New York Homicide Squad rode down Fifth Avenue with me in a steam-calliope, which was being played by Chief Inspector Riley, and we harmonized on 'The Minstrels Sing of an English King.' When the police celebrate, my dear Baron, I assure you that no citizen is safe."

"I noticed," remarked von Arnheim, "that the police were celebrating last night."

"You refer to my little dramatic sketch with Miss Reine?"

"And others. Madame D'Aunay, Sir Marshall Dunstan—"

"Damnation! You saw everything. Well, Baron," said Bencolin, deprecatingly, "I am sorry if you were shocked, but young people will be young people, and—"

Von Arnheim set down his coffee-cup. "It was confoundedly, fiendishly clever. We shall have to put them up for questioning. But what did it prove? I never imagined that Madame D'Aunay or young Dunstan had anything to do with the murder in any case."

"That, my friend, is not the point. What I did prove was something you do not yet see, but it should be glaringly apparent to you. And it is one of the most important things in the whole case."

"Bah!" said von Arnheim, making a gesture of impatience. "A mean assignation by the river…"

"You come closer, my friend! That is the point. I told Miss Reine that those two were not concerned in the murder, to set her mind easy—but are we so sure? You say, 'an assignation by the river.' The point is, where did they go? They were coming up the steps from the landing-stage. Down there are nothing but steep banks, and they certainly didn't hold their amorous tête-à-tête clinging to the trees on the slope…"

"The motor-boat," said von Arnheim, softly.

"Precisely, the motor-boat! It was heard only *twice* on the river that night. Once when it crossed to Castle Skull between nine-thirty and nine forty-five. And once when it returned, after Hoffmann and Fritz had seen the mysterious man with the torch. It returns—and Sir Marshall Dunstan comes up the steps from the dock. Well, remember that Alison himself had to cross that river. The question is, Did Dunstan and Madame D'Aunay go with him?"

Flinging his napkin on the table, von Arnheim got up and strode to the window, where he tapped impatient finger tips on the glass. At length he turned. Bencolin was carefully buttering a roll.

"I am not pig-headed," the German asserted. "I insist that I am not pig-headed. But I tell you you are taking the wrong line. You do these flashy things—yes. But you neglect to go to the root of the matter. There is something in those newspapers which has given me a clue. If I could verify one thing, I could solve the whole case. The people here know little about Alison's stage-work. Even his sister paid small attention. To find somebody who knew him in that way I would give much…"

"I can tell you exactly the man," I said.

Then I told them of my encounter with the reporter, Brian Gallivan, on the boat the day before. Von Arnheim smote his hands together.

"'Gallivan,'" he repeated. "Yes, I recall the name. It is signed to one of those articles in the newspapers about Alison's work. And Maleger's press-agent, you say? Good! Very good! For once the stars fight on our side." He glanced at his watch. "Nine-fifteen, and the house not up yet. I must go to Coblenz and look in at the police headquarters to see what they have done about the watchman's body. Let us postpone our questioning until the others are up, and take a run in there... Can you phone this man, Mr. Marle?"

So presently I rang up the Hotel Traube. After a long interval I heard Gallivan's sleepy voice; he snapped to attention when I told him. I cautioned him, however, about sending any word to his paper. We arranged to meet in Coblenz. Bencolin and von Arnheim were waiting with their hats in the hallway when I returned. Together we descended the steps to the landing-stage, where Fritz had run the launch out from the boat-house. As we swept out into the bright river, I looked back at the walls and towers of Castle Skull for the first time in full light. It seemed that a singular radiance illumined the top of the domed head. I pointed it out to the others.

"Pardon me, sir," Fritz interposed in his excellent English. "It is glass. I am told that the very top is occupied by an enormous room with a glass roof like a conservatory. We are often troubled by small boys trying to climb up and look in. The tourists make themselves unpleasant, too."

"I should like a look at that," commented von Arnheim, shading his eyes with his hand as he looked behind. "Yes, we must certainly explore it thoroughly."

We said no more as the boat sped towards Coblenz. Many craft were out that morning. A scull, propelled by a solitary oarsman with a naked powerful torso, slid past at easy strokes. One of the Rhine steamers towered above us in gusts of black smoke, its white sides gleaming and its rail crowded with passengers, who waved and shouted to us according to the genial custom of the river. Bencolin and I were having a fine time returning the salutations, but von Arnheim sat studying his newspapers without seeming to notice. A launch full of girl hikers—those muscular thick blondes with bare legs and packs on their backs—went by on its way to Stolzenfels, the girls singing lustily. Before many minutes we turned into a straight stretch, and we could see on the right bank the grey fortress of Ehrenbreitstein piled against the bright sky. Coblenz was on the left—white houses whose windows were gay with red geraniums.

Gallivan waited for us on the dock, an eager, impatient figure in grey flannels, his Punchlike face poked out over the rail. He was obviously very much impressed; but one squinted eye took on a belligerent gleam when von Arnheim was brusque to the point of discourtesy. Von Arnheim then said he had to visit the police station, and asked us to wait somewhere.

"It's a warmish day," said Gallivan, moistening his lips. "Meaning that there's an open beer-garden at the end of the promenade, about a quarter of a mile down in the direction you came from…"

"It will do," nodded von Arnheim. "I know where you mean. I will see you there shortly."

We tramped along the cool and shaded promenade, Gallivan whistling, scuffling grey dust from his feet, and telling us how damn swell it was of us to let him in on this. In the beer-garden, tall trees arched far over tables laid with red cloths, and beyond a stone railing shimmered the Rhine. A waiter lumbered out of a kind of *châlet* as we took a table beside the balustrade.

"*Drei Pils*," said the reporter. "And take the collar off mine, will you? You know." He made a level motion in the air, and then sat back judicially. "They have a quaint habit of piling up the suds six inches for artistic effect," he explained to us. "Many's the time I've come up looking like a mad dog. Mr. Marle said you wanted to see me. That right, sir?"

"It is Baron von Arnheim who wants particularly to question you," answered Bencolin. "But I should like some information, too. You understand that nothing is to go to your paper without his permission?"

"'Fraid so. But I'll play ball."

"You were for some time press-agent for the magician Maleger, I think?"

"Three years, 'ten to 'thirteen. Up to the time he died."

"A good employer?"

Gallivan accepted a cigarette, shaking his head. "He was particular hell. And it was his tour-manager who hired me; he wouldn't have anything to do with it. Still, it was an easy job. Almost anything the old boy did was good copy."

"I see. Did you know him well?"

"Eventually, yes. He learned about my interest in the supernatural. And I swear the man had the largest library I've ever seen on subjects like that—particularly demonology and witchcraft. He'd read about some particularly horrifying piece of magic an old-time sorcerer was said to have produced; then he'd labour for months to work it out as an illusion. I swear it made your hair stand on end! Have you ever been in that Castle Skull of his?"

"In just a few of the rooms. Why?"

"Br-r-r-r!" said Gallivan. The beer had arrived, and he solaced himself with a long pull before he resumed. "What I mean, I have old-fashioned ideas of hospitality, myself. I don't think it's especially funny to turn all your guests into candidates for the loony-bin. He was a sort of ghastly Peter Pan; with all his brains, he never grew up from the soul of a kid who gives you a doughnut stuffed with cotton or squirts water in your eye from a flower in his buttonhole. He had a genius for devilish effects, and he liked particularly to work on drunks and neurotics... Maleger. *Maleger!* Yes, the name suited him, all right..."

"It wasn't his own, then?"

"O Lord, no! Have you read Spenser's 'Faerie Queene?' Maleger is the name of a ghostly presence who wears a human skull for his helmet, and whose horse turns into a tiger when he hunts to kill. He had the tigers, too, *this* Maleger. I remember there was one charming effect in particular, in which a gigantic Bengal tiger bursts from a fiery cage—and takes a terrific spring straight over the footlights for the front row of the audience. Maleger fires a pistol, and the tiger (believe it or not) disappears in midair. Goo!" said the reporter, making expressive gestures. "But he got into half a dozen lawsuits with hysterical patrons, and had to withdraw that one. Lord knows how he did it. I suppose nobody ever will."

"Mirrors?" I suggested. "Like the talking-head trick?"

"Mirrors," said Gallivan, "me eye. There weren't any mirrors when he turned the thing loose on *me* when I was sleeping at the castle one night. I mean—a joke is a joke. If I hadn't been so unholy interested in everything he did, I'd have chucked the bloody job then and there. And I told him so." Moodily Gallivan sipped his beer. "Imagine six-feet-two of stringy muscle. Imagine huge deep eyes that sometimes looked grey and sometimes black; imagine dark eyebrows, an immense bulging forehead, and moth-eaten red hair worn halfway to his shoulders— which were stooping, with long dangling arms like an ape. Imagine a smile, yellow teeth, and a cigarette in his fingers. That was Maleger. May he burn where he belongs, and like it."

Setting down his glass with a thump, Gallivan sat back and watched the sun edging the filmy green of the trees beside the Rhine.

"But," continued Bencolin, after a pause, "what do you know about him personally? His real name? His origin? His nationality?"

"Not one thing! He came from Africa with a fortune in 'ninety-nine: that's all. He'd travelled everywhere and seen everything, so that was no indication. Spoke ten languages perfectly, and—well, sir, a man who reads Spenser, Sir Thomas Malory, the Beowulf poems, and James I on witchcraft has no stevedore's command of English, let me tell you. But when you get to messing with Vitoux, Delacroix, Baissac, and Florian-Parmentier in French—"

"How the devil," interposed Bencolin, "do *you* know of those people? Delacroix's *Les procès de Sorcellerie au dix-septième siècle* is so little known that…"

The slouching reporter pulled his battered hat down farther on his head. Little deep wrinkles suddenly appeared round his mouth, and he squinted at the sun.

"Oxford," he said, shamefacedly. "I was at B. N. C. a long time ago; that was how I happened to land over here. And at the Sorbonne. And I thought I was a writer, once. Yeah, write little books for the portly matron from East Ham to learn what the sights are…" His finger traced aimless designs on the table. "Ah, nertz! Never mind me. Wouldn't think I was forty-six years old, would you?… We were talking about Maleger."

"So we were. You know nothing more?"

"Well… women? Like to hear about his private life?"

"I was coming to that."

"I can't tell you how much is hearsay and how much fact, and I know a good deal about it. He had a wife and a mistress; both of them were fiercely hushed up. It was easier to do then than it is now. I believe he had a child by the mistress when he first appeared in London. He chucked her, and she died somewhere. That was before my time—I wasn't more than a young un when I was his press-agent, you know. About the wife, I don't know; I understood it was a secret marriage, because her family objected, and I don't think they ever lived together. It wasn't long before his death, anyhow."

"He had a child by the mistress," Bencolin murmured. "H'm. Who was this mistress?"

"Don't know her name. You could probably find out... But I saw her once, years after they'd broken up. It was in 'eleven, I think, and in Paris. I was with a friend of mine; chap who worked on the Paris *Herald*. We were sitting at some café or other—don't remember where—and he nudged me and said, 'There's your friend Maleger's *amie*.' She was drinking absinthe at another table; looked pretty far gone and almighty shabby. But she had been a stunner—gorgeous blonde, with long hair."

"And the child?"

"No idea... Wait a minute, though!" Gallivan was pounding his fist slowly against the table, his face grotesquely pinched in groping for a memory. "It seems to me... Not very long ago I was talking to Dick Ansil, who does that nosey gossip-column. One of those chaps who know so offensively much about everybody's business that you want to give 'em a poke in the eye. It was at a press dinner or something, and we were both pretty cock-eyed. He said: 'Listen. D'you remember that mysterious kid of Maleger's everybody was speculating about years and years ago?' (It was a kind of legendary mystery, you see.) I said, 'And a bloody good thing *you* weren't alive then, or nobody could have had an illegitimate child in peace.' He said he'd found out the name; told me all about how it would surprise everybody, and gave that nasty little chuckle of his. I told him to shut his head or I'd whang a bottle at it. But I have an impression that he did tell me, anyway. The name was... Oh, hang it!... Nope. It's gone. Was it very important?"

"It may be. I am not certain."

"Well, I can always cable Dick, if you really want to know." He looked behind us down the promenade. "Hullo! Here comes Baron von Arnheim, and he looks like the cat that swallowed the canary. H'm. Now I wonder what he wants of me?..."

XII

THE TORCH THAT WAS ALIVE

GIVING US A SHORT BOW, VON ARNHEIM SAT DOWN AND ORDERED beer. He still carried his old newspapers, which he placed beside his chair. Then he folded his hands on the table and spoke crisply:

"Mr. Gallivan, you are the only journalist on the premises now?"

Gallivan winced at the word "journalist," but he nodded.

"Unless," he said, "the German papers are giving it a whirl. I know half the crowd on the Continent, and I haven't seen anybody about. I'm just supposed to be doing local colour, you see, but if you could let me in on any developments…"

"There are developments," interposed von Arnheim, "but nothing must be said of them now. If you so desire, you may have the entire story very shortly. You will now give out only the statement that von Arnheim, of Berlin, has taken charge of the case, and that an arrest will be made within twenty-four hours. There are no 'buts' or 'ifs' or conditional clauses. An arrest *will be made* within that time."

There was a pause. Bencolin lighted a cigarette thoughtfully.

"The real story, sir," said Gallivan, "is the presence of you two in—in co-operation. Er—"

"If you obtain my friend Bencolin's permission," von Arnheim told him, "you may also use that." He smiled in his tight-lipped way. "As a matter of fact, the arrest will be made tonight. Now to business. Mr. Marle gives me to understand that at one time you were well acquainted with Mr. Myron Alison. Is that correct?"

"Oh, not very well. I knew him."

"A pleasant sort of person?"

"He was with the press. *I* always rather liked him. I mean—champagne dinners, and calling you by your first name; he liked to stand in well with us. They say he was dead mean and spiteful, but he was always fine to me because I boomed him so much. Lord knows, I don't think he was a great actor, but I've a weakness for that cloak-and-sword stuff…"

"He was quite a friend of the magician Maleger, I am told?"

"H'm… Well, that's what they say, but it always looked to me like a close association of mutual enmity. Here was the point: Alison was handsome as all hell; he'd a fine voice, was an idol of the women and a splendid mimic. In plays calling for the acrobatic-Douglas-Fairbanks business he had no equal, and he had, above everything, a fine stage-sense. But he wanted to be thought a great actor. And Maleger singled out that one little sore point to get a knife into him…"

Birds squeaked, and a flutter of them fought shrilly in the branches over our heads. A steamer bell clanged on the bright river. Over Coblenz the sun was whitening into cloudless still heat; you could pick out fiery windows in white houses on the opposite bank of the Rhine. Von Arnheim's beer-glass tilted slowly…

"I'll never forget," said Gallivan, "the first time I ever saw Maleger. It was in nineteen-ten, about six months before I began to work for him. And it was the opening night of one of Alison's big successes.

"The play was one of those things that used to send shivers up my spine. You know, the Scotch highlands in the days of the Young Pretender. The lost cause, the bagpipes of the clan, and voices offstage singing the 'Skye Boat Song.' The last charge at Culloden—hah! Alison played Bonnie Prince Charlie, and brought down the house.

"I had seen it in rehearsal, and I was so ecstatic that Alison invited me round to his dressing-room after the performance. There was a huge crowd in white ties, but I got in. Alison sat at his dressing-table before a mirror ringed round with electric lights, wiping the grease-paint from his face. He still wore the dagger and jackboots, and he had a cigarette in his mouth. The place was a jumble of flowers and telegrams; stuffy, full of babbling voices and a smell of powder. He kept beaming, 'How did I do it? How did I do it?' like a nervous prima donna, and everybody assured him he was magnificent. Then, all of a sudden, the whole place went silent.

"Somebody knocked the door open. A huge man in a long black cloak, with red hair and an old-fashioned black stock, stood there lean-ing on a gold-headed cane. He had gold seals on his watch-chain, and an evil long face. He wasn't really any taller than Alison, but he seemed to fill the room. Alison's eyes lighted up, and he sat back blowing smoke at the ceiling and trying to conceal his exultation. 'Hello, Maleger!' he said. 'Like it?' The other man just looked at him. Finally he said: 'It was sickening. I couldn't stand the play past the first act. And you were worse. You'll never be anything but a rotten actor as long as you live.'"

Gallivan shook his head slowly. He laughed a little, but he was so heart and soul in the recital that I think he hardly noticed our presence at all. He flipped his cigarette over the balustrade.

"It was funny. I remember how Alison's hand flew to his dagger, just as though he'd really been living in the eighteenth century. And the way the lights shook when Maleger slammed the door as he went out. Then Alison laughed, making light of it, and all the sycophants fluttered round again. But it was always that way—Maleger insisting what a poor actor he was."

Eyes narrowed, von Arnheim nodded. "But," he said, "so far as you knew there was never an open clash?"

"H'm… Well, on one occasion there nearly was."

"And what was that?"

"A private theatrical for a bunch of swells. Alison gave an imitation of Maleger on the stage—costume, make-up, and everything. It was uncanny. I told you what a fine mimic he was. He gave such an uproarious and fiendishly clever burlesque that everybody was roaring with laughter. And then somebody noticed Maleger himself standing at the back, taking snuff and watching it."

"Well?" said von Arnheim, eagerly. He leaned forward, rapping his knuckles on the table. "What happened?"

"Nothing. He just took another pinch of snuff and said, pleasantly, 'You'll regret this, my dear fellow.' But for a second I had a horrible fancy that he would wave his hand and that we would all be turned into swine or something. I looked again, and he was gone—just like that."

Gallivan snapped his fingers. There was a little creaking of chairs as we settled back. The waiter brought another round of beer.

"The curious thing was," the reporter said, moodily, "that their natures were in so many ways alike. They were bound together. They were like Siamese twins fighting a duel with swords, and each knew the other's guard and attack so well that neither could penetrate. But Maleger's was the greater spirit, I think. I don't understand this new atom-and-molecule thing, but you had the impression of a towering mass of life-force, and it shook you like big hands. Even death, you felt, would only liberate it in the air. It might be snapped back together again, suddenly, like those flying arms and legs of the man in 'The King of the Golden River.' If he had a son…"

Gradually, almost imperceptibly, Gallivan was speaking less and less like the slouching hack-writer I had known yesterday. He wore the air of one studying something under a microscope. A fisherman's skiff idled past on the river beyond the balustrade, with that mysterious secret air which belongs ever to the solitary angler. Gallivan took off his hat, revealing a mop of wild sandy hair; he squinted at the trees, at his glass, at the river, everywhere searching under the hot noonday. Von Arnheim said:

"We are not here to discuss science or metaphysics. There are facts…"

"Quite," said Gallivan, snapping alert. "Sorry. Fire away, sir."

"I have here," went on the German, "a number of old newspapers, detailing past plays of Myron Alison. Some of the accounts were written by you. In all of them there is mention of a certain ambition long held by Alison. He states that it is the dream of his life to produce a certain play…"

"Yes, sir."

"A play from the German of Heinrich Erckmann-Wolff, called 'Bronzebeard.' It is so spectacular that it could never be played on any ordinary stage; I do not think it could ever be produced at all. Thousands would be required in the cast. It is laid in the time of the Roman Emperor Nero. And I have read it…"

"Of course I remember," said Gallivan. "He spoke of it often. I never read the thing. He could never get anybody to back it, or the gigantic sum necessary to produce it himself. But he always said it would be his greatest effort. It was almost an obsession."

Von Arnheim consulted the papers. "He states that he wishes to play the part of Cantanus Lupo, a young Roman aristocrat who becomes leader of the Christians and is eventually sentenced to death by Nero. Is that correct?"

"I don't remember. But I suppose so… Oh yes! I remember there was an amphitheatre scene in it which would have stumped even the movies…"

Von Arnheim could not quite conceal his gratification. He folded up the papers meticulously; triumph seemed to accumulate inside him like air pumped into a tyre. He said:

"Very good. I thank you very much, Mr. Gallivan, for your information. I thank you also for the very illuminating insight you have given into the characters of certain people. Here!" Tearing a page from his notebook, he scribbled on it and tossed it across to Gallivan. "Present this to Magistrate Konrad, and he will supply you with all the facts you may need for your—your story. You say you are familiar with the inside of Castle Skull?"

"Find my way round it in the dark, I think."

"Good." He looked round the circle of us with the utmost complacence. "Gentlemen, I am planning for this evening a little entertainment. I can promise you as much excitement as you are ever likely to see... Mr. Gallivan, will you be so good as to present yourself at the Alison home this evening after dinner? I suggest that you bring an overnight bag. Our entire party will be spending the night in Castle Skull. For the present, that is all."

Bencolin had not uttered a word since the beginning of the questioning. Now he tossed his cigarette over the balustrade and roused himself from his obscure meditations. He glanced at von Arnheim, opening his eyes wide; then he shook his head as he looked at me, and his wry expression said, "I told you he was going to do this, Jeff." But quite abruptly he observed, aloud:

"Maybe that's the best way..."

"What is the best way?" demanded von Arnheim, whirling on him.

"I spoke to myself. An error, Baron. Pardon me."

"You follow my train of questioning—about the play and such matters?"

Bencolin was not acting now. He was genuinely puzzled, and von Arnheim knew it. The Frenchman said:

"You have me, my friend. I confess I don't."

Von Arnheim rose and buttoned up his coat. His grey felt hat was set at a jaunty angle on his cropped skull. "*Sic volvere parcas!* You did not see the crucial point. Well, well, it is about time I indulged in a little private mystification on my own account. Now, if you are ready, we can return to the house and clear up some of our difficulties."

The two of them walked ahead down the promenade, with Gallivan and myself following at a distance. The reporter's stooped shoulders were swinging, and his long arms dangled out of their sleeves. He was whistling cheerfully; he had almost gone through the skipping, haunting tune when I realized with a shock what it was—"Amaryllis!"

"Where the devil—?" I said.

"Oh, I read the papers," he informed me, grinning sideways. "They made something of that thing being played during the murder. Some violinist or other; can't remember the name; don't think they mentioned it—was sawing it out." He nodded up ahead. "I'm keeping quiet, but... what's the betting?"

"On those two?"

"Right. I'm no fool. They'd cut each other's hearts out if they got a chance. It ought to be a good show, at which one Brian Gallivan will be present to see the vivisection. And, if I may say so, how. Well—I'm hopping into the hotel to send a cable. Thanks, and see you later."

It was queer, walking along that promenade. Part of it is shadowed by a vast stone wall, vine-grown, which is the back of terraced gardens leading up to the old summer palace of the Saxon kings. At one point the promenade runs under the tall arch of a stone footbridge, and in it hangs a box lantern which by night burns yellow above a cool and whispering tunnel. There are many echoes in Coblenz by night, for you must not be deceived by a bravery of geraniums and villas into forgetting the old decaying gables crowding up behind. Bells have rung, and men have died, since Cæsar here threw his bridge across the Rhine.

But now it was bright daylight—though dusky in the tunnel—and I distinctly heard somebody walking just behind me. Gallivan was striding along, whistling "Amaryllis." The gravel crunched. I glanced over my shoulder. It was an illusion, some trick of echoes, here in this cool dim place. We were alone with that idiotic whistling...

Even when he left me, and I was nearly run down by a trolley on the Rheinstrasse, the illusion persisted. A wing had brushed me. The footfalls (I recalled distinctly) had been long and steady and swinging. I had a rather horrible fancy that they might have been conjured up by the whistling of "Amaryllis." When I asked Bencolin and von Arnheim to wait, and went into a shop after cigarettes, I even tried a few experimental bars of the tune. The screen door on the shop banged. I bought my cigarettes and went out, feeling relieved not to have heard any more footsteps. Some children ran past, shouting. In a shop window were little souvenir models, in brass, of the William the Great equestrian statue, which the pale sun set gleaming in a white deserted street.

The chugging launch bore us back again. I heard Bencolin's voice:

"—Suggest that we let Jeff question Dunstan; not as obvious questioning, of course. One of his few abilities, Baron, is an uncanny knack of getting people to talk to him, and it is the reason why he is useful. We can handle Madame D'Aunay. But Dunstan needs to be drawn out. I think he'll speak of his own accord, but not otherwise... Why the daydream, Jeff?"

I mumbled something. Fritz had put up the tarpaulin against the sun, and the rear of the boat was shady and pleasant. We sat for a long time in silence, von Arnheim with his chin in his fist, and we were in sight of the Alison landing-stage when the German spoke.

"There are no intruders now," he said. "I am going to tell you something."

His voice was portentous. The water swished creaming past our bows.

"I will show you what escaped you," continued the voice behind my ear. "We face a terrible murderer. We face a very Wagner for sensational effects. Listen! You remember that Alison wished to play the part of the Christian leader in 'Bronzebeard'?"

Bencolin did not reply. I twisted round to look at the set face whose monocle was edged with sun. Against the motor-chugging I said, "Yes…"

"And that he was, in the play, condemned to death?"

"Yes."

"And how did Bronzebeard notoriously serve his Christian enemies?"

"Why… the lions," I said.

The monocle became a fire eye. He leaned forward. "*Yes!* And how else?"

"Why, he had pitch poured over them, lighted it, and used them as human torches to… O *my God!*" I breathed, and half jumped to my feet.

There was a silence. Von Arnheim said, "Alison got his wish."

Our launch slid in and bumped to rest against the landing-stage.

XIII

DUNSTAN TALKS—AND D'AUNAY LISTENS

L UNCH WAS NOT A VERY MERRY MEAL THAT DAY. LEVASSEUR, Dunstan, and the Duchess came down for it, but none of the others appeared. Miss Alison's voice boomed pleasantly in our ears, without our hearing it, to cover the conversational gulf; she and Bencolin exchanged sallies across the table. She drank a vast quantity of wine and got a little tipsy. Dunstan hardly touched his food—he was the most worried-looking man I have ever seen, and once he upset a glass of water all over his lap. Levasseur ate with all a Frenchman's absorbed interest in his food, and scarcely lifted his dark face from his plate. Von Arnheim's quick eyes roved everywhere about the table, which did not improve Dunstan's morale in the least. Then the Duchess told a dirty story, which was a very funny dirty story, and I was interested in seeing the various ways they took it. Bencolin roared. Levasseur permitted himself a brief appreciative smile and continued to excavate roast duck. Von Arnheim did not seem to hear it at all. But Dunstan got a bit pale. He was obviously shocked and embarrassed, but more—his hands could hardly hold his napkin. It had been another of those tales wherein the *cocu* husband comes home unexpectedly...

Afterwards the Duchess drew up her squat figure, thumping her cane, and challenged Bencolin to a game of chess. I knew that they were going to sit upstairs and exchange stories, of which the Frenchman had an inexhaustible fund, and that they would be out of the way for a time. Levasseur excused himself immediately. Von

Arnheim, nodding almost imperceptibly in the direction of Dunstan, wandered upstairs. The young man did the thing I hoped for. He started to go upstairs, hesitated, and went to the library; presently he came out with a book and sought the veranda. I was scheduled for a little informal interview with him, while von Arnheim prowled round Isobel D'Aunay.

They had let down a vast red-and-white-striped awning over the porch. Dunstan sat sprawled in a wicker chair in the corner, staring out over the river. He wore an old cricket coat, with colours, and had a scarf knotted at his throat. One leg moved ceaselessly up and down across the other. Beside him lay his unnoticed book. He had got a Bradshaw's Railway Guide in mistake for Heaven knows what, but I did not appear to notice that.

I said: "There isn't a tennis-court hereabouts, is there? I could do with a couple of sets."

He said into his scarf: "By Gad! I wish there were! Like to whack a few just to—to whack 'em." The leg continued its restless swinging. "There's a gym, but who wants to swing an Indian club? I should bung it at somebody. Don't know what else, unless... I know!" he suggested, and looked at me in an inspired way. "Let's get tight."

He was very, very young, but I knew exactly how it felt to be in that mood, and I could sympathize. So I said, cheerfully:

"Too early in the day. If you get tight on a summer afternoon, the sun hurts your head and your eyes, and it's worse than anything I know."

"Jove! so it is! Hadn't thought about it that way." This new idea distracted him for a moment, and he turned it over in his mind, but gloom settled again. The foot resumed its jumping...

"We might borrow the launch and go for a run up to Stolzenfels," I suggested. "That is, if you can drive one of the things. I can't."

"Oh, I can drive it. Got a little beauty of my own at home—" He caught himself up and glanced suddenly at me, but I was scanning the horizon in an absorbed way. He snapped: "But I won't go near the beastly boat, do you hear? Hate 'em. Never touch 'em."

We discussed the dullness of billiards and other matters, and finally I proposed a climb in the woods behind the house. He agreed. There was, he said, a path which left the landing-stage steps and wound up beside the house into the hills. It was as though he could not keep his mind off that path by which Isobel D'Aunay must have returned to her room.

We descended the steps until we found the path; then we went up ridges deep cut in the earth. Along the side of the house, I noticed, it ran close to an outside staircase communicating with a second-floor balcony. Presently the path entered a cool tunnel of trees, whose under boughs were still heavy with rain. We emerged at last on a flat promontory bounded by a stone wall, but long before that I had satisfied myself on one point—Dunstan and Isobel D'Aunay had not come up here on the night of the murder. The path was—even when not, as now, befouled with mud—steep, rocky, and treacherous; it was overgrown with brambles and Spanish needles, and at one point it edged a gully tumbling sheer fifty feet down the hillside. It was hard climbing even for me, and in daylight. No woman like Isobel D'Aunay could have managed it at any time, much less at night.

The promontory was a little shelf against the slope, shaded by beeches and lindens, through whose trunks you had a magnificent view out over the river. It was a green twilight filled with the odour of moss and wet earth. Mysterious rustlings stirred and fled at our approach. Dunstan sat down on the low stone wall, nursing his knee and staring up at the intertwined boughs. Some of the ugly wrinkles were smoothed out of his face. From the brush rasped a querulous cawing. A woodpecker tacked faintly. All the quietude of the Rhine was about us, breathing in sleep. We discussed one thing or another, idly, and then I said:

"Pleasant place to bring a woman, this, if it weren't such steep going to get here…"

"Oh!… I dare say," he replied. He turned his head away; he thought that a vulgar remark.

"Much easier to go across the river, though," I pointed out, thoughtfully. "If you had a boat, there's doubtless a little cove over there somewhere."

I had an impression that the wood noises had suddenly been withdrawn; that no breath stirred in the ferns any longer. I was not watching him, but I could see his long fingers tighten round the edge of the wall. That terrible silence! Sitting down beside him on the edge of the wall, I took out my watch.

"Late," I said. *"Two o'clock…"*

"Nonsense!" he jerked, breathing more freely when he thought I had changed the subject. "Why, my watch says half-past—"

He stopped. I did not look up, but the sun cast a shadow of him across the glass face of my watch. Its steady ticking was unnaturally loud. He knew; he knew, and his stiffening was a terrific, inaudible gasp. Anger boiled slowly, gathering and darkening. He got to his feet…

"Steady," I said. "I could throw you over that wall without half trying, you know."

"You damned swine!" he said, heavily. "You wrote that note."

"No. No, I didn't. If I had, I should be inclined to agree with you."

"Who did, then?"

No attempt at concealment. The doors had been knocked in on a secret place; he stood at the breach, his hooked arms shaking and his nostrils dilated. The arms of the blue cricket-coat were bulged by his slender, ineffectual muscles. I shook him by the shoulders, rising to look into his eyes. They were dark and rimmed with red.

"It was a filthy trick," I told him. "Who did it doesn't matter now, does it? We've got to find you a way out."

"A way out? My God! that's funny! I suppose the whole house knows."

"Nobody knows," I lied, "but Bencolin and myself. And—that's his business. If he told all he knew, there are a good many people in France who wouldn't sleep a wink from now on. But he never does. Wake up, man! You're not the only one who's ever been in that position; it's nothing new."

He looked at me curiously, for I was speaking as one might to a child who is afraid the police will get him for stealing jam. With a shuddering breath he sat down again. "You're sure," he persisted, "it isn't known? I've had rather a ghastly time since—"

"I'm positive."

"What—what did you mean," he asked hesitantly—"it's nothing new?"

I said this and that, shrugging. He looked puzzled, with a dawning wonder, and he was obviously so reassured that his brain faltered. But he flared, "Then *why* the devil—!"

It was no easy task to convince him that the important issue was the investigation of a murder, and not his affair with another man's wife. He could not see that being caught in adultery was more desirable than being hanged. I stressed the damning evidence of the motor-boat, but I also stressed that, if he could demonstrate his innocence, any erratic behaviour need never be mentioned. And I knew I was going to hear the story; he had to get it off his chest sooner or later…

"Look here," I concluded. "You and Madame D'Aunay really were out in the launch then, weren't you?"

"I don't mind telling *you*," he said, "but I can't tell that detective. I swear I can't! I don't know why—"

"Well, I'll handle that part of it. You don't need to see him at all."

For some reason this eased his fear tremendously. "Besides," he muttered, "there are parts of this you don't understand at all. Oh, it's a mess! The fact is, I—I'm mad about that woman. I can't give her up, and I don't mean to. Do you hear?" He struck the wall with his fist, turning to glare at me. "If you knew what she's been through with that rotter—!"

The old sweet song. How merrily (and, for all I know, how truthfully) it has been sung, from the well-known mountains of Greenland to what the hymn-writer somewhat fantastically calls Afric's sunny fountains! There was a rhapsody coming, to which I listened in solemn attention. Life runs true to melodrama; there was even the statement, "If he'd only beaten her—!" I do not know why it is that the wives of cruel husbands always prefer their husbands to beat them, and seem annoyed when the beating does not occur. Anyhow, there it was. And I could sympathize, because—judged by old-fashioned standards— Jérôme D'Aunay was not a bad husband at all. He was what is worse; he was just petty, overbearing, and mean.

"… I met her a year ago in Brussels," continued Dunstan, "and I thought I'd forgotten her. Then, last week, I came here to see Alison about designing some sets for his new play. I didn't know she was to be here. I don't even know how it happened, exactly, except that she handed me a teacup, and all of a sudden I touched her hand and got all red and panicky. I know it sounds so damn silly. But it wasn't."

He was talking faster now, almost incoherently.

"And the worst of it is, you see, I'm supposed to be engaged to a girl who's here now! Didn't know that, did you? The little one— Sally Reine. I say, you won't peach on me, will you?… I can't go on with it, and I haven't the nerve to tell her. I knew I couldn't go on with it all the time; but I just got in deeper. I can't stand women who joke with you! Never know whether the dashed girl is serious or ragging me…

"Well, the night—the night of the murder, old D'Aunay took his drug and she knew he was asleep. She came downstairs. At first, you see, we'd only intended to sit on the porch and talk. Then I—I rather went out of my head. I said, 'Let's take the boat and go across the river.' You see, there's a path which leads to a little grove on the hillside, and easy to reach. We took the boat…"

"Wait. Did Alison go across with you?"

Jerked out of his recital, he looked at me blankly. "Alison? O good Lord, no! Who said anything about Alison?"

"Look here," I said, "getting sore won't help me any, but I can't help it. I've been trying to drive it into your head all afternoon, and now you calmly tell me, 'Who said anything about Alison?' Damn it! that's the crucial point! He went across the river somehow, and the boat was heard only once."

"Oh!… Oh, well, he could have rowed it, you know."

"There was only one rowboat, and it was used by Hoffmann and Fritz."

"And I tell you," cried Dunstan, "he jolly well didn't go with us! Do you think I'm dotty? Do you think I'd have taken—"

He stopped to look at me suddenly, for I must have looked so dumbfounded that it penetrated even his fog. I rose slowly from the wall, and in that instant I *saw*. I saw in one vivid flash, which was like a blow across the base of the skull, how Alison had really crossed that river. Oh, stupidity! Stark, incredible imbecility for not seeing it long ago!

"The shoes," I said aloud; "the shoes—"

"What shoes?" demanded my companion.

I did not answer, but the explanation became increasingly clear. Those pairs of walking-boots plastered ankle-deep with mud and green slime! Alison did not get it going up the path to Castle Skull, for, as I had observed, even in the wettest weather my own shoes had accumulated only a little black mud. I remembered now where I had seen stuff like that with which the shoes were caked. It was at the draining of a pond on my grandfather's estate. The river-bed... there was a way under the river.

Castles like that had in most cases an underground passage, by which the lord could escape in time of siege. This one ran beneath the river-bed, and had another exit in Alison's house. And the missing evening-slippers! Alison had obviously removed them just after entering the passage, and put on his heavy boots—so that when he returned he could put on the slippers again and avoid staining the floors with that messy mud. Meticulously neat as always: only, he had not come back. Everything dovetailed. The disreputable coat hanging in his closet. The locking of his door, ostensibly to work on his memoirs...

All these things flashed through my mind in an instant, though they seem long-drawn-out in the writing. And other details flashed into place, too. The mysterious man with the torch, whom Hoffmann had seen on the battlements. They tried to tell us that he had run out from the castle gates and gone down the hillside, to drive the boat back before the servants arrived. Sheer lunacy! He could not have come down the path without meeting them; and, had he tried to force his way down that tangled brush-grown steepness—even without almost certainly breaking his neck—he must have roused such noise that they could not avoid hearing it. No. He had returned by way of the passage under the river. Things which had seemed so meaningless now took on an appalling clarity. I recalled the alcove between Alison's sitting-room and bedroom; I recalled a disarranged rug and a greenish mudstain on the floor. The entrance to the passage! More, a mudstain obviously not left by Alison—but by the murderer when he returned. Somebody had seen Alison enter on that terrible night. Somebody had taken the pistol from his bureau, followed him under the Rhine, performed the fantastic deeds, and come back. Bencolin had seen all this... but he had seen it last night, immediately, without groping. We had been misled by the returning motor-boat, which bore back only Dunstan and his paramour...

"... Whatever is the matter with you?" the young man was demanding.

"A brainstorm," I said. "Please go on."

"But, hang it, what do you want to know? I've admitted what we did. We drove across and I tied up the boat at the dock... Oh, my hat, are you off again?"

In a sense I was. For, in the new revelation, I remembered Hoffmann's testimony that he had seen the launch tied up at Castle Skull's dock, and it was placed on a different side from that used by occupants of the house. Obviously Alison had never gone across in that boat, not even as a passenger. That must have been what gave Bencolin his surmise of the truth.

"... Lord knows who he was or what he was doing," I heard Dunstan say, "but when I saw that man come up out of the ground, I—"

I whirled on him. "When you saw *what*?"

"The man who came up out of the ground. It put the wind up me, I can tell you! For a minute I was frightened out of my wits. He was dragging some kind of bundle. Probably a poacher. I suppose he didn't come up out of the ground, really, but—"

"Tell me about it. The whole thing."

Colour crept into the young man's face. He looked at me pleadingly, and then his jaw hardened with anger. "But—No, I'm hanged if I do! What good can it do you? Confound you, it's—it's *sacred*," he blurted, "and it's none of your—"

"I understand all that," I told him as patiently as I could. "Never mind the details of the beautiful romance. What I want to know about is the man who came up out of the ground."

"Oh!—Well, you see," Dunstan explained, after several false starts, "we were in a little grove, as I was telling you, a very little way up the hillside. It was bright moonlight. We were—were sitting in the shadow of a huge beech tree, on a kind of sloping bank, and I was—O God! I was crazy, and shaky inside, and the whole place turned around in front of my eyes!... D'you know?" he demanded, fiercely. His hands were shaking now. "The trees, and the night, and the feeling of being away out there miles from everybody; then the terrific knowing—right in your heart—that you were closer to that woman than you'd ever been to anybody. That's what it is!" His hands clenched. "And then afterwards feeling as though all your bones were broken... I remember, my face was in the grass, and all of a sudden, for no reason at all, I looked up.

"It was horrible. About twenty feet away, behind some bushes, a man seemed to come right up out of the ground. His back was towards me and he was bent over a bit. I could hear him dragging something heavy along the ground—it tore and dragged in the brambles—and the man was humming a tune to himself.

"Then he disappeared. I don't know where he went. I thought for a second my heart had stopped. And Isobel was afraid somebody had seen us; she was nearly crying, and she was moaning, 'We've got to go back, we've got to go back.' But we were even afraid to do that. We waited and waited, talking about all sorts of terrible possibilities, when we heard those screams...

"That finished us. We could hear them plainly, and we looked up and saw that ghastly blazing thing running. But Isobel was so terrified she couldn't stand up. I tried to get her back to the boat. At last I had to carry her. We made a terrific amount of noise, because it was hard to keep myself from falling. Just when we got to the dock I saw the rowboat putting out from the other bank. We waited in the bushes until Hoffmann and Fritz had arrived, and once I was afraid we were discovered, because they kept flashing lights all about. When they were safely up the hill we got into the boat and streaked it back. Isobel went up the path, and I up the steps to the porch. Thank God, she got in without waking her husband…"

It was just at this point that we both became conscious we were not alone. Subconsciously, I suppose, I must have heard a rustle in the ferns or the roll of a pebble some seconds earlier. Under a big linden tree at the edge of the path a man stood motionless, watching us.

Jérôme D'Aunay.

XIV

THE WAY TO CASTLE SKULL

I DO NOT KNOW WHAT SORT OF EXPLOSION I EXPECTED. HE MUST have heard the entire latter part of Dunstan's speech. After the shock of seeing him there, I remember glancing quickly over the low stone wall and noting the wooded ravine below. A man could break his neck if he fell over there. For a long time nobody spoke. A fan of dappled shadows waved slowly back and forth across this clearing; one point of sunlight lighted a mud-puddle beside D'Aunay's foot, and the woodpecker continued his tapping, distantly.

Then I saw a queer thing. D'Aunay remained still, dusky and sinister, with his chin a little lowered and his hands in his pockets. But the man was almost smiling. His big face was smug, his mouth twisted in a kind of thick complacence, and the lids were lowered over pleased eyes. A breeze moved on tiptoe, softly, through the leaves...

Dunstan broke the quiet by saying: "Well? Get on with it!"

"Ah, good afternoon, Sir Marshall Dunstan," D'Aunay said in English. His pronunciation was bad, but he did not lack fluency. "I have been looking for you. Hoffmann told me you two gentlemen had started in this direction. Yes. I have just had a talk with my wife."

He moved a few steps forward. He was dressed offensively in a mottled golfing-suit, with stockings of loud red and green. Still we did not know what was behind his manner.

"Herr von Arnheim," he continued, "was questioning her. I walked in on the middle of it. I heard enlightening things."

Dunstan was a little pale, but he looked back steadily. "I should have had to tell you sooner or later," he said.

"Forgive me," D'Aunay requested, raising his hand in a curiously unctuous gesture. It did not go with his bluff face. "I wish to ask a personal question. I feel I have a right to an answer. Yes? Do you love my wife?"

"Yes." Dunstan was trying to be so dignified that he almost gulped.

"If she were—free, you would marry her?"

"Yes."

"Ah," said D'Aunay. "Very well. You shall have her."

He rasped out the words. The unction left his ploughshare jaw and his cold, watchful eyes. He said: "You save me much trouble. I have felt for a long time she was not good to be head of my household. Vain. Wishful of clothes. Wishing to go on trips where I have business. Not clever to receive guests in my house. And—I am frank—she cannot have children. In short, a bad wife. I wished for something like this, but I thought she was too virtuous." He smiled, without humour. "I could have had her put out of the way. But it might damage my reputation."

He examined the tips of his sport shoes, reflectively.

"It's a quarter to three," I observed, looking at my watch. "I've taken entirely too much time. If you gentlemen will excuse me—"

"Thank you," said D'Aunay. "If you will be so good. I wish to discuss certain details with my friend from England…"

I left them standing by the wall, Dunstan stiff and D'Aunay reflective. Tramping down the path, I bestowed a few well-chosen doubts on D'Aunay's origin and parentage. But, after all, I reflected, why be angry? He might be of canine ancestry, but his attitude had saved a bad situation. Had he chosen to play the heavy husband, it might have become insupportable. Somebody, I thought wearily, was always trying to start a fight around this place. Now everybody was happy.

Everybody, that is, but a little, wryly humorous, puckish girl named Sally Reine...

But—here was an idea—suppose D'Aunay had sensed that affair, had watched it and fostered it? Suppose he had not really taken the veronal, and was shamming sleep to make sure of his suspicions? With his wife out of the room, we had no proof that he had been peacefully sleeping all the while. In any case, I must hurry down to see Bencolin about this new feature: the man who had "appeared from the ground" on the other side of the river.

There seemed to be nobody about when I entered the lower hall-way. I went upstairs, and heard a murmur of voices from the Duchess' sitting-room. Bencolin's voice said, "I'll see that and raise you five." Levasseur announced regretfully, "I am out," and the Duchess growled, "I'll read 'em, you devil-faced old crook." I knocked.

They were seated at the card-table by the window. As I entered, Bencolin was laying out the cards of a club flush. He had before him rather a remarkable stack of blue chips. Levasseur regarded the cards in a hurt, polite fashion. The Duchess viciously finished off a Long Tom Collins, lit a cigar, and made sundry references to thieves and burglars, with comments on the probable conduct of a man who fills a flush on a two-card draw.

"Come on in, laddie," she greeted me. "This blighter with the funny-looking whiskers," she explained, pointing a stubby forefinger at Bencolin, "has won everything but my corsets. My God! I haven't had a good hand all afternoon! Sit in, laddie. Five-mark limit. Here—pull up a chair."

She paused in the act of holding out her glass to a wooden-faced girl in a maid's cap, who stood behind her chair.

"I say! I do believe the kid's discovered something!" she cried. "Here, Frieda, mix me up another gin sling. I need it.—Look at him, though; he's all puffed up." She turned to Levasseur and let out a gust of laughter. "Levasseur, he's got you, you old murderer. Better confess."

Levasseur smiled. "Please, mademoiselle," he said, "I do not think you ought to joke about such things. It is quite obvious…"

"Go on, man! I was only pulling your leg!" At this juncture she really reached out and pulled it. "Y'know, Devil-face," she told Bencolin, "I can't resist the temptation to rag that man. I'd like to see his hair mussed. I'd like to see him spit on the floor, or get squiffed and fall downstairs. He looks like what the well-dressed man will wear even if it hurts. No, wait; don't get your back up, Levasseur… I say, has the kid heard the news?"

"What news?" I asked.

Bencolin paused in the act of dealing cards. He glanced up with wrinkled forehead. "We have all been invited," he returned, "to be present at a little show under the auspices of Baron von Arnheim. It is to be held in Castle Skull, where we are to spend the night. Miss Alison here has suggested something further—a state dinner, to be held there in Maleger's dining-room—"

"So long as our friend Glass-eye insists on being dramatic," she put in, "we'll do it up right and give the servants a little work for a change. The whole staff is over there now. Oh, wait! What's this about the reporter chap you saw in Coblenz?"

"Gallivan?" I said.

"Gallivan; right," she nodded. "Glass-eye's damn inhospitable with my house. Look here, laddie. You just phone him and tell him to be in on the dinner. If he hasn't clothes, give him some or tell him to come the way he is. I like those reporters and I don't like Glass-eye. He's another one who needs to get drunk… Now deal 'em out, deal 'em out! And for God's sake give me some *cards!*"

At this juncture there was a sharp knock at the door. Von Arnheim appeared, and he was excited.

"Pardon me," he said, curtly. "I should like to see M. Bencolin and Mr. Marle in private, immediately. It is important. No, wait." He regarded the Duchess speculatively. "You may be able to help us, Miss Alison. I have practising to do now, if you will draw—?"

"Most assuredly," murmured Levasseur, rising. His dark, sharp face was concerned and he bowed to our hostess. "I can settle with the bank later, Miss Alison. I have practising to do now, if you will excuse me."

The Duchess motioned her maid to go. When the four of us were alone, she said: "Right. Now what is it?" Her manner was impatient.

"Miss Alison," von Arnheim went on, "I have just learned of the possible existence, in this house, of a secret passage."

It was out! Bencolin smiled and applauded soundlessly. For the first time the Duchess was really surprised.

"Secret passage?" she said. She regarded von Arnheim with a sour eye. "Somebody's been kidding you, Glass-eye. I never heard of any secret passages *here*. Might be one across the way; probably is… Who told you that?"

"Nobody told me. But I have evidence of the fact."

She frowned. "Well, I've been in this house nearly eighteen years, and it's news to *me*. By damn! Wouldn't that be just my luck, though, if there really was one and I didn't know about it? Where is it? Where does it lead to?"

"I have reason to believe," answered the German, "that it is in your late brother's rooms and that it leads under the river to the castle." He turned to Bencolin sardonically. "I see your point now, my friend, about 'muddy shoes.' I too have been investigating."

Agatha Alison whistled. With narrowed eyes she muttered, "By the Lord, that may be!… Well, maybe so. If that's the case, Myron had it built. It would be like him; he built this house."

"I dare say the passage under the river is many centuries older," said von Arnheim. "I have ascertained that the castle was built by a fifteenth-century nobleman who was eventually executed for sorcery. He was continually besieged, and almost made his escape at one time by what the records say was some secret way out… And, my friend Bencolin, I now see your point about the elaborateness of the ancient defences in the castle having something to do with this case."

"Yes," said Bencolin, "I mentioned it to you last night. It seemed probable that a fortress with so many devices must be equipped with an underground exit. That it runs under the Rhine was a precaution against besiegers guarding the river…"

"I see also the reason why you wished to spend the night in those rooms," the German snapped. For the first time animosity showed in his face. He struck the back of a chair. "This is no time for foolery, my friend! Did you find it?"

Bencolin absently dealt himself a poker hand. "Oh, it's in the alcove between the rooms, of course," he sighed. "But I defy you to find a way to open it."

"Well, what are we waiting for?" cried the Duchess. "Let's go and have a look at the thing! I'm damned! A secret passage, in this house! Why, in the Lord's name, couldn't Myron have told me? That's the funny part. I—"

"Mr. Alison had a reason, I think, for telling nobody," von Arnheim said, quietly. "He kept it from all of you. Oh yes, he had a reason."

"And how does this new discovery square with your theories, Baron?" asked the Frenchman, cocking up an eyebrow as he dealt the cards.

"It is the confirmation I needed," snapped von Arnheim. "Come!"

The four of us went out into the hall, the Duchess stumping on her cane and muttering to herself. The hall was flooded with sun, but it did not longer seem very cheerful. An eerie, ugly note had crept in. Downstairs Levasseur was playing again. It was the Hungarian Dance, No. 5, of Brahms, but the skipping music, the leaps and trills and patterings, suggested an older, deadlier dance. And as we passed towards the wing, I thought I could distinctly hear a woman sobbing in one of the rooms. I could not tell which, but it sent a queer wrench through me; the sunlit hall, the cheerful Rhine, and those faint, gasping sobs…

"Listen!" said Bencolin.

We were at the angle of the wing, and we all stopped involuntarily.

"It's that fiddler playing again," said the Duchess. "Sometimes he gets on my—"

"No," said Bencolin. "It's somebody in Alison's rooms."

Upon me then crept the deadly fear which was to materialize fully that night. The Hungarian Dance rose on a shriller, wilder note. I think it was von Arnheim who started to run. We hurried down the corridor, and the German flung open the door of Alison's study.

Only the sun, entering from high windows. There were dust-motes dancing in it, and the light gleamed on the nickel-work of Alison's dusty typewriter. There, still across the arm of the easy-chair, lay the smoking-jacket he had put off when he entered that strange passage. It was very warm…

The German made a savage gesture. He ran through the alcove, and we heard him opening doors in the bedroom. He emerged, stamping heavily on the floor.

"Nobody," he said. "Nobody now. But there was…"

I watched the pattern of dust on the window-panes, I traced out the brown-and-dull-gold design in the carpet. It was warm, but I shivered.

You could still hear the violin. Throwing back the alcove curtains, von Arnheim scanned the oak-panelled walls inside.

"It must be here," he went on, knocking; "but it *feels* solid. It feels like a brick wall. If there's a secret entrance here—and there must be, damnation!—it's cleverly concealed. We must try to find the opening."

"You could get an axe," suggested the Duchess, "and smash the whole wall in."

"Too thick," said Bencolin. "There's a beam somewhere there; you might bring down the roof. And, besides, that really is brick inside. Here—let's try it systematically."

We tried for fully three-quarters of an hour. We pressed and probed and sounded; we twisted at corners, ran fingers along panels, and used every bit of ingenuity we possessed; but it was of no avail. The oaken wall remained. At last the Duchess, very red and flustered from the unusual exertion, stumped out into the study.

"Bah!" she said, disgustedly. "I think you're all potty. I'll get some axes and crowbars, if you like, but I'm through with it."

"We must get the entrance from the other end, that's all," snapped von Arnheim. "We have a clue. The torch! The torch thrown in the passageway by the man Hoffmann saw on the battlements! It must be somewhere near there. Or in the watchman's rooms—probably the latter."

"Wait!" I chimed in. Excitedly I told the story I had heard from Dunstan; I was careful not to mention the name of the person who told it, but I gave a high-coloured description of the mysterious man dragging "a bundle" in the moonlight. Von Arnheim almost danced for joy.

"That's it," he agreed, rubbing his hands together. "I questioned the—the woman, as you may have heard. But she said nothing of the man from underground. *Ach* yes! It all fits! The end of this passage is on the other side of the river. There is another passage going from there up into the castle. They could hardly tunnel one underground burrow all the way over and up the hillside; the weight of the hill would bring down its roof. Now—for the other side."

"*Hey!*" protested the Duchess, waving her cane. She glared at us, the eye-glasses coming all askew on her nose. "Damn it all, give me a chance! What's all the funny business? Who saw this? Who was over on the other side of the river? You detectives give me a pain. You—"

We soothed her with half promises and half explanations. She rumbled and thundered and shook her stick at me, saying that I was a young scalawag who ought to be spanked, and that any unmentionable people who broke up a perfectly good poker game in order to seek out non-existent gory secret passages in a bleeding wall were off their respective chumps.

Von Arnheim tried to persuade us to accompany him across the river. For a reason I did not fathom, Bencolin declined. Oh, but von Arnheim was in a gay good humour! He knew he was approaching his goal—whatever it might be—and he was becoming the least bit patronizing. The meeting broke up. The German hurried out to get his hat. Agatha Alison departed for her room—to break some chairs, she said. Together Bencolin and I descended the stairs towards the porch. The long afternoon sun was slanting across the Rhine. We dropped into two wicker chairs.

Bencolin drew a long breath. "Whew!" he said. "Have a cigarette, Jeff. Those two gave me a bad time, for a while. Once or twice I was actually afraid they would find it."

I sat up and glared at him. I said, "You knew where the—?"

"Oh yes. But I spent most of last night searching for it. The rest of the time I spent exploring the secret passage."

I made various remarks.

"It's in the alcove, right enough," he told me, soothingly, "but the means of opening the door I discovered in the bedroom. It's very ingenious. You turn one of the gargoyles on the wall, and the door in the alcove opens. It's an entire slab of stone on a well-oiled mechanism, and it may be locked from either side."

"Well, then, why the devil didn't you tell us?"

He tapped his fingers on the chair-arm. "Because, Jeff, I didn't want them to see what is down there. When von Arnheim flung his solution in our teeth, they would both have known it was wrong, and somebody would give the show away. Let everybody continue believing in von Arnheim's solution. It will be best."

"I don't understand this," I remarked, despondently. "Maybe I'm not over-intelligent, but I don't understand it."

"Ah, but you will. Now I am going upstairs to do a little work. Don't ask me what it is. I shall require only a broom and a pair of heavy shoes."

I sank back into my chair as he rose, grinning, and left me. And the long afternoon light crept in flat brightness across the Rhine. And faint blue shadows moved under the trees, drawing slow veils upon that brightness. And I did not understand why the warm breeze seemed to have become chill, or why an unaccountable start ran through me in my lethargy when I heard the mellow, deep gong sound for tea.

XV

THE WEAVING OF THE NETS

L OOKING BACK OVER THE EVENTS OF THAT NIGHT, THERE IS ONLY one thing I cannot understand. That is the mad gaiety with which we were all imbued. Throughout the evening—from the time the hangman's cake was baked to that final terrifying scene in the room with the glass ceiling—we were possessed of a reckless and hilarious mood which was all the more appropriate for being grotesque. It struck us simultaneously. Our separate humours were such that we could plunge in with abandon, even though Death sat in a high-backed chair at the queerest dinner we had ever attended. But he was a suave Death, rather like von Arnheim, I fancied, with monocle and evening clothes, and he made a good dinner guest.

We drank too much, too, in that fascination of sitting down at the table with an unknown murderer. And the weird surroundings helped in no small measure. There may, of course, have been individual reasons. It was precisely the sort of situation which would make Bencolin glitter at his best. The Duchess was always ready for any form of roystering. Von Arnheim, seeing the game in his hands, expanded and became as genial as a watchful cat: I could fancy his mouth stretching in a grin of bristly blond whisker, and the round smile of his yellow-green eyes. Levasseur's philosophy of life and death made him breathe with quick satisfaction in this hobgoblin atmosphere. D'Aunay, the cold reasoner, the cunning game-maker, could watch in fascination. Dunstan was alarmed, but intrigued and tipsy; exuberant, too, that his way was clear to Isobel D'Aunay. And, with the realization that she was no longer to be mistress of D'Aunay's household, Isobel D'Aunay became subtly metamorphosed; that night, of all nights, she was a gay and beautiful woman. Gallivan's love of ghosts and murders had its perfect cumulation in the death dinner. But the maddest of all was Sally Reine... No more suitable group of people could have held up glasses for a toast.

All afternoon there had been bustle. The launch and the rowboat went back and forth, back and forth, carrying Hoffmann, Fritz, Frieda, and two or three other servants I had not previously seen. The caterers and butchers came from Coblenz; linen and silver and bedding, fruits and wine and flowers, had to be transported; they even got a chimney-sweep somewhere, though the energy of the late watchman made too much cleaning unnecessary.

It was going to be a perfect night: a cool, moist night, with a pulsing of crickets. Dull streaks of silver, laced with grey cloud, lay behind the dark pine-tops in the rise of the moon. While I dressed, I could hear subdued activity bustling all through the house. I brushed my hair more carefully that night than usual; I paid more attention to the wings of my tie, and even included the rather flamboyant diamond studs which some impulse had prompted me to bring from Paris. According to directions, I packed an overnight bag and left it at the foot of the bed for Hoffmann to gather up on his rounds. We were to dine late; it was well past nine when I went out of my room. Something, seen through the front windows of the hall, drew my attention. I looked out...

It was a breath-taking sight to see Castle Skull illuminated in that fashion, and I have no doubt that night-travellers on the Rhine gaped up at it. The vast death's head lifted itself to stare with light. The eyes were enormous oval windows of violet-coloured glass; the nose was triangular and yellow, as were also the arches of the gallery forming the teeth; and all of them shone out with a devilish and sardonic blaze. As the lights moved or fluttered in the least, different expressions played over the face of the skull. Now it would wink an eye slyly; now its grin would expand; now suddenly a look of cunning and ferocity would freeze its dead glance motionless. Cressets flamed along the battlements, pin-prick gleams were in the windows of the towers, and I could see figures moving there. I could not understand the shining of the hats on these figures until I realized that the hats were the black metal helmets of policemen. All this stood out on the sky, the vast skull grown silver-grey against the streaks of moonrise. It watched, and it waited. For centuries it had looked down on the Rhine, but it was endowed (you knew) with a savage sense of humour. It appreciated in its old age the little people who were to walk inside it, literally like creatures in its brain, and who were to tread, as phantoms in its poet's mind, the steps of the red quadrille. Ah, Baron von Arnheim, but you were a showman! Your French enemy should be humbled in a setting of which he himself would approve...

I went downstairs. Somebody was ruffling the keys of a piano in the music-room, and from the library I heard the satisfying rattle of a cocktail-shaker.

In the library, more surprises. I caught, on entering, the feverish spirit which was to carry us along, a beat of excitement strangely like the noise of that cocktail-shaker, typifying our modern world. I felt the closeness of the companionship we all suddenly cherished for one another. We were all passengers on a fantastic ship, and the first place we sought was the bar. But surely this was not Isobel D'Aunay who was manipulating the cocktail-shaker! Flushed, brown eyes dancing and head thrown back, she was swinging it with quick jerks of the wrist...

She wore a low-cut black gown, gleaming with sequins, and it showed the beauty of slim and polished shoulders. A little strand of pale hair fell over her flushed cheek. The spectre had come to life. She cried:

"Do come in, Mr. Marle! Come in and sit down and have one of these cocktails. They're called Golden Dawns, and I've always wanted to mix them. You use two parts gin, one part orange juice, and one part apricot brandy."

"Immediately," I said. And then I noticed others.

Sally Reine, in a green gown, waved a delighted hand at me from a deep couch. One eyebrow had travelled higher than the other; she balanced, somehow, a glass on two fingers. "My adored!" she greeted. "Come over and sit beside me. I think you're a perfectly lousy writer, but I like your hair-cut. Oh, and you know Mr. Gallivan, don't you?"

Gallivan, too, was a surprise. His evening clothes were flawless; they even gave grace to his lanky figure, and he was shaven and groomed, with a sleepy smile on his Punchlike face. He flipped a cocktail back into his mouth with a capacious gesture like a shark swallowing a thimble; for a moment it alarmed me with the idea that he had swallowed the glass. The drowsy smile appeared again.

"Don't goggle, young man," he told me, wagging an admonitory finger. "You're wondering where I got this rig out. I'll tell you. From an undertaker in Coblenz. The Gallivans were ever poetic. I—"

"Yah!" said Sally Reine. "I know. Bribed him with a promise of work. I say, that was thoughtful. Give me a drink."

"In fact," continued Gallivan, taking her glass, "I would have you know that I possess all the social virtues. I got them from taking those courses advertised in the magazines—the kind that work while you sleep. 'Last week they shunned me. I was a wallflower, and about to lose my best girl, because I could not speak a word of Latin. How they laughed when I offered to recite!—but their grins changed to

spellbound amazement when I quoted four books of the Æneid.'
Brilliant stunts of magic astonish my friends and cause them to lock
up the silverware every time I step into the house. Easy lessons in
etiquette, during spare time, have taught me not to throw soup in
my hostess' face or appear in public without my trousers. I can play
the saxophone, take people's fingerprints, or do any of those things
required at the ordinary social function. I—"

"Oh, *do* be sensible and have a cocktail," urged Isobel D'Aunay. "I
don't think that's funny. I—"

"You read the magazines," I said.

"So do I," Sally Reine informed me. "My old man gets heaps of
them from the States. I like the detective-story ones, where the characters aren't allowed to swear, and the Chicago gangster cries, 'Good
gracious!' It's nice to see the tough racketeer become a pathological
case at one sweep of an editor's blue pencil…"

She hesitated. Jérôme D'Aunay had come into the room. I was
taking a cocktail from his wife's hand at the moment, and I felt it
tremble ever so slightly. Her eyes travelled over her shoulder, then
back to me, and there was something breathless in them. I realized
that, quite abruptly, she was not afraid of him any more.

"Good evening, my dear," D'Aunay said in French. "You look
charming tonight."

He was smiling. The danger which momentarily had brushed us
was gone. She replied coolly in English: "Thanks loads. Won't you
have a drink?"

The effect of her words seemed to please her, for a deeper flush
came into her face, and she looked about affectionately. He walked
over to take the cocktail she poured; she gave him a little tight-lipped
smile; he took the glass, bowing. I thought that at that moment I had
never seen a more lovely woman. But I hastened to present Gallivan.

And I saw a queer look come into the reporter's face as he and D'Aunay exchanged nods. D'Aunay seemed puzzled.

"Have we ever met before?" he asked, stroking his big chin.

"I hardly think so, sir."

"H'm," muttered the Belgian; "probably not, probably not. You remind me of somebody, that's all; I can't think who—"

"Cocktails? *Cocktails?*" bellowed the voice of the Duchess from the door. She floundered in, her bulk compressed into a tight black gown which caused startling bulges in extraordinary places. She could have been strangled in her own pearls, and her hair was piled up like a wedding-cake. Her gusty entrance set everybody talking at once. The place became a babble.

Most distinctly you noted the tilt of the cocktail-shaker, gleaming and gleaming again. It was a big one, but it had to be filled almost immediately. The lighted pictures of Myron Alison looked down gravely from the walls. Dunstan entered—a little apprehensive, I thought, and not quite knowing what to do with his hands. His glance flew to Sally Reine, whom I now discovered sitting on the arm of my chair, trying to give me a drink, though a moment before she had been on the divan. Then he saw D'Aunay. D'Aunay came over and greeted him effusively, sardonically, which made him more uncomfortable. He tried to keep his eyes from Isobel D'Aunay, who was gulping down a drink, but he could not quite manage it. I remember thinking: This party's determined to get drunk, and that D'Aunay woman had better watch her step. Again I had the vision of a fantastic ship moving out into dark waters and fog...

Sally Reine pulled the lobe of my ear, and made determined efforts to sit farther in so that she could more conveniently spill my drink. She said, "You're not listening to me, and you've jolly well got to—!"

Bencolin and von Arnheim appeared at the door, resplendent. The German was in fine feather, savagely gay, and his almost invisible blond moustache had been waxed until the points stood out like the whiskers of a cat—a lean, chuckling, prowling cat. Bencolin, Mephistopheles in pearl studs, elaborately offered von Arnheim a cigarette. The other accepted and said something in a low voice, at which Bencolin nodded. They went over to get cocktails. It looked like a challenge of some sort. By the Lord! this tension, this whirling mad spirit, had caught them, too! Solemnly they touched glasses.

"Look here, darling," I heard Sally Reine saying. Under the babble her voice was low and rather fierce. "You've got to pay lots and lots of attention to me tonight. I don't want to make a silly ass of myself…"

The Duchess lumbered past in a heavy backwash of perfume. Gallivan was telling her a story about a Scotchman. At last Dunstan had drifted round to Isobel D'Aunay's side, and they were exchanging remarks in the stiffest possible tone—about the weather, I am willing to swear. Hello! Bencolin and von Arnheim had filled their glasses again. I sincerely hoped, for the glory of the Berlin police, that the challenge had not been a challenge to a drinking-bout. One night, in Payne's London bar, I had seen Bencolin in a titanic contest drink under the table a red-faced Englishman they called Bloogey—who appeared, when we carried him home, to be Lord Somebody, or Earl of Something-and-Something, but who was anyway known as the thirstiest fish in Paris.

The weird boat, with its queerly assorted cargo, had weighed anchor. I heard her fog horn. But it was not; it was only the voice of the Duchess, crying:

"Look here, draw it mild! We've got a few cocktails to deal with when we get across the way. What about starting now?"

"An excellent idea," said D'Aunay, who had been examining the portable gramophone, apparently to see what made it work. "I am hungry. *Pardieu!* I am hungry! Are we all here?"

There was something in his tone which caused everybody to look up. The words, "Are we all here?" were innocent enough; it was the sudden lifting of his voice, the slight ooze of ugly implication, which quieted down the turmoil. Sally Reine had twisted her green-clad body about on the arm of my chair, so that I could no longer see D'Aunay's face; but I know that his tone made me jump slightly. His wife and Dunstan sat on one of the broad window seats. At their feet was a disarranged Ispahan rug. Bencolin stood with von Arnheim near the tabouret of the cocktail-shaker, von Arnheim with his glass half lifted. Gallivan bent across the arm of the Duchess' chair, and in his hand was a copy of his book, *Legends of the Rhine*. Silence.

Somebody said, "All but M. Levasseur."

Like a polite and graceful, but deprecating, reply, a long note from the violin slid to our ears. Somehow there seemed to be a difference in it, but while we sat there in silence it began to play a tingling tune. Each note beat with the sharp curtness of a dance-step, emphasized by the swift finger-work. It played "Amaryllis."

Sally Reine upset her glass when she put it down. For the first time it was fully borne in on us that we were absorbing cocktails in order to avoid too much thinking about horrible things. There was a small decisive *clink* as von Arnheim deposited his own glass on the glass top of the tabouret. Dunstan's muffled, "I say!" was an incoherent protest, but none of the rest of us spoke. What the man Levasseur was doing, what mad intention prompted his playing that song, I could not conceive…

The folding-doors of the library were pushed open. Levasseur walked in. The unseen violin still hopped and skipped in its rhythm.

Somebody said, "O my God!" Jérôme D'Aunay began to laugh horribly.

But I was watching Levasseur, and I saw that he was cool and unruffled. In fact, he was smiling. That fact struck me in the mental chaos engendered by his appearance. The light gleamed on his polished black hair, on his emerald stud, on his rings as he spread out brown, deprecating hands.

"It is a Heifetz record," he said, clearly, "played on an orthophonic Victrola in the music-room. I put it on myself, in order to demonstrate that I had nothing to do with this crime."

He advanced a little. His narrow brown face was turned towards D'Aunay.

"Some people," he continued, "suffer from too great a sense of melodrama. This afternoon M. D'Aunay had the impudence to suggest to me that I was provided with an alibi because, behind locked doors, I had a gramophone record playing while I did—certain things." He twisted a deprecating wrist. He laughed. "I am aware that it is so familiar a device of melodrama that I was not surprised. I pass over the obvious silliness of the idea in any case. I pass over the insulting suggestion that, were I to commit a murder, I should resort to such a shabby trick. I pass over the fact that the Victrola would not obligingly continue to play disks of its own accord for several hours…"

In a profound hush he pointed a finger at the door. "But," he said, "I wanted to show you that anybody who believes such a thing has no knowledge of how records are made. You have only to listen, and you will hear the difference. You will hear the piano playing a musical accompaniment… And now," he concluded, smiling again, "will somebody be so kind as to offer me a cocktail?"

You did not need to strain your ears to hear the difference, but we all did listen. I think that from the beginning some dim suspicion of that sort had been at the back of several minds, and Levasseur had dispelled it with a single gesture. We were still silent. D'Aunay stood motionless and Sphinxlike, but his fists were clenched. Isobel D'Aunay got up hastily and poured Levasseur a cocktail. He took it, and his rings glittered as he held up the glass, and his bright dark eyes shone mockingly over the rim.

XVI

DEATH TAKES A COCKTAIL

N OW THE FULL WEIRDNESS OF THE THING HAD TAKEN POSSES-
sion of me.

I stood on the battlements of Castle Skull, hatless in the cool breeze. Directly in the centre of the gallery whose teeth were arches, they had opened doors I had not seen before—doors which were iron, painted grey, and invisible in the light of our electric torches the other evening. But it opened up an unsuspected world, as I had seen when our party arrived here a few minutes before…

That swift rush across the river in the scented night! I recalled the white fur collar of Sally Reine's dark wrap, crowded against my coat in the swaying launch; I recalled the gold slippers of Isobel D'Aunay, the high moon dappling the water, and, most of all, the great lighted skull staring with purple-coloured eyes from its height. Madness! Above the chugging motor I heard the Duchess' cracked voice singing, "… for many a stormy wind shall blow—!" Another boat had begun its mysterious journey. There were torches at the landing-stage on the other side. Somebody had mentioned the Styx, and the women had put on goloshes over their light footgear to climb the hill. There had been a great deal of shouting and laughing and panting and terror…

Cressets burned on the battlements around me now. Down at the end I saw duskily the green uniform and black helmet of a policeman. I turned and went back into that central hallway, revealed when the iron doors were open. The hallway with the coloured window and the curved stair, which we had seen the other night, I now knew for only a small side-effect in this house.

This central hall was large, but severe. At the back was a broad staircase, dividing into two galleries at a landing far up against the wall. Floor and staircase were muffled in thick black carpet. Candles burnt in wall-brackets along the length of the galleries, but here below were no lights. Against the wall at the stairhead stood a suit of black Milanese armour, fifteenth century, gilded and inlaid. The candlelight glimmered in the slits of its visor. It leaned on a broadsword and looked at me.

I do not know why I shivered, ascending those stairs. I noted again that in daylight the place would be illuminated only by the yellow-glass window constituting the nose, behind which now hung a gigantic cluster of candles hanging from iron chains in the ceiling. The place was too vast, it was too eerie, it too much suggested a ghost with red hair. At the landing, something stirred beside the armour, and I shied.

"I've been looking for you," said the voice of Sally Reine. "Why did you run out? The crowd is upstairs—getting tight. Here!"

She looked very small in the shadow of the black armour. The yellow light looked queer on her painted mouth; enormous dark eyes stared up at me steadily, and she had two glasses in her hands. She handed one to me. I tossed down its contents, another Golden Dawn, which warmed me pleasantly.

"It's finished," she whispered from the shadow of the armour. "He's drunk, and he told me. I—I don't think I care much, really."

I put down the glass on the pedestal of the armour, and took her face between my hands.

"Be careful," she said without winking. "I'm not going to get burnt again."

During a pause I felt a stab. You couldn't play with this girl; for all her ways, she was always in deadly earnest. And to play now—

"Let's go upstairs," I said.

More flights of steps, past another floor where the dining-room was located, and we emerged in the room which made up the entire crown of the skull. Noise rushed out at us; noise buffeted the ear-drums, swirled you again into that half-sick tensity of waiting. I saw that the roof was of glass in the shape of a dome. That there were carven pillars of ebony soaring to support it. The floor seemed to be of a black-and-gold mosaic in circular patterns of zodiac sym-bols, but I could not see what symbols because it was strewn with animal-skin rugs—strangely like the hall of Alison's house—and the animal-heads opened white-fanged jaws like an uncanny dead menagerie. People were tripping over them in all directions. Four immense crowns of candles hanging from the roof gave a fiery glow to the mosaic floor, but, even so, the room was not well lighted. I could make out no details; shadow lay everywhere outside the candlelight.

Isobel D'Aunay and Levasseur sat on a Turkish ottoman in the middle of the room. They were pouring drinks out of a big purple-glass wine-flask—the sort you buy at the stalls in Tunis—and Levasseur, noticeably more merry, was shouting compliments at her. She was laughing, crimson in the face, and telling him to hush. Also, she was having a fine time. Dunstan, a glass in his hand and an expression of the utmost determination on his face, was wandering about the room—apparently looking for something, but not quite sure what it was. Somebody started to bang the keys of a piano in the shadows; it was badly out of tune. Voices commenced a song fervently. They were the voices of Bencolin, Gallivan, and the Duchess. Sang the voices:

"Oh, the general got the *croix de guerre, parlez-vous,*
The general got the *croix de guerre, parlez-vous—!*"

I had never seen Bencolin plunge with such spirit into an occasion like this; it was unlike him, and I wondered what scheme (there was always a scheme) he had in mind. The voices explained, with feeling, what they thought of the general, and recounted some astounding biological adventures of a versatile young lady from Armentières. I wondered what all this was coming to, sooner or later, and decided that I ought to have another little drink. Over in a corner, by a solitary candle which burnt on a lacquer cabinet, I saw von Arnheim standing motionless, his arms folded.

Sally Reine let out a delighted cry, and ran from my side towards the group at the piano. I walked to where von Arnheim was standing under the candlelight. Then a shiver went through me. The expression of the man's face—it was cold, dead, watchful. His green, narrowed eyes went slowly round the room. Standing alone in that yellow pool, against high bookshelves, he was miles removed from the roaring noise; I felt uneasy at the contrast between the raucous voices at the piano and this watcher on Darien. His absurd edge of blond hair on the shaven head grew full of subtle menace. I was a little afraid of him. A curious, terrible idea came to me as I approached...

"Your party, Baron von Arnheim," I said, "seems to be a success."

He turned his head slowly. "It has already been a success, during the short time we have been here," he said. "It will be more so before the evening is ended."

A silence. Dunstan went wandering past us, holding his glass with the utmost care. He tripped over the head of a tiger, paused, examined it gravely, and continued his progress. The blatter of noise beat against my ear-drums; they were singing again. Dunstan approached us again, like a planet in its orbit. He stopped and said, very distinctly, "The beautiful blue Danube." Then he went on. Von Arnheim—of all people—was getting on my nerves horribly. Somebody had left a glass, full of greenish liquid, on a teakwood table. I tasted the liquid, and found it was *pernod*; I drank it. Von Arnheim continued to study the room, his arms folded.

"Tell you what!" This was Gallivan's voice across the uproar. "We've got five nationalities represented here—English, German, Belgian, French, and American. We'll sing national anthems. Sing national anthems. M. Bencolin, you're the only one with a good voice. You be courteous. You lead. Now! '*Die Wacht am Rhein!*'" Somebody applauded. There was a riffle and plink of keys. I heard Levasseur shouting into Isobel D'Aunay's ear, "Absolutely exquisite! Absolutely adorable!" Then a stately thunder began to give curious dignity to that badly tuned piano…

I looked about. "Well," I said, "if it's this way *before* dinner… Isn't it almost time to eat?"

"Hoffmann will be here to announce it any minute," he answered.

"Well, I suppose everybody's ready." Some one was missing, and just then I discovered who it was. "By the way," I asked, "where is M. D'Aunay?"

Again the narrow green eyes were turned on me. Gravely von Arnheim looked me over.

"M. D'Aunay," he said, "will not attend the dinner."

"Not attend the dinner?"

A horrible premonitory chill began to crawl through me as the German nodded, in a thoughtful and impersonal way.

"No," said von Arnheim. "M. D'Aunay is dead."

… I make a pause here because there really was a pause in my thoughts, even in sight and sound; a sudden severing like what must occur when the guillotine knife falls on one's neck. The stomach rose up inside me, and the lights became, for a moment, a blur. Next I saw von Arnheim's rim of blond hair, and by some evil chance I heard thunderous blended voices singing "La Brabanconne"…

"You will please be quiet about it," said von Arnheim. "Nobody must know."

"You mean," I said, trying to keep my voice steady, "there's been another mur—"

"No. It was his heart, which, they tell me, was in bad condition. I tried a little test on him. I did not expect it to have such consequences."

"But where—when—?"

"Keep your voice down! Nobody must know. We are going on with the affair; I will make an excuse. And we are going to have the murderer before you get to the coffee…"

"Then D'Aunay wasn't—isn't—I mean, wasn't guilty?"

"Not of killing Alison, no. Say nothing, do you understand? The body is in another room, covered. We will tell them afterwards."

He walked away. Still the whole appalling idea did not take possession of me: that we were expected to sit down and make a gay meal with one of our number lying—"covered"—in another room. "Covered!" How meticulous von Arnheim was! Out from under the glass roof had gone (shall we say) a mortal soul, while the piano banged, and the cocktail-shakers tilted, and Levasseur yelled, "Exquisite! Adorable!" into the ear of Isobel D'Aunay. The great financier, the high khan of money-changing, had become silent like a stopped tin clock. He was "covered"; the damned, expressive word recurred again. Presently the Bourse at Brussels would go crazy, and bloodshot eyes watch the ticker-tape, and franc-bags tilt on that foolish see-saw called the stock-market; but, for this moment, the great lord's corpse must not interrupt our fruit and wine. He would rest—covered.

Feeling rather sick, I wandered over to the table where innumerable bottles were stacked. I was looking for more of that spiritous tabasco sauce called *pernod*, and I found the bottle, together with a glass, a syphon, and cracked ice. The labels—Amourette, Amer Picon, Dubonnet, Byrrh; they had been taking no chances on thirst. And then I saw a picture, a framed photograph propped against a bottle of gin…

Maleger! The face jumped out at me, though I had not seen it since I was a child, at a theatrical performance. Maleger of the red hair; and with him, in this ancient photo, was a woman. I remembered what Gallivan had said about his mistress in the old days, and about a child. His mistress—a beautiful face, a striking face, with dark hair piled up after the fashion of the day. In the prime of life then; say thirty-five…

By God! Something was familiar in that face. A child—a child—a child which looked like its mother: the face reminded me of somebody here. The child of Maleger had grown up; I had seen that face only a few minutes ago. Boy or girl? Boy or girl? My hand trembled as I gulped down the drink. I wondered how the picture had come there. It was very dusty. Somebody had resurrected it…

Dunstan wandered past. He fixed me with a stern eye and asked whether I was drunk. *He* was drunk, he pointed out. I tried to shoo him away, but he was not satisfied until he had seen me pour out a huge one and watched with a critical eye while I drank it. Then he nodded and passed on. I racked my brains over that photograph; but by this time that terrific *pernod* had commenced to take hold. The whole crowd had now gathered round the piano, even Levasseur, and I was alone with the mess of bottles. The face of red-haired Maleger swam before me, and there occurred lines out of a forgotten book: "For I am Abaddon, Lord of the Bottomless Pit, and though I be destroyed, yet my image lives in another whose hand shall be swift to strike, and will guide the flame and thunder on the six weird roads of Death…"

"*Drunk last night,*" roared the voices at the piano, "drunk the night before! Gonna get drunk tonight if I never get drunk no more!"…

But they were not, as I discovered when Hoffmann came to announce dinner. With the exception of Dunstan and Isobel D'Aunay, nobody was more than pleasantly mellow; they were strung with excitement instead. And D'Aunay's wife carried it remarkably well. She was displaying unexpected talents that night, of graciousness and poise, and her new-found beauty lent to even her least intelligent words a tinge of wit. Just how she would take the death of her husband…

"I am very sorry," von Arnheim was saying, "that M. D'Aunay will not be able to start the meal with us. He has been suddenly summoned on the long-distance telephone…"

Which, I suppose, was true enough.

I saw von Arnheim's face when he made this remark, suavely; it was not a pleasant sight. Nobody commented. They shared my own very vague ideas on the habits of money kings, and it seemed reasonable. I tried to recall when I had last seen D'Aunay that night. It seemed to me that he was walking along the hallway of the suit of armour, and that von Arnheim was walking beside him, genially, with his arm about D'Aunay's shoulder.

The dining-room, as I have already indicated, was on the floor below in front. It was approached by corkscrew passages of marble and blue-plaster fresco in which, I noticed with a start, were hung some really remarkable paintings, as carelessly as though stacked in a lumber-room. I saw a sleeping Venus by Correggio, the lost "Sappho" of Rubens; chiefly nudes, in fleshly and languorous lure. Then through grilled iron gates we entered the dining-room…

Black! But for the great oval windows of purple-coloured glass, sable velvet draperies swept up to an arch of incredible height. Fully a hundred candles, swinging from the roof in lamps fashioned as fighting dragons of blue porcelain, threw a wild blaze on the white tablecloth, the silver, the service of Sèvres china, and the single vase full of scarlet blooms in the centre. Incense-burners in the four corners of the room curled up a thin mist of sandalwood...

The table was an oval, set for ten, and with seating arrangements thus:

von Arnheim

Myself   Bencolin

Sally Reine   Isobel D'Aunay

Gallivan   Dunstan

Levasseur   D'Aunay

The Duchess

The hush which usually falls on a dinner ensued when we sat down. I noted that the blue ceramic vase in the middle of the table contained—of all outlandish flowers—poppies. From the corner of my eye I could see, high up, those purple oval windows acquiring a ghastly sheen in the candlelight. A few candles make a table soft with pleasant illumination, but too many, as now, flame with a harsh, nervous, jumpy glare. Bencolin was examining his caviare impersonally, and the array of wine-glasses before him. Isobel D'Aunay glanced sideways, in a somewhat betraying fashion; her humid eyes ran over the face of Dunstan. But Dunstan—with one lock of his hair protruding upwards, I recall—blissfully contemplated the prospect of wine. With a gesture like a gladiator, the Duchess whipped out her napkin and regarded with a somewhat fishy eye the pleased dark countenance of Levasseur. I could not see Gallivan's face, but I saw that his freckled hands were nervously playing with the silver.

"Look!" cried Sally Reine, so suddenly that we all jumped. "I say, look! That's a bit thick!"

She was indicating the centre of the table, beside the vase of poppies. I saw for the first time a large cake, with white icing and a grotesque row of blue forget-me-nots round the edge. On this cake some craftsman had reared, in white icing, the figure of a gallows. It was, as she said, thick. I realized how stuffy it was in the room; my collar seemed tight, and the sandalwood reek had grown oppressively. I glanced from von Arnheim's thin smile down the table to the empty chair, the high-backed chair in stamped Spanish leather, where Jérôme D'Aunay should have sat…

Isobel D'Aunay laughed. She leaned white elbows on the table and looked across demurely. "But don't you know, my dear?" she said. "*I'm* the one they want. I'm guilty. Yes, really! I killed Jérôme, too; that's the reason why he isn't here…"

It broke the tension; whether the cocktails had spoken, or whether she had deliberately chosen to revitalize us, I do not know. In any case, everybody laughed and began talking at once. Levasseur, flashing white teeth, swore with uplifted hand that he had committed the murders and had just recently thrown Jérôme D'Aunay over the battlements—because, as he pointed out, he had the utmost reason to do so. The Duchess said she had always thought so, anyway, and appealed to me for corroboration. D'Aunay's chair remained empty, and suggestive. They thought it such a good joke that somebody should conceive of D'Aunay as dead. Great lords of the Bourse do not die, any more than archangels…

The soup course arrived. *Bisque d'écrévisse*—very delicious if you could eat it, which, regarding the empty chair, I found difficult. With it the wine was Montrachet, 1915. The dinner became a vision of flunkeys, curiously like cats, tilting scintillant bottles in a panorama past the shoulders of the people opposite. The steam of dishes rose subtly and mingled with the odour of sandalwood and poppies. With slow voluptuousness, as into a warm bath, our spirits sank into it. I began to be less and less afraid that the unoccupied chair might be visited by Banquo. In some high hall of this high house D'Aunay would remain, "covered."

The dish-clatter grew louder. The fish came, a sole Dijonnaise, with a satisfying Sauterne. Sally Reine was entertaining me with a discourse on the singular possibilities of being amorous with an octopus; vivid in her green dress, with eyes too bright. Snatches of conversation swirled about the candles. Booming: "—what I mean, Levasseur, God damn it, I like songs with tunes in 'em! Now, f'rinstance, you take 'Mary of Argyle—'" "—and the beautiful Blue Danube, Isobel; gonna sail beautiful blue Danube—'" "—won't you hush please, Marshall?" "—ah, but, Mademoiselle Alison, you would not like just one note played over and over again; it would drive you insane. Why, then, like two or three notes played over and over?"

Abruptly, with the entrée, the break. Somebody had knocked over a glass (I think it was Gallivan), and in the unexpected pause Sally Reine spoke.

"I have it!" she cried, snapping her fingers. "Listen, everybody! It's just come to me—the solution. And a fiver it's the right one!"

The well-known intuition of woman, Levasseur exclaimed, was—

"No, but really! We've been accusing one another, but the person farthest from suspicion is always guilty. It's Baron von Arnheim! He arranged this party just to get up over the dessert and confess…"

A babble broke out. Behind it was a curious sense of shock, as though blasphemy had been uttered. I had a feeling of topsy-turvyness, and I shot a glance from the empty chair down towards von Arnheim. He sat with his chin in his hand; his eyes had narrowed slightly…

"Besides," continued Sally, "where *is* that funny Mr. D'Aunay? The last time I saw him was with Baron von Arnheim. There!"

She obviously meant it as a joke, and yet laughter died. Everybody became conscious, even in the warm mists of wine, that he had taken far more time than was necessary for any telephone-call. Sally's loud voice still shrilled in our ears; I caught her arm and blurted, "Be still!"—which only made matters worse. The vacant place grew to distorted size. In the middle of the silence, while I saw Isobel D'Aunay staring over at her, the tipsy voice of Dunstan dropped like a stone into a pond. He leaned across the table with a jerk, as of one falling; he pointed a finger at von Arnheim's shaven head.

"When," he demanded, sternly, "did you have your last hair-cut?"

Somebody let out a hysterical giggle, immediately silenced. Isobel D'Aunay cried, "Please!" but Dunstan shook off her hand.

"I want to know," he went on, firmly, "because night murder was committed I was over here on this side river. Quite." He beamed. "Saw somebody come up out of ground, you see? Right out of ground—boppo!—dragging something. It was a body, that's what *I* think. Never thought of it before. Just remembered…"

He knocked his knuckles against his head. Isobel D'Aunay breathed fast.

"Now," he went on, "just remembered something else. I could have told you, all along, murder wasn't committed by any of *our* party at Alison's. Man who came up out of ground… couldn't have been… our party…"

In the midst of an uncanny silence, Bencolin spoke for the first time. He asked, "*Why?*"

Dunstan drew himself up and beamed about the table.

"Because," he said, triumphantly, "the man had red hair."*

---

* At this point in the first edition, readers were offered a refund from their bookseller for returning the book without having broken the physical seal to reveal the subsequent pages of the novel, on the basis that they should now be able to "guess the criminal" with the clues supplied.

XVII

"WE SHALL SEE THE MURDERER
BEFORE THE COFFEE"

VON ARNHEIM SHOT TO HIS FEET. EVEN THE EFFECT OF THAT announcement did not detract from the fact that he was in command of the situation—a small, wiry figure with head bent forward and green eyes raking the table.

"Yes," he said, distinctly, "the murder was committed by a man with red hair. It was committed by the magician Maleger."

Something went round our circle, a weird sound which was not a gasp or a moan, but was as though half a dozen secret black fears had been dispelled in one shuddering release of the breath. Sally Reine's hand jolted against her wine-glass, and it clattered over on her plate with a tingling crash which vibrated away to stillness. Curiously enough, I happened to be looking at Levasseur then. He was pale; he had been so afraid of being accused, I sensed, that relief left him aquiver. Out of the shock emerged only the staring eye-glass of von Arnheim. He stood very straight, fingers outspread on the table. His hypnotic voice, speaking in English, would not let us even turn our heads.

"I want nobody to move," he said; "I want nobody to say so much as a single word until I have finished. I brought you over here to show you something which will presently appear. A French friend of mine, a very intelligent gentleman who nevertheless sometimes allows himself to be misled, is, at bottom, the cause of this dinner.

"I respect M. Bencolin, and I know that he respects me. But once upon a time, when we were engaged in more far-reaching duels than this two-penny affair, he made a remark which has stayed with me…"

He looked at Bencolin. The Frenchman's face was utterly impassive, and his eyes looked steadily into the shadows beyond my shoulder. Satan on trial.

"He said to me," continued von Arnheim, "'My friend, you have talents. But at the end you will fail, because you have no imagination.' I never forgot it. I mention this now, because its moral is the solution of the very riddle at our door."

Von Arnheim struck the table with his fist. "The course of a life, the course of success or of madness, is determined by some careless remark directed at a weakness; and this remark brews poison long after it is forgotten by those who made it. Boys at a military school ferociously deride a scarecrow Corsican, and thus are forged the guns of Bonaparte. We laugh at a stammerer, and thus is born Demosthenes. Men do this, because at the bottom lies the horrifying fear that the sneers are true.

"Just twenty years ago, a magician named Maleger walked into a dressing-room of a theatre where Myron Alison had scored a triumph. He told Alison that never in any time could Alison be an actor. It was the eternal terrible struggle between them; and on some stifling bed in his own brain Alison always tossed in a nightmare…"

Von Arnheim made a slight gesture.

"I do not need to give you details. But Alison had already a good reason to loathe Maleger. Maleger, invariably victorious, had cheated him of a fortune in diamonds, as Maleger had cheated Jérôme D'Aunay. This afternoon I obtained the whole story on a *dossier* sent from Berlin; I need not bore you with it now. Yet it was not the loss of the money which brought Alison his particular sort of madness. It was merely a repeated sneer.

"D'Aunay was practical. Maleger had cheated them; there was no proof; *ergo*, they must get their money. D'Aunay was coldly sane, and Alison wildly visionary, and together they determined on the crime of murder. And this *I* know, because—I have no imagination."

I was not watching the others, because I was too intent on the white, grim, powerful face of von Arnheim. The great purple windows were behind him; the sable draperies and the candlelight above. He towered.

"They determined on the most cunning, devilish scheme of murder ever perpetrated. It was sheer genius. It satisfied both D'Aunay's cold reasoning and Alison's hectic love of drama. Because I have no imagination, it suddenly flashed into my mind what this plan was. You know the circumstances. Maleger was riding alone on a train. There was a train-guard to swear that nobody had been near him. He disappeared, and later his body was found in the river. It might have been accident, it might have been suicide; *but under no circumstances could it have been murder.*

"And yet it was. Several nights before Maleger was to die, they trapped him in his own Castle Skull. He lived mysteriously; he travelled mysteriously; he was so strange that none of his movements, his absences, or his foibles were ever questioned, even by his own servants.

"They trapped him, and they tied him in one of the countless secret places which he himself had constructed in this castle. They took from him his rings, his watch, his seals; even the luck-ring with which he would never part. The man's own mode of life, his own genius, had allowed them to keep him a prisoner in the place where he lived.

"Do you now see who the man really was who got on that train in the afternoon? Do you know whose diabolically clever impersonation of Maleger had once—"

"*Oh, my God!*" Gallivan cried out. "Alison! I see it! I see—"

"Alison," said von Arnheim, "who rode alone, and whose impersonation had to pass muster not under the eyes of people who knew him—for nobody knew him but D'Aunay and Alison—but of a train-guard, of half a dozen people who had seen him only on the stage in grease-paint and make-up. Alison the acrobat, who could easily swing out of the train window, alight unharmed, and remove his disguise. Then a corpse from a dissecting-room, or from a rifled grave, already prepared with rings, watch, and seals, could be thrown into the Rhine that night by Alison and D'Aunay...

"They had proved that no murder could possibly have been committed. And Maleger's will; do you recall that the two witnesses were Myron Alison and Jérôme D'Aunay? Do you see how easily it could have been forged? Well! Had the original plan been carried out—had they killed Maleger then and buried his corpse deep in the stones—they would have been safe. But Alison was not satisfied with this. He must do a more mad, dangerous, evil thing, and satisfy the traits of character which made him wear cloak and sword on the stage only because he had been born centuries too late to wear them in life. He must act with the childish savagery of his real age."

Still nobody moved or spoke. Even Dunstan had been stricken sober, and blinked with queer bloodshot eyes at his plate. I looked across the table at Bencolin, and by the Frenchman's expression I knew von Arnheim was right.

"My imagination," continued the German, "leads me to fantastic lengths, as you perceive. And yet I seem to see a wild night on the Rhine, and figures—perhaps in this room. It is after the funeral of the supposed Maleger. The coffin has gone out, borne by solemn hands; the silk hats have been reverently doffed; the smell of floral wreaths is still thick in the air; and two sorrowing friends have paid the priest.

Shutters are raised on Castle Skull. But Maleger, kept a prisoner, is still alive.

"Cunningly the friends have waited. There must be *no* chance of a slip until the last hymn is sung and the last prying questioner satisfied. If they fail, Maleger is still alive—and a horrible practical joke (but only a joke) has been played by them on one who notoriously plays horrible jokes on other people. They were paying him back, they could say to the police. He is not harmed; he has only been given a good lesson. Ha!

"I see, then, this room, with the purple windows, the high black draperies, and a single candle burning on a vast expanse of polished table. The guests and servants have gone; there remain only the neatly stacked camp-stools, and a smell of flowers. It is night, and there is rain on the windows. (How, friend Bencolin, does my imagination work *now*?) D'Aunay sits alone by the candle, with a brandy-bottle before him. Alison has volunteered to go down into the pits, down into a secret passage under the Rhine, and *finish the work*.

"So D'Aunay sits there, and he does not drink much. He does not need courage; logically he has reasoned it out. He waits for Alison's return. Presently there are returning footsteps. Alison appears—through that door—smiling. D'Aunay looks at him inquiringly. Alison, always the actor, turns out his wrist, and unconsciously he quotes, 'I have done the deed.' The castle is still silent, but for the rain on the windows."

Suddenly, with a choking noise, the Duchess pushed away her plate. She did not say anything; but, after all, von Arnheim had been speaking of her brother. I saw Levasseur's glittering, fascinated eyes, and I saw the set white face of Isobel D'Aunay.

"Alison knew he must tell D'Aunay he had killed their victim," snapped von Arnheim; "he knew that D'Aunay logically wanted the pig-sticking over once and for all. But the mad idea's buzzing drowns out logic for Alison. He is obsessed.

"Then do I need to tell you how for nearly seventeen years Maleger was kept a prisoner? The locked and guarded castle? The visits of Alison by night, through a tunnel under the Rhine? The room in the tower, without windows, with a sliding panel in its massive door; with manacles, *freshly oiled*, hung from iron staples in the wall? The old newspapers, each telling of a triumph for Alison, which Alison read to his captive to accentuate the torture? The half-crazy watchman and jailer who brought Maleger his food and cleaned his cell?

"My imagination works again. I see *why* Alison kept him there for seventeen years; why his madness grew and corroded instead of decreasing with the years. I see why—as many times he must have wished—he did not finish off his enemy with a merciful revolver-shot and end the danger of his grisly secret. I see why he renounced his British citizenship to come here even during the war. Because he could not break Maleger's spirit!

"He could keep Maleger chained like a dog to the wall. He could shut him into a windowless cell, lost and airless; give him dry bread and filthy straw; crush his body and darken his sight. But he could not banish the laughter, or trample down the defiance, which were as the laughter and defiance of the fallen Lord of Light. He could not, for the briefest instant, triumph over that titanic mirth.

"It is night. Lanterns move up the damp tower stairs and make cartwheels of light in a blue devilish gloom. The sliding panel in the door is partly open, for no cries can be heard beyond the thick walls there. Bauer, the watchman, leans against the wall and chuckles. Alison bends close to the sliding panel. A newspaper crackles, and his white lips move in the lantern-light. '… thrilled us with the power and passion of his portrayal… spellbound… surely one of the great actors of all time...' Then, from within, first a rustle of straw, a clanking of fetters, a foul odour. And presently, struggling, the boom of laughter. 'Oh, go to hell,' whispers Maleger, 'you cheap barnstormer.'"

Von Arnheim paused, bowing his head. He seemed to be shaken by his own recital, and his white knuckles supported his weight on the table. In my mind swam the tall figure of Maleger, unconquerable...

"Kreuger! Lieber!" cried von Arnheim. "Bring him in!"

He had extended his hand towards another door of the room. Three figures were coming towards us; two of them wore the green uniforms and black helmets of policemen, and were supporting a third between...

I do not know what I expected to see. For me there was only one image—the huge man with the ape's arms, the matted red hair, the powerful grey-black eyes, swaggering in his old-fashioned clothes. And now the policemen were approaching in the candlelight... Involuntarily I pushed back my chair and rose, as did Gallivan and Levasseur. There was a sinking sensation at the pit of my stomach.

The thing those policemen supported between them was, I suppose, a man. They had tried to clean it somewhat, and give it respectability. It wore a baggy salt-and-pepper suit, many sizes too large. A celluloid collar, also too large, was twisted halfway round on its scrawny neck. And it wore very new and very large shoes of a horrible bright yellow, which squeaked loudly in the silence as it shuffled towards us.

The red hair, thickly streaked with grey, had been trimmed a little round the neck. Its face was all heavy, dusty folds, collapsing at the chin, and it was drawn shiny over the cheek-bones. Only the nose jutted out, but even this seemed to droop above the lower lip. The eyes were sunken so far in the head they always seemed wriggling to emerge, like hideous shiny bugs—but you could tell that there was little sight in them. It blinked and blinked. The policemen supported its stumbling footfalls; its blind turns to the right and left, and the shaking palsy of its shoulders...

The yellow shoes squeaked loudly across the luxurious carpet. The man was mumbling, turning his fallen jaw and his bleary eyes alternately at each policeman. Maleger the unconquerable. Maleger, the fallen Lord of Light...

Dunstan sprang up, his face twisted, and indicated his chair. Isobel D'Aunay shrank away suddenly, choking. One of the policemen drew out Dunstan's chair, and the other gently lowered Maleger into it. He did not protest, but his head kept bobbing and bobbing uncontrollably. They sat him down at the rich table, before the Sèvres china, the silver-woven glasses, and the vase of scarlet poppies. His dim eyes seemed to be trying to understand what he saw. Slowly his mouth drooped open again, like a window which will not stay closed at the top. Loss of teeth had sunken his jaws, so that with each breath a sucking sound hissed on the stillness.

"You need not be afraid to speak," von Arnheim said, quietly. "His mind is gone, and his sight almost gone, too. He does not know where he is. That last terrible effort, where he carried Alison to the battlements, broke him. It is a miracle—of hate—that he was able to do it at all."

A sort of terrifying amiability spread itself over the decaying face; the steady shaking of Maleger's head seemed to be nods agreeing with von Arnheim. His vacant eye lighted on the cake which bore in white icing the figure of the gallows. A small flicker of interest came into it. He stretched out a shaking claw, with finger nails torn off it and blue cords standing out against grimy white...

"Pretty!" he croaked. "Pretty!"

"Maleger," said von Arnheim, loudly, "can you hear me?"

The man's head turned slightly, but he only looked puzzled. "Pretty!" he said, nodding again, and seemed pleased. Under the hot stuffy reek of the room I noticed another odour, a ghastly and unforgettable thing I had known only once before, at a certain hospital in New York. I found that Sally Reine's arm was about my neck, her face buried in my shoulder, and she was crying inaudible words, "Take—him—away—! Oh, take—!"

"Von Arnheim," I said, "has he—?"

"Yes," the German answered. "It is cancer. He will never go to prison; he will not even go to an asylum. It is too far gone."

Still the jerky nodding of Maleger's head, and the pleased look.

"My God! and you let him sit down at the table?" cried Isobel D'Aunay. She was behind Bencolin's chair now. Dunstan went to her and without further ado put his arm about her waist. In Dunstan's eyes there was a queer fierce pity...

"You let him alone!" suddenly roared the Duchess from the foot of the table. Her broad mouth was pulled down, and her eyes huge and fierce behind the glasses. "He'll sit at this table if I say so! Hoffmann, bring some wine! Bring the best! Bring—"

"It is cancer of the stomach, Miss Alison," said von Arnheim, gently. "And you need not be afraid, Madame D'Aunay," he smiled, "that it is contagious. We will remove him shortly..."

"Most interesting!" said Levasseur.

"You see it now," continued von Arnheim. "His energy lived until he had accomplished his purpose. You may not know of the play which Alison wished to produce, starring as the Christian leader who was burnt by the Emperor Nero. But Maleger knew of it, and Maleger lived to give him his wish..."

At the word "Nero," a flicker of struggling comprehension seemed to come into Maleger's eyes. A sort of half-cry gurgled between his toothless gums. He was like a man trapped in the middle of a heaving floor.

"Maleger!" he said.

Slowly his bleary eyes wandered about the room. Some inaudible conversation seemed to be going on in his brain. One fluttering hand tapped his chest, and his jerky bobbing grew to real comprehending nods. He tried to throw back his shoulders...

Before anybody could stop him his claw shot out and grasped Dunstan's glass of Burgundy. He spilled the red wine over his mouth and collar, but he drank a little of it. Now he was tottering on his feet, trying to regain some of that great height in his shrunken frame. His gaze was terribly intent, though his face seemed to dissolve and grow ludicrous. The celluloid collar was skewered round on his neck. He looked out over invisible spaces. His hand moved up in a twirling gesture.

Then he saw it. The Duchess had left her handbag lying on the table beside her plate; it was open, and it showed the pack of cards she carried always in the hope of a poker game...

"What's he doing?" Sally Reine demanded, hysterically. "Stop him!"

With infinite pains he edged his way along the table. His dull eye was fixed and his trembling shook the glassware. He plucked out the cards...

"Maleger!" von Arnheim yelled.

A mumbling burst from Maleger's jaws. He turned, twitching up one hand. A fan of cards appeared in his fingers, and the dull gaze gleamed with dawning triumph. But only for an instant. His shaking shoulders, his bobbing head, his palsied clutch spilled the cards in a shower over the table...

He stared at them uncomprehendingly for long minutes. Then he let out a sort of sob, a high-pitched gurgle. Two large and ludicrous tears appeared in his eyes, and the life washed out of him. For a moment he stood shaking. Then he sank down, slowly, across D'Aunay's chair.

XVIII

THE LAUGHTER OF VON ARNHEIM

"I'VE GOT TO HAND IT TO YOU, GLASS-EYE," SAID THE DUCHESS. "You had it right. And, somehow, I had my money on the other man…"

The Duchess, von Arnheim, and I sat alone in the room with the glass roof. Where the others were I did not know; but I expected Bencolin and Gallivan back at any moment. There were too many wild memories of the scene in the dining-room after Maleger had collapsed. It was very late. The clocks had gone two. Some of the candles had burnt down to guttering masses of wax, which we blew out; and now only a few of them threw over us a flutter of yellow light. Above the gulf of shadows you could see stars through the glass roof.

Von Arnheim sat back against the many-hued cushions of a divan, watching the starlight throw blue gleams against the ebony pillars. A glass of cherry brandy was at his elbow; he was affable, almost deprecating, and he smoked a cigarette luxuriously. The Duchess absently shuffled her deck of cards.

"I do not know," said von Arnheim, "what the ideas of my friend Bencolin were, even yet. But I am afraid he did not use his imagination. From the first he consistently deprecated the suggestion that Maleger was alive. He consistently, I am afraid, tried to lead me in the wrong direction."

Quizzically von Arnheim blew a smoke-ring. He continued: "But whatever else he may be, he is a sportsman. He congratulated me warmly.

"Of course, the conclusions were not very difficult. The starting-point was the mysterious man seen on the battlements with the torch. He clearly could not have run down the hillside after the murder, without being seen and heard by the two servants. It was not a very far-fetched conclusion to assume that he had never left the castle…"

He shrugged.

"Even the finding of the secret passage did not lessen this probability, in my mind. Who would be more likely to know of this passage than Maleger, who knew every nook and cranny of his castle? On the contrary, it supplied the link I needed. It supplied the means by which the pistol could have been returned unseen to the coat hanging in Alison's wardrobe.—By the way, you recall this afternoon, when we all heard somebody moving in that room but could catch no one? Maleger, of course, on his rambles. Immediately after, I crossed the river to find the other entrance. With the aid of several policemen, I found it without difficulty.

"It is beneath a skilfully concealed stone slab on the hillside. Steps go down to a stone-arched passage entirely under the river—it is not very deep at that point, you know; but how those masons in the fifteenth century must have laboured! They built those things to last, in that day. It was foul with slime and mud. Almost at the foot of the stairs, I found Maleger lying in a faint. He was done for. He has not spoken two consecutive words; the police surgeon assures me he will not live through the week."

"Well," said the Duchess, grimly, "he'll have the best of care while he *does* live. That brother of mine…" Clenching her hands, she stared at the cards. Her lower lip was folded over. She shook herself, as though to banish sentimentality. "Wait a minute! Did you go to the end of the passage on our side and see how the devil we overlooked it after all that searching this afternoon?"

"Unfortunately, I hadn't time. I was interested in trying to question Maleger. Useless, of course. But..." he hesitated.

I said, "Well?"

"There was one curious thing I did notice in the distance I penetrated along the passage. The floor, as you must have decided, is so slimy that one's feet sink to the ankle in it. I noticed Maleger's footprints; but farther along towards our side of the river I noticed a sort of trail of churned mud, as though Maleger had been over it with a broom, trying to efface his footprints."

"A broom!" I said, startled.

He turned his head slowly. "Why, yes, Mr. Marle! Is there anything very strange about a broom?"

"No. Oh no," I hastened to say. "Just something that occurred to me. Won't you continue?"

"I also found three ejected shells from the Mauser. The actual shooting, obviously, took place in the underground passage. The sequence of events is fairly clear. In some fashion, Maleger's chance to escape came at last. How, we shall never know. Perhaps the watchman relaxed his vigilance for a time; a door carelessly left unlocked is most likely. The skull of the watchman, you recall, was somewhat battered before he was shot. Presumably Maleger sprang upon him from behind and left him unconscious...

"Maleger must have meditated long on his vengeance; he must have prayed for many years to get this chance. So, once free, he started for the secret passage leading to his enemy's house..."

"One moment, please!" I interposed. "There are two secret passages, are there not? One leading from the castle itself down the hill, and then the other from the hillside under the river?"

Von Arnheim nodded, savouring his brandy. "You recall," he told me, "that passage between the walls—the one with the dummy window—which Ben—which we discovered the night we found the watchman's body? The entrance to the underground tunnel going down the hillside is in the closet of the watchman's room. Maleger came down between the dummy walls (that was where he found the kerosene-can) to the watchman's closet. Then he descended, first under the hill, and then the river. He had no need of a light; he had lived so long in semi-darkness that light would only have blinded him. The years had brought him only one demoniac idea. Whether he had meditated on burning Alison to death, once he got free, or whether the ghoulishly poetic conception came to him when he stumbled over the kerosene-can—that, of course, we cannot say. In any case, he entered the lowest passage."

Another candle burned to its socket, flickered, and puffed out. Deeper shadow crept around us, and the stars brightened in blue mysterious heights above the glass roof. I was fancying then the lean, red-haired spectre, staggering along under his last desperate strength. Von Arnheim's cold eyes grew dreamy again.

"We see the evil, mouldy passage under the river. We see the walls thick in green slime, and the arches which for four hundred years have borne the weight of the Rhine. We see this, because Alison's flashlight is approaching. Some whim has seized him this night, of all nights, to see his captive. Maleger hears the footfalls sucking and sloshing in the mud. He crouches back, and suddenly the light finds him...

"What wild yell did Maleger voice then? What agony of disease, of black years and bloody sweats, of torture and scurvy, all came boiling up into one awful shriek of insanity and triumph! And Alison—I think his heart would stop, and his knees turn to water, when his light suddenly picked out that red-haired horror hurling apelike arms at the roof. He sees death in a slimy tunnel under the Rhine. He carries always a pistol on these visits, but there is hardly time to draw it before Maleger is upon him. I do not think the shots were even fired deliberately; I think they were fired in the scuffle…"

"Look here. Go easy on the word pictures, won't you?" put in the Duchess. "What I mean, Glass-eye, he was no especial favourite of mine, Myron wasn't, but—" She fidgeted uncomfortably.

Von Arnheim caught himself up. He inclined his head, again all cold and deprecating politeness. "I am sorry," he said.

"What I mean," growled the Duchess, "you sound like a damn shilling shocker, Glass-eye. 'Tisn't so thrilling when it's personal. Well, and we know he was carried back; and I suppose Maleger shot the watchman to make sure of him. H'm." From her bag she took a cigar and struck a match, immodestly, on the heel of one shoe. "There's just one funny point," she scowled; "why, *why* did Maleger take the pistol back to the house and stick it in the pocket of Myron's coat?"

"What went on in that man's brain, Miss Alison, we shall never know…"

"And I have wondered," I interposed, "why, if D'Aunay was concerned in this thing, too, Maleger didn't go after him, also."

Von Arnheim turned to me in mild expostulation. "My dear Mr. Marle, how could he have known D'Aunay was there at all? He didn't prowl through the house and look at the guests. And he wasn't omniscient. After the murder, he could only lurk in hiding in Castle Skull. He could only hang the body of the watchman up where *he* had been imprisoned…"

He paused. The door into the hallway, a tall pointed door, was opening slowly. Against yellow light the figure of Bencolin took form; his shadow slanted across our dusky room and in his very poise was portent. He beckoned to von Arnheim. The German finished his brandy and rose.

"You wished to know," he said to us, "what really happened to D'Aunay. Come with me."

We went out into the narrow hall at the side, where a corkscrew stair descended under the dome; we went down another staircase to the gallery overlooking the main hall. Even the Duchess walked lightly. And at the side of the gallery we paused. All the candles had burnt low, though none had gone out; sodden masses of wax raised trembling flames on the iron chandelier behind the window of yellow glass which was the death's-head nose… The gallery made three sides of a square, with the broad staircase, carpeted in black, in the centre. A draught ran along the candles in the wall-brackets at the back of the staircase. The suit of black Milanese armour seemed to clasp its gauntlets more tightly about its broadsword; its gilt-work shimmered, but it remained impassive. Down in the huge gulf of the hall we saw a procession descending the stairs.

Two policemen carried a lacquer screen which had been folded together so as to form a stretcher. There was a body upon the screen, because we could see its patent-leather shoes, but a huge silver-work shawl had been thrown over this man. The gaiety of that body stood out against the sombre hall. Beside it walked Isobel D'Aunay; her pretty, vapid face was still uncomprehending, and with one hand she pressed a futile handkerchief against her chin, staring blankly at the screen. At the head of the stairs Dunstan hesitated; then he ran down after her. I noticed that Gallivan had joined our motionless group.

Von Arnheim spoke softly: "I tried an experiment, to verify my theory. I casually led Jérôme D'Aunay for a tour of inspection about the house. I took him with the utmost friendliness into one of the rooms, where there were no lights. He was lighting a cigarette, I recall. I cried out for lights, and two of the policemen entered the room bearing candles. Then M. D'Aunay saw Maleger sitting in a chair, looking at him… His heart, I fear, was not so strong as his will-power."

I was still leaning on the bannister, staring, and the Duchess had put a heavy hand on my shoulder. Von Arnheim nodded to us in farewell, and hurried down to oversee the transporting of the body to the other side of the river.

"Shall we go upstairs?" Bencolin suggested from behind us. "Mr. Gallivan, may I see you there shortly? There are certain details which should not be given out in your story to the press."

How those patent-leather shoes gleamed as they took Jérôme D'Aunay into the wind which was blowing through the front door! It would, I reflected, be a job to get him down the hill. The last impression I had was of Dunstan's seizing Isobel D'Aunay's hand as they both went out. One of the candles flickered and expired—a small one. The suit of armour was not impressed.

Back we trailed in the candlelight, up to the room with the glass roof.

"I never liked that man," said the Duchess, thoughtfully, "but, what the hell! He's dead. And I'm sleepy. And it seems to me that there hasn't been anything but a double-dose of the horrors ever since—oh, ever since ages! Would—would anybody like to play some poker?"

She and Bencolin and I entered the glass-roofed room, where now only two or three sturdy candles clung to life. The moon emerged from behind a cloud and threw wan light slyly across the animal-skin rugs; I had an impression that the ebony pillars were moving in slow procession. With a wheezing sigh the Duchess took out her cards and looked at them, and I was weary too.

A silence ensued with the closing of the door. We seemed floating in space, under glass open to the blue night, where a fantastic ship had completed its journey. Bencolin was looking up at the pale moonlight, his eyes curiously pinched. Then he looked down with gentleness at the shapeless figure of the Duchess, fumbling the cards in her pulpy hands.

"Tell me, Miss Alison," he said, gently, "why did you kill your brother?"

XIX

THE BLUE-WASHED SKY, THE TORTURED CANDLES, THE FLABBY hands manipulating the cards. But they manipulated cards no longer. They sagged. The fingers grew nerveless and trembled, and in a slow, tumbling cascade the cards fell about her feet. One solitary eight of diamonds remained in her lap.

Silence. Presently she looked up, aged, with the moon edging her grey hair. She squinted through the eye-glasses, curiously.

"D'you know, Devil-face," she said, with a sort of speculative detachment, "I kind of expected that. I knew you—well, I knew you were too clever to miss it. I couldn't help pitying old Glass-eye, there. He was so cocky. And so sure he knew. And a lot of it was right…"

"Yes," Bencolin said, quietly, "a lot of it was right."

"I'd been waiting for it all evening," she went on in that detached way. "And I don't mind. Hell! I'm old. I'm no good. I've had heaps of good fun." She squinted up at the moon. "And I don't even care anything about Maleger, any more… But I thought surely that when Glass-eye went down in the secret passage he'd find my footprints. I asked him whether he looked, and he said he only went a little way…"

Bencolin shook his head. In that instant I knew that he had conceived a sort of queer affection for this woman, as near real affection as his nature would permit. Satan in the moonlight.

"He wouldn't have found them in any case, Miss Alison," said the detective. "I took a broom, and a good pair of heavy shoes, and I messed them up beyond recognition."

"Eh?" she said. It was not an exclamation; it was a slow loosing of the breath; and she blinked at him with near-sighted eyes.

Bencolin chuckled. "Come! The thing isn't serious, you know. I can keep your secret, and I'm certain Jeff will, too. After all, why not? It was Maleger who carried the body up to the battlements and set fire to it. He can never suffer for what he did, and he did it so justly that nobody will blame him. Is there any reason why you should suffer?"

His forehead wrinkled in wry interrogation, Bencolin sat down. Abruptly I discovered that I had already sat down; that the smash of this final surprise had acted on me almost as a ghastly surprise had acted on Jérôme D'Aunay. Agatha Alison had bent over blindly, and started to pick up the scattered cards; for a time her asthmatic breath was the only noise. At last she sat up again, her hand shading her eyes.

Silence. The fantastic ship swam far out among stars.

"Devil-face," she said at last, "God knows I don't want to—to be sent up for putting bullets in—him; I don't want to, really. If I'd been sensible, like I've always told everybody else to be, I'd never have let things run away with me…"

"Funny, ain't it, laddie?" she suddenly demanded of me. "Yesterday I was sitting up in my room and telling *you* how to grow old nice and graceful-like. And I was the one that couldn't forget… No, it wasn't that, exactly; I *had* forgotten, d'ye see. It was just when the thing hit me in the face—and I discovered Myron had been keeping him over here. Y'see, I was—"

"You are Maleger's wife, aren't you?" Bencolin asked, quietly.

"There's no keeping anything from you, is there, Devil-face?" she demanded, rolling about in her seat almost gaily. "Now, then, how did you know that?"

"I discovered a photograph," replied Bencolin, "when I was ransacking your rooms. I apologize! I was looking for something else, but when I found the photograph it rather decided matters. Gallivan had told us, you see, that Maleger had been secretly married to somebody, and that it was being kept quiet because her relations objected. (Your brother *would* have objected, wouldn't he?) Well, I brought the picture over here because I thought it safer out of your rooms... Jeff, I believe, picked it up..."

Now, ludicrously, I knew why that woman's face in the photograph had been so familiar; it was the face of Agatha Alison in the days of her beauty. But I had got mixed up thinking about a son who resembled his mother. I blurted:

"Then that picture wasn't the mistress of—!"

"Damnation, Jeff!" said Bencolin. "Don't you remember Gallivan distinctly telling us this mistress was a blonde? The hair of the woman in that picture is very black indeed, as you must have noticed. Oh yes, Gallivan spoke of the secret marriage..."

The Duchess blew her nose violently on a very large handkerchief. "I told you," she said, "I was a good-looker in those days. After Maleger died—or I thought he died—I didn't much care. I—Oh, damn! Devil-face, you old crook, gimme a cigar!" She glared at him. "How did you get on to me?"

"That's better," said Bencolin, extending his case. "My suspicions at first were the same as von Arnheim's. I got his own—imaginative flashes, also." He smiled obscurely. "Particularly in the case of Maleger's supposed death. That train journey, which was so purposeless; the travelling entirely without attendants, which was an unheard-of thing for Maleger—"

"But you said," I protested, "that the theory of a fake death was untenable, and—"

"Oh, on the contrary, Jeff, I said nothing of the kind. All I said, if you will remember, was that Maleger had never *planned his own fake death*, which was perfectly true. I said it was not so simple as that. I said it was much more devilish. Then von Arnheim's undoubted imagination led him to assume the guilt of Maleger. Maleger was, obviously, alive. Maleger carried the body of Alison from the underground tunnel up into the castle, downstairs, and then hurled it flaming out on the battlements. But Maleger's finger never pulled the trigger of that Mauser."

The Duchess bit off the end of a cigar. "Sound teeth," she growled; "not a false one in me head. Get on with it, Devil-face! I—I want to know."

Bencolin handed her a light. The flare of the match lit the amusement of his long inscrutable eyes. "I am surprised," he continued, "that Baron von Arnheim overlooked one point which he himself indicated for us at the beginning. The person who fired the Mauser wore gloves. Maleger would never have taken the trouble; and at the time he was imprisoned the fingerprint system had not even come into use. What is more, don't you remember about the short finger, which could not reach across the trigger? No man so gigantic as Maleger..." He shrugged.

"When we saw in this castle the bloodstains on the whitewashed wall I was already convinced that *two* people had acted—one who shot Alison, and one who dealt with him afterwards. I had already turned my suspicions towards the secret passage also. The *height* of the bloodstains, which I carefully emphasized to you, Jeff, showed that a very tall man had carried Alison down those stairs. Alison was tall, but, carried over his captor's shoulder, Alison's arms were able to reach no closer than three feet to the floor. It did not square with the short gloveprint on the gun; it confirmed my belief in two persons..."

The Duchess examined her own stubby fingers, turning them over curiously, with the cigar stuck at an angle in her mouth. She sucked at it noisily.

"Somebody in that house was clearly guilty. I knew it when I found the gun at the first. No human reason, not even von Arnheim's poetic imagination, can give any explanation of why Maleger should have put the Mauser in the pocket of Alison's coat—"

"I asked him that," I said, grimly. "He couldn't."

"And," continued Bencolin, "there was only one small mudstain on the floor near the secret passage's entrance in Alison's rooms. Maleger didn't carry two pairs of shoes, and change them after he came the length of that sticky passage; had he come up into the rooms and put the pistol in the pocket of the coat, the place would have looked like a pig-sty. Even Magistrate Konrad could not have overlooked it.

"But reflect again! If the murderer were somebody in the house, he—or she—was scarcely *a guest*. We will even grant the unlikely possibility that a guest might know of the entrance to the secret passage; we will even grant the unlikely possibility that a guest knew Alison kept a pistol so conveniently in his chest of drawers; unlikely, since, with the exception of D'Aunay, all of them were guests who had never even been in the house before! Remember, they had been there only one day when the tragedy took place. But recall that, when Alison went into the secret passage, the outer door to his rooms was always secured with a heavy, fancy lock. The murderer had to get into Alison's rooms before he could get to the secret passage. A duplicate key could be made, of course, by taking a wax impression of the lock—but it could not conceivably be obtained by somebody who had been in the house only one day! Alison had, remember, only one key.

"And there one significant, glaringly obvious fact seemed to escape you entirely—even, I regret to say, the good Baron von Arnheim. When Alison went into the secret passage, he naturally locked the outer door to his rooms. And when his body was brought back here the door was *unlocked*; otherwise, how did Hoffmann take the burnt shoes and throw them into his closet? Who, then, unlocked it in the meantime? The answer is, clearly, somebody in this house who opened it with a duplicate key and followed Alison into the secret passage. Inferences: (1) the murderer came from this house, and (2) the murderer was not a guest, but lived here."

Another candle went out. There were only four or five left in the huge room. The Duchess sat staring at Bencolin, motionless, in a kind of fascination...

"Nevertheless," I said, "those conditions go for everybody except D'Aunay. D'Aunay was an old friend who might have known all these things. D'Aunay could have had a duplicate key. D'Aunay had short fingers. D'Aunay's wife was out of the room, and he had no alibi. D'Aunay tried to wreck his car and kill you on the way here—"

Bencolin nodded. "Yes, I thought of that, Jeff. My first impulse (you recall?) was to suspect him. But I considered. Knowing the story as I felt it must be, I could not imagine—can you?—anything more wildly impossible than D'Aunay working in co-operation with *Maleger*? Don't you realize that if they had seen each other in that secret passage either D'Aunay would have killed Maleger, or Maleger would have killed D'Aunay, or somebody would have died of shock; in any case, I can safely say that the meeting would not have been amiable. No, Jeff. D'Aunay thought Maleger was dead. He tried to wreck the car because, as I told you, he suddenly realized that I knew the truth about Maleger's 'death.' Some little cord snapped in his brain—just for an instant. He lost control of himself and..."

The detective made an impatient gesture. "But what the devil! We sit here arguing the thing like a chess problem! If I already suspected you, Miss Alison, when I went down into the secret passage I had proof. Your shoes are rather distinctive, you know; and, besides, the prints of your cane in the mud were there also. I found the muddy shoes in the closet of your bedroom—you changed them for carpet slippers, didn't you, when you came out of the passage again?—and I took the liberty of throwing them into the Rhine. That was where I found the photograph, too, and supplied myself with the motive, which, as I informed Jeff, I lacked…"

The Duchess took the cigar from her mouth. "It's funny," she remarked, heavily, "sitting here listening to this. I had the swellest kind of alibi, too; I was sitting playing poker with Frieda when the body was seen afire. Y'see, I was only gone maybe fifteen minutes; I wasn't playing poker *all* the time… Funny! Honestly it was! Tonight when Glass-eye got poetic and began to describe how Maleger had killed Myron in the secret passage—Devil-face, I swear I damn near got hysterical! At my age, too." She squinted across at him. "I bet, old timer, I'm the queerest-acting murderer *you* ever handled. Hell! I don't feel any different!…"

She sat like a squat, bespectacled Buddha, breathing asthmatically. The red end of her cigar winked, and smoke drifted up to the brightening stars. I could see that her flabby face was a little twisted, but it was with a sort of intense groping after some fact that eluded her. She held out one hand, twitched the fingers, and clenched it.

"Look," she said. "That hand took a gun and shot a brother of mine. I ought to go off in hysterics or something. And yet, I'll swear, it was just like shooting at a big scarecrow hung on wires; you know—no life in it, like! And to me that's just what Myron was. I know now he was human—oh, no end human! But I just thought of him as a kind of walking phonograph; you wound him up, and he recited, and squawked when you let him run down. Or d'ye think I'm loony?" she demanded. "When he turned around in the passage, and we put our lights on each other, and he saw the gun in my hand, he just went to pieces like a scarecrow. I—I don't feel guilty. I just feel—kind of—tired…"

Her head, with its elaborately waved grey hair, sagged slightly.

"No," she went on in a whisper; "I'd better tell you…

"Once, y'know, I was rather fond of Maleger. I think I was the only person who ever knew him. Sounds funny, hey, from me?" She rubbed a hand across her nose. "He was bad, maybe. I didn't mind that. He had hell's own fire in him! He would have been great at anything he tried, and I—I was thirty-five then, too, mind you—my insides just turned to water, somehow! Seems queer, now. I don't feel it any more; I haven't felt that way for twenty years. And I didn't feel it when I shot Myron. Y'see, Devil-face"—she hesitated, her face pinched up—"it was just something I *had* to do.

"I discovered the secret passage by accident, less than two weeks ago. Myron was away for the night, and there were guests due to arrive the next day. I wanted to get out a necklace Myron kept in a wall-safe in his room, so I could have it restrung. I remembered his safe was in the bedroom, behind a panel, but I couldn't quite remember how you opened the panel. I got to pulling things, and I heard a noise, and out in the alcove the door opened…

"Of course, at first I didn't suspect anything. But then all of a sudden I remembered all the queer things—Myron's visits, the funny shoes, and everything I knew something was *wrong*. All the peculiar incidents…

"Devil-face," she said, slapping a hand decisively against her knee, "I went back to my room. I got a pair of heavy shoes, and at the mouth of the passage I put them on. I knew Myron kept a gun in his chest of drawers, and I took that gun and a flashlight. Still I didn't know what to expect. Believe me, I went entirely under the river, and up the steps on the other side. Mebbe I'm psychic, but somehow… well, it wasn't any trick to find the entrance to the other secret passage, under the hill. It *was* a trick to go up all those steps; God knows how I did it. I couldn't do it again for any amount of money. I called myself a fool, but I felt cold all over, and something kept urging me…

"Well, sir, up I came in the watchman's closet, so out of breath I had to support myself on the wall. I was muddy and my side hurt. But then I noticed where I was. All of a sudden I heard somebody talking—crooning, like. D'ye know about the dummy wall, where the coloured-glass window is, in the wing? I could see right up those stairs from where I was in the corner of the closet, and I saw Bauer going up them with a lantern. He was nearly deaf, and he sang to himself. At the words I heard, I—"

She ran her fingers up to her hair and clutched at its edges.

"Devil-face," she said, breathlessly, "he was saying, 'Food for Maleger, food for the dog,' and he was carrying a tin plate and a cup. He was singing it, d'ye see? and his voice was dreadful. I followed the lantern. I knew he couldn't hear me.

"We went on up and up. My side hurt like all hell, but I followed. When we got up to the top of the tower he set the lantern down in front of a big door with a panel in it, nearly closed. Bauer pulled it open, and he started to laugh, and whistle to somebody inside, like a dog. He talked, and rattled his plate. Then he took out his bunch of keys and opened the door. He went inside. I could hear chains. And, Devil-face, I *knew*. It all came over me just like that. I didn't even need to look inside when he set the lantern down and took a long stick and started to prod a filthy thing in some straw…"

(Oh, how different, Agatha Alison, *this* recital from the polished pictures conjured up by von Arnheim! She hardly raised her voice and her cigar had almost gone out. But she was talking to Bencolin now as though everything in the world depended on her being understood.)

"I thought I was going to be sick. You know how you feel when your stomach gets cold and you feel sweat all over? But right then I got just as calm, just as firm, as though I'd been deciding on how to play a poker-hand. D'ye see? And the queer thing—d'ye know what I was thinking about at that minute? I was thinking about a night—oh, twenty years ago!—when I went to a dance in London with Maleger. He never danced, of course; he just watched. But, anyway, I remember I was in the ladies' dressing-room, looking at myself in a mirror, and the women were all chattering, and outside the orchestra was playing a waltz. And I had on a yellow gown with red roses at the waist, and I was all flushed up, and I *knew* I was pretty...

"Just then I must have made some noise, for Bauer looked up. I could see his face over the lantern. And my hand was absolutely steady. I shot him twice between the eyes.

"Devil-face, honestly, I must have gone potty or something, because I don't remember anything more until I was kneeling over Maleger and nursing his head. He was in a stupor and breathing badly. At first I thought, I've got to get him out of here and over to the house. Then I knew that Myron was behind this, and I knew, just like that—I had to kill Myron. D'ye see?" she demanded.

The wheezing of her breath was loud in the dim room. "And—funny!—the next thought I had was that Maleger mustn't see me the way I am now. A hag. A washerwoman. That's what I look like. Ah, hell! Why try to explain it? I remember I unlocked his manacles, rolled Bauer's body into a corner, and left all the keys near him. Then I went downstairs and got a huge lot of good food and stacked it up beside Maleger. Y'see, I didn't really think he was ill. You couldn't imagine him ill. And I resolved—calmly, Devil-face—that Myron was going to die.

"So I went back. I could hardly manage the last flight of steps. It's ages long, you know; it goes clear from our house down under the Rhine. I got back, changed my shoes again, and put the gun back in the drawer. I was careful to wipe it off again. And I lay awake all night.

"I wonder what Maleger thought when he woke up next day?... Anyhow, I got a soap impression of the lock on Myron's door, because I knew he kept it locked when he was 'working.' And I was going to wait for him to go back over there so I could catch him in the secret passage and show him I knew. I couldn't go the whole distance again.

"You know how I got my opportunity, Devil-face. Soon after he'd gone to his room, about nine o'clock, I went upstairs with D'Aunay and to my room. I'd told Frieda not to come in for a while. All I was afraid of was that Myron might look at the gun and see some bullets missing. But—that was where Glass-eye was wrong—he never carried that Mauser. I got other shoes, a long coat, and a flashlight. There was nobody in the hall. I opened his door, got the pistol, and waited until he was well down before I followed him.

"He went faster than I had thought. He was a goodish bit over when I—I was running again, and stumbling all over myself; pretty, hey?—came to where he could see my light. He turned. He had dinner-clothes on, and huge shoes, and his trousers were turned up. He yelled, 'Agatha!' I was cool, Devil-face. His voice sounded like a cannon in there. I said"—she choked suddenly—"I said, 'You bastard, this is for Maleger,' and I started shooting at him. The noise scared me, it was so loud, and there was so much smoke I got blinded; but I could see him beginning to spout blood, and he screamed. My God! Devil-face, how he screamed! He doubled up like a knife, and fell against the wall. Just then I heard footsteps splashing, and I saw Maleger with a lantern coming towards him."

She shivered. "Glass-eye wasn't so far wrong, at that, the way Maleger looked. He saw he was going to get his revenge at last. He let out a yell, too, and he was filth from top to bottom—queer how Glass-eye hit that right. I switched my own light off, and started to hurry and stumble back. I didn't know what was going to happen. I heard voices booming back there. Maleger kept yelling, 'Nero, eh? Nero, eh?' And there was a sound of somebody thrashing around…"

The voice died to a whisper. "Well… I got back all right. It was hardly turned half-past nine when I got back. I had sense enough to change my shoes. I dropped the pistol in a pocket of his coat in the closet; I thought they might overlook it there. That was a potty idea, but I was pretty potty myself; that's why I thought of it. Nobody saw me go back to my room. I changed my muddy skirt and threw the shoes into the back of my closet. When Frieda came in I was playing solitaire by the window. I'd had about six drinks, fast, in the meantime, and my hands were steady again. At ten minutes past ten that thing across the river…

"Devil-face," she said, softly, "we'll never know what Maleger said to him, or what Maleger did with him, between nine-thirty and ten past. And I think it's jolly lucky we'll never know it…"

An expiring candle-flame leaped for the roof and vanished. The stale smell of burnt wax was heavy about us. She sat with her flabby chin cupped in her hands, the cigar still stuck in the fingers. I was sunk in a phantom world in the shadows under drifting stars; I was seeing Maleger prowling about with the watchman's body on his back. The Duchess' panting breath slowed down. Peace crept into the room, subtly, as after an exhaustion of tears. Down tumbled an anchor, soft-gurgling through mysterious waters, and the ebony pillars were as spars of the weird ship riding calm at last. Now I could not see the Duchess' face, but only the hair of her bent head.

"You're safe," said the voice of Bencolin. Suddenly his voice became sharp. "Quick! Buck up, Miss Alison! Somebody's coming!"

The mysterious water was ruffled as at the splash of a stone. Bencolin jumped to his feet; I heard him fumbling about. He was striking matches rapidly, and he had found a bundle of fresh candles on a table. By the time the door opened, he had put them into the prongs of a seven-branched candelabrum, and he was lighting them on a table beside the ottoman where the Duchess sat. I gave her a quick glance. She drew a deep breath; her lower lip folded over, and she rolled her eyes towards me.

"Well, laddie!" she thundered. "My God! Can't I get *anybody* interested in a poker game?—Hullo, Sally! Come in! Want to play poker?"

Sally Reine came slowly into the candlelight. She looked tired; her green gown was mussed and she looked listlessly about.

"I suppose I might as well," she said, without interest.

"Ho!" exclaimed Agatha Alison. Setting herself, she raised that maternal eyebrow and pursed her lips. "Something wrong, m'dear? Your young man, maybe? You just tell me about it? A little poker'll do you good, hey?"

"You wouldn't understand," Sally answered, dully. "Never mind."

"Give the little girl a drink!" urged the Duchess. "Laddie, you just pour out four good stiff snorts of *pernod*, with a little seltzer and lemon. Now, here. Clear the table. I want vengeance on Devil-face. Where is everybody?"

"Baron von Arnheim," said the girl, "is telling the press all about it. I think our friend Levasseur has found a violin in one of the curio-rooms, and he's in ecstasies. Isobel and Duns… Well, everybody's occupied. For God's sake," she cried, her voice rising shrilly, "give me the cards—give me a drink—anything! I want to get stewed. Oh, damn! Levasseur's playing that violin again…"

She hurried over and slammed the door, but you could still hear tunings and plinkings from somewhere below. The Duchess had spread her bulk out in a chair at the table of the candles; she was riffling the cards, and did not spill one of them. "I've got chips," she informed us. "Carry 'em with me, like cards and cigars. You never can tell when you'll need 'em. M'dear, m'dear, calm yourself!"

Again she beamed maternally as I put the glasses of the four drinks I had been mixing at the table. Viciously Sally Reine pulled out a chair. A wandering melody had begun to float up from below; a queer, lost, sad song which suddenly sent a sting behind my eyes. The forces, fiercely repressed, which burnt in this room! That melody touched them lightly, with a cool and haunting insistence. Bencolin drew out his chair as the Duchess arranged the chips before us. With a curious emptiness in my chest I sat down.

"I'll deal the first," said the Duchess. "Dealer kicks in. Jacks or better to open…"

"What *is* that tune?" demanded Sally, pausing with her glass lifted. "I've heard it before! It—"

"Don't know, m'dear," said the Duchess, smiling complacently as she dealt. "Tush! Wake up! D'ye hear?—jacks or better to open. H'm."

"It's all very well for *you* to talk," snapped the girl. "You don't know. I wish I'd lived in *your* generation. Nice little mid-Victorian emotions and nice little ordered lives. Pah! Give me a cigarette. I—"

"I'll open it," said Bencolin, pushing a white chip to the centre. His eyelids were drooping; the candlelight caught the grey patches at his temples, and the queer twist of his mouth between small moustache and pointed beard. The violin song crept softly…

"That tune," I said, inspecting the two queens in my hand, "is called 'Humoresque.' I'm in this pot, too."

"I'll stay," said Sally, and knocked a white chip across the table. "Nothing ever disturbs *you*, Duchess. To think of you in the position I'm in... It's different. This is a new age; young gentlemen can treat things more casually than they did under good old Victoria. Bah! Who's in this?"

"Quite," said the Duchess, taking a long drink of *pernod*. "Well, I'm by. Cards, ladies and gentlemen?"

THE FOURTH
SUSPECT

I T HAS ALWAYS BEEN A MATTER FOR WONDER TO THE PARIS
newspapers, which adore the spectacular, that M. Henri Bencolin
did not rise to higher rank in his profession, and that he was not
head of every detective bureau in France. The sober ones shook their
heads, opining that it was because he had far too much imagination, so that he worked out his cases with an eye to the dramatic
rather than to the truth. They cited, for example, the murder of
his countryman Jules Fragneau, which had caused so much of a
stir in England. True, the little Frenchman had solved a problem
which baffled the best heads in Europe, but he introduced so much
unnecessary theatricality that his man almost escaped. On the other
hand, more knowing people decided that the innate sentimentality of the man worked against him; at odd moments he might be
found dreaming at the opera, or buying wine for Bohemian friends
on the left bank, or consorting with beggars whose obviously false
tales drew large sums of money from him. He, whose business was
truth, never seemed able to detect a falsehood which was practised
on himself. Nevertheless, when a member high in the War Office
wired for help in a matter which had kept the lights burning late
in the departments of government, there came the reply: "WE ARE
SENDING YOU THE BEST IN THE BUSINESS."

High up burned the lamps that night on the Quai d'Orsay, over the
black Seine and the tracery of lights, the singing lights of Paris, as mur-
murous as an old waltz. Like all good Frenchmen, Bencolin loved his
Paris. He loved the pink-and-white-flowered trees, the hurdy-gurdies,

the gaiety that is almost sadness. And something of it all touched him when he entered Villon's office in response to his superior's order.

In the big oaken room sat Villon behind a great plateau of a desk. He claimed descent from that other Villon who had once grinned over Paris like a gargoyle, and he had an odd intent expression now on his face—large and bald, with a loose underlip. His eyes were all pupil points. The capacious head was said to contain more information than that of any four men in France, and it was likewise said that he never forgot a fact. He merely sat and stared at the door until Bencolin's knock roused him. Then he rose.

The little detective came shambling in with his rather apologetic air. Bencolin's eyes were kindly and squinting; Villon could picture the stooped figure, black beard, high nose, all redolent of cigar smoke, even with closed eyes. Bencolin had a top hat stuck rather rakishly on his head; his cloak sagged after him when he advanced to the desk.

"M. le Comte," he said, "my greetings. Your agents found me listening to Mme. St. Marie's singing. I gathered that the message was urgent."

"Sit down, monsieur. A cigar? My dear Bencolin, I sent for you for obvious reasons. We have not forgotten your work on the 'newspaper' murder of the Rue des Marchands, nor your more recent adventure in England (though we were forced to deprecate your assumption of authority there, monsieur)." Villon nodded his big head slowly, like a wooden mandarin. Then he said abruptly: "You did well to listen to Mme. St. Marie, my friend."

Bencolin sat down and lighted a cigar. The office was silent awhile, almost as though it were empty under the brilliant light.

"She sings divinely," Bencolin remarked, blowing a cloud of smoke.

"Bah! I must correct you there. She has no great voice; she will never appear in the opera. She is only a gypsy, a winking red-haired gypsy whom men want to kiss because the sight of her affects one like the touch of her. And yet, my friend, last night I thought that she was guilty of murder."

He spoke unemotionally. Bencolin shrugged, and waited. His companion looked faintly disappointed, the pinpoint eyes blinked, but he went on:

"In these days after a great world war, it is almost ridiculous to speak of spies or espionage. Yet there is such a man near Paris. He is a spy exactly as von Stumann was a spy ten years ago. For what reason, or in the employ of what nation, we do not know; that is the worst feature. Why does one have spies in peacetime? Who should be interested in knowing what goes on in our councils? What of our finances, our battleships, our code signals? We do not publish such information broadcast, yet this man has it, because we have detected him. And we cannot punish him, monsieur, because the world is at peace. Such information may be even more deadly to us now than ten years ago. Italy, England, America, Germany... You have often been called upon to investigate the spy of war, my friend. Now you are called on to investigate the spy of peace."

"And you want me to discover who he is?"

"No!" Villon said triumphantly. "We know the man. But you have been summoned because he was shot through the head last night. Listen to me, Bencolin. The person who called himself LaGarde had a brilliant mind, a mind handsome as his face was handsome, but he was indiscreet. He carried with him constantly some paper whereon was written his commission, *and the name of the government which commissioned him*. We know it because we have a letter, in a very childish cipher, boasting of its possession. Some say he had an accomplice, a woman, but we do not know. Don't you see? Living, LaGarde with this commission was a danger. But dead, he may be fatal. That commission has not been found. If it chances to be found, and published"—he was growing excited, so that the big form underwent an odd alchemy, like jelly into stone—"published, it might mean war. There is an international etiquette; publicly, France could not overlook such a breach of it. And France does not want war. Let us suppose, M. Bencolin, that a nation, which we shall call X, were for some reason prying into our secrets, and that every newspaper in France carried news of it—or that it even got outside the proper channels. Ah, you see the consequences?"

For a long time Bencolin looked at his cigar.

"M. le Comte flatters me with his confidence," he said.

"For an evident reason! You must find that slip of paper—identification card, if you will—and bring it to us. And when you do that, monsieur, you may be able to discover who killed LaGarde. This time, as in the Fragneau case, you will be dealing with a vanishing assassin. Your department boasts that you have never been beaten. But here I think that you will be beaten at last... Because, my friend, it is all as simple and baffling as life. We have seen this incredible thing occur, yet we cannot conceive of an explanation. Someone shot LaGarde, after which the murderer disappeared. There was no trickery, no stealing away in half light or any such mummery as the Englishman Garrick perpetrated. He merely vanished... Let me tell you the story."

Villon rose heavily and lumbered to the wall. He turned off all the lights except the desk lamp; when he returned to his seat Bencolin was in shadow. But the official sat there motionless as a monstrous bald idol while his lips fashioned the words slowly and clearly, and the pinpoint eyes did not waver in their stare.

II

If you know Mme. St. Marie (said Villon) you may possibly know M. Patrick O'Riordan, the drunken Irishman who is her husband.

Sometime we shall be forced to give O'Riordan his dismissal from the secret service bureau; when he is sober, there are few better men in the department, but his erratic conduct cannot be pardoned by that. He saw three years of the most horrible blinding fighting on the western front; after a series of insane stunts he was railroaded to Paris, full of gas and shrapnel. He had the Cross of Honour, but he had no right arm...

I saw him once in the Bois, quite thin, with eyes wretched because he who was so handsome had his right sleeve pinned across his chest. He was riding on a fine black horse, and beside him rode a girl with blood-red hair bound around the white of her face. It was Mme. St. Marie. I said she had no great voice, but ah, my friend, who can forget the night war was declared, when she, very young, sang "La Marseillaise"—with her wild hair streaming and every beautiful vibrant thrill in her body! That night, monsieur, one heard again the drums of Jena and Sedan.

O'Riordan met her on one of his rambles about Paris, as I have said. They were crazily in love, but they did not marry for a while, because he volunteered for intelligence work. He wandered all through the Balkans, the great tall Irishman with his drunken grin; he got through the German lines on sheer nerve, and once he was seen in Constantinople, riding like a lord in a German general's motorcar. When the armistice was signed, he came up from the East, singing, and married Mme. St. Marie.

Now I must gather up the narrative. I suppose you have heard enough of the man LaGarde to consider it natural that since he has been in France he should have paid attentions to Mme. St. Marie. Handsome man—hands like a musician and eyes like a poet, but slightly fat. Women used to rave over his beautiful hair; yes, and I did not know that it was a wig until I saw it slipped partly off, while he had a bullet hole through his head. He had an establishment some few miles up the Avenue de la Défense; literally, the house used to be full of women. Last night he gave a masked ball.

I warn you that you are going to meet odd characters in this affair. Had it not been for one of Patrick O'Riordan's two guardian angels, O'Riordan and I might not have gone out to LaGarde's house. At least, we should probably not have gone that night. Of these two guardian angels, one is a little Turk named Gomboul, whom O'Riordan brought back from the Balkans—a chocolate-coloured fellow with shiny eyes and teeth like a tame tiger. O'Riordan frisked him out from under somebody's sword, so that Gomboul is annoying in his constant attention on his master. He waddles around after him, fanatically fearful that somebody is going to hurt him, all daggers or smiles, mumbling, "Yus, master." He will throw back his head and intone long passages from the Koran like a dog crying to the moon... Then the other person is even more of a religious fanatic, in a way. It is a dried-up woman, a crooning soul who has been housekeeper for O'Riordan. Her name, to be exact, is Celeste Gratin; she has the air of a stone virgin, with a slight moustache like such women, and eyes that follow one around in the manner of a picture. She is religion-crazy. Sometimes, O'Riordan has told me, you will see a wild ridiculous scene, with her shrieking the Ten Commandments at the heathen, and he bawling out his Koran with head back, while O'Riordan sits in a corner applauding and drinking brandy.

Well, then! For nearly a month O'Riordan has been away on a government mission. It had to do with LaGarde; specifically, he has been attempting to discover what government sent him. No success, my friend! And in the meantime, all very cleverly, LaGarde has been doing his own secret service work. He has hunted the hunter, and he has stalked the hunter's wife. You see the trend of affairs?

I met O'Riordan at the Place de l'Etoile; he was flushed and despondent, but he talked with eagerness about seeing his wife again. He had returned unexpectedly, with only a wire to me, and he planned on surprising his wife…

I shan't soon forget his expression when we arrived at his apartment on the Avenue du Bois du Boulogne. In the dusk it was quite empty, but shadowed with blowing branches and filled with the scent of flowers from the trees outside. You could almost feel someone stepping lightly over the carpets. But she was not there. Instead this moustached, grim-eyed woman sat in the middle of the drawing room, telling her beads.

"She is gone," said Celeste Gratin, rising and clenching her mannish hands. "May the good God have mercy upon her soul for hurting you! She has gone with M. LaGarde, to his house, and she has taken a valise."

III

Subsequent events (continued Villon) are confused in my mind. I remember that O'Riordan sat down to wait; he steadfastly refused to believe that Mlle. Gratin spoke the truth. He said, trying to smile, "She'll be in, Villon; she'll come in from shopping—There! Isn't that her laugh in the hall? Of course!" But she never came. Celeste Gratin went out, mumbling; I heard her rifling among drawers in the next room, and presently she stalked out of the apartment.

It grew later and later, until O'Riordan's talk of shopping tours became a rather ghastly farce. He paced up and down, smoking cigarettes. Nor had he bothered to turn on any lights, so that I could hear his steps go padding about in darkness, or see his spectral figure move across the moonlight in the windows. I must have fallen into a doze.

When I awoke he was shaking me by the shoulder. He had turned on every light in the room, and was standing with a big black cloak billowing around him, a weird and lofty form with white, staring face.

"Get up, Villon!" he muttered. "Get up. We're going to LaGarde's place. By God, I can have it out with him in more ways than one! I'm going to get to the bottom of this thing if I have to kill him, and I'm going to find out about Sylvie... Is your car still downstairs?"

That drive was a stormy, roaring race. O'Riordan was at the wheel of the roadster; I can remember only a stream of lights, the screech when he jumped on the brakes, the people scuttling past us like chickens—black silhouettes on the windshield. We turned right at the Boulevard des Lannes, then left up the Avenue de la Défense. I was wide enough awake when we got out on the open road. White road, rushing in the car lamps, and the scarlet A's on the stop signs reeling and falling behind, with the call of the horn screaming before us like a battle cry.

Presently we smashed in through a tapestry of trees, eerie and ghostly like flying clouds. The wet perfume of gardens, the swish of leaves, the gleam of a statue—we mounted past them and stopped lone as on some deserted windy height. There it stood, forlorn under the stars: the house and the gardens, which were strung with vague lights. Yes, I tell you the gardens glowed all naked, but the house was black except for one illuminated window. And the rustling branches, and the gravel drive rutted with car tracks, all looked uncanny, as though an army had passed. It was then that I remembered: LaGarde had given a masked ball that night. It must be near dawn, I decided, for the guests had gone. Nothing moved in those lighted gardens.

We got out of the car; we moved over the lawn rather breathlessly. Then, close to the house, we saw it, full black on the yellow oblong of the window. It was a shadow, rearing up like smoke, and it was the shadow of a woman. O'Riordan muttered something...

We were almost at the steps when we heard the sound of the shot. It was unmistakably that, and it had come from the room of the lighted window. O'Riordan broke into a run. He leaped the porch stairs, he had knocked open the door of the house before my wits were aroused. When I reached the front door I saw him in the hallway, terrifying as a cloaked god, and he was surging his shoulder at one of the doors. When I heard it tear open, and saw him half fall inside, I noticed another thing in that blank corridor, where a single lamp beamed high. It was a little brown figure, gibbering like a monkey under the lamp: it was Gomboul, the Turk.

I went quietly to the shattered door. O'Riordan was leaning against the jamb, and his head was bowed.

"I thank God," he said, "that we are too late, monsieur."

In the middle of the room, partly facing the door, a man sat throned in state, except that his legs had a curiously sprawled look. He was in velvet and satins, white wig of the eighteenth century, all white in the sombre furnishings of the room. Incongruously, one hand lying on the table beside him held a lighted cigarette, from which the smoke went up very straight. Just that lonely figure, head on one side, looking at us through the eyeholes of a white mask. But in the centre of the forehead, like another eyehole in the mask, there was the round red blot of a bullet mark. Then, as we looked, a little streak of red shot down from it across the white mask.

From the doorway O'Riordan suddenly asked, *"Where is she?"*

That was a last bitter tangling of strings. There was nobody else in the room except that grotesque dead man—nobody else. I examined it with care. No one hiding. There was one full-length window, fastened on the inside with sliding bolts and a catch. Obviously it would have been impossible to step outside and lock that window from the inside. And as for LaGarde locking it after he had been shot, that was just as impossible; death was instantaneous. We had both been watching the door of the room, and we had seen nobody leave. Certainly the person who killed LaGarde could not have left, *yet that person was not in the room*. Secret entrances? Quite out of the question, as we discovered; besides, my friend, that is a sheer wild device of melodrama, and one does not find such things in prosaic country houses. Suicide, then? Again out of the question, because there was no weapon.

Name of a name! The whole matter was appalling. And it was so aimless. I remember what a horrible significance small details had: O'Riordan, in a sort of daze, meticulously taking the cigarette from the flabby hand and squashing it out on an ashtray—it was a homemade cigarette, and it crumbled; then Gomboul, sidling in with a scared look. In the doorway behind him a lot of faces had begun to peek in like curious chickens—servants. The insanest gabble went up, and when we took the mask off LaGarde's face, so that the eyes peered out, Gomboul began singing out his religious chants. O'Riordan cursed him into silence, after which he demanded in English, what the hell Gomboul was doing there.

"Master say, 'Take care Sylvie,'" the Turk answered. "I haf followed. Master, she go in this room, after she dance. Master, she not here now."

O'Riordan's slow eyes moved as though they alone were alive in his face, from Gomboul to me, and then to the dead man. Then he made a little sniffing, shrugging motion, after which he turned his big back and went toward the door.

When I followed him to the porch, the dawn was brushing out over the trees, drowsy on the eyelids. The garden lights glowed on the grey. There was a faint rustle of birds. And in the middle of the lawn, like a figure in mist, stood a lone woman, looking at the house. It was Celeste Gratin... O'Riordan sat down on the steps.

"I'm tired, Villon," he said. "I'm so tired..."

IV

Quite suddenly M. Bencolin realized that the quiet voice had stopped speaking. The little detective had sunk so far down in his chair that his elbows over its arms looked like wings. His cigar had gone out.

"Well!" grunted Villon, drawing a long breath. "What do you make of it now?"

Bencolin accepted another cigar. He got up and went wandering about the room, his head forward and bobbing on his shoulders. Then he paused.

"With all this evidence," he remarked, "why has not Mme. St. Marie been arrested?"

"Because, my friend, she has a perfect alibi!"

Bencolin struck the desk. "Monsieur," he said wildly, and he flourished the cigar, "are you now so blind as to doubt the existence of a God? It was the one chance for which I had been hoping. Ah, yes; you are going to tell me, are you not, that she was seen outside the house before the shot was fired?"

"If I doubt the existence of a God," replied Villon politely, "at least I cannot doubt the existence of a devil. How does monsieur know? Yes, she was seen getting into a motorcar on the other side of the house just as we approached. She must even have seen *us*. We have witnesses in the form of a couple who were coming over the hill behind LaGarde's house, and who met her face to face. We shall not pry into the reason why they were abroad at that hour, this man and woman; they are lovers, and their business was at least honest. We are withholding their names; monsieur sees? But they are well-known peasants. Mme. St. Marie has bought milk from one; she recognized her, and called on her today for identification. Yet," said Villon, "I think that all three are lying. The thing is incredible! How did she leave the room, if she did not shoot LaGarde, with the Turk guarding a bolted door, and the windows locked? And who *was* the woman in LaGarde's room, if not she?"

"Ah! Well, M. le Comte, how did she leave the room even if she did shoot LaGarde? As for the second question—stay a moment! This matter of the paper with LaGarde's commission: you searched for it?"

"We searched the house from cellar to attic; we have been through all LaGarde's effects very carefully. No, monsieur, we have not found it. The paper *must* exist—"

Bencolin laughed. He seemed very lively now.

"Yes, of course… My friend, a great American once wrote a story… No matter! Now tell me, if you will, where was the window of this room?"

"It faced the lawn, opening on the porch. As one entered the room, it was on the left-hand side, at right angles to the door."

"You see the significance of that?"

"No."

"And the cigarette? Monsieur does not see the significance of that? Of course not; being on the scene, you were blinded." Bencolin put on his hat thoughtfully, hunching his shoulders under the cape. Then he went to the door.

"M. le Comte," he said, "I have a theory. I do not know whether it is true, and there are parts of it which are as puzzling to me as to you. I shall want time: And now may I bid you good evening? I shall want to walk the streets a long time to think. Paris at nighttime! Is it not fit subject for a dark romancer, another Villon with singing heart and swinging tankard?"

Villon was annoyed. He blinked his eyes slowly. "No," he admitted, "I have no theory, because I am a man of facts. I can conceive of none whatever to fit this business. Can monsieur suggest any?"

"There are many, many theories," responded Bencolin, with his hand on the door. "Consider! There is the theory that while O'Riordan was rushing into the hallway ahead, M. Villon himself went along the porch and fired through the window, using, let us say, a Maxim silencer, and that afterwards he locked the window on the inside, unnoticed."

"Ridiculous! What of the shot we heard? What of the woman in the room? You do not imply that I am telling an untruth…"

"Naturally not. The idea is, of course, ridiculous. But M. le Comte de Villon has said that there could be no theory. I know that it is not the true one; nevertheless, it is a theory."

"But who," cried Villon, rising up like a mountain behind the desk, "was the woman in the room?"

"I may be wrong," answered the little detective, "yet I think that it was Celeste Gratin."

"It means, then, that she is guilty?"

"No, my friend, nothing of the kind," said Bencolin. "It means that she is innocent."

And he bowed politely as he backed from the room.

v

In the springtime of Paris, which is a blue dawn over a city of old ghosts, there was a window in the Avenue des Bois beyond which white trees moved. And framed in the window sat a girl all in white, except for her unbound red hair. Hers was a paleness like ivory, with drooping eyelids and a slow curving smile. But something of the lift and defiance of the falcon's poise was in her profile, the falcon as well as a frightened bird, so that her blue eyes were truly as those of one who explores the sky. Beside her there knelt a tall quiet man, with his dark head bowed, so that in the peace of it all there was something closely akin to a shrine.

When M. Henri Bencolin entered through the portieres, a trailing apologetic figure, the man rose.

"Come on in, old top!" he said, and the voice had a thrill that woke the picture to life, as though tapestries assumed vital form. "I was expecting you, after our conversation this morning."

He stood there, vibrant with his laugh, and the empty sleeve was almost unnoticed in that warm light. Sylvie St. Marie smiled too.

"M. Bencolin? Of course I know you! Who does not?" she added, shrugging. "Please sit down! I should hate to consider you a police officer." (The falcon, head back, gay, defiant, poised.)

"Do not inconvenience yourselves," said Bencolin rather fumblingly. He glanced round at the maid in the doorway, who was retiring. Then he sat down. Patrick O'Riordan seated himself beside his wife.

"I bring bad news," Bencolin continued, "but I bring you news that will set you free. I know the truth about LaGarde's death."

He said it simply and quietly, blinking at them. Sylvie St. Marie looked at him with unmoving eyes. (The frightened bird, steadying for flight.)

"When I left you this morning, M. O'Riordan, I discovered something—I learned that the woman Celeste Gratin has killed herself. Let me finish, please. She drowned herself in the Seine. They got the body out this morning, with a little silver crucifix twined about the neck. She had already written a note which she just addressed 'To the Police

Department,' confessing that she had shot LaGarde. She confessed to a crime she did not commit."

Bencolin was leaning forward, speaking in a low voice which held the others motionless. The wind-touched bright room, the shadows of white blossoms, the little black figure who addressed them very gently.

"She thought that she had killed LaGarde. Listen, she meant to kill him. She loved both of you, but she loved M. O'Riordan best, for she could not see him suffer, and she could not let go unavenged this thing which she considered so blasphemous. When M. O'Riordan returned, she got a pistol from the next room. By hired car she went to LaGarde's house. The guests were departing. Through the window she saw LaGarde and Mme. St. Marie in that room…

"You perceive it? She waits, praying there with the pistol in her hand, driven to a frenzy, moving in the moonlight. LaGarde is talking, at his ease with mask up and lolling over a chair in his white-stockinged finery. The last car has gone. She raps on the window!

"No," cried Bencolin, "she does not know that a wife, playing alone against LaGarde, has been attempting to find out from him what she knows her husband is attempting to find out in another country. She enters the room, this maniacal woman, and at pistol point she orders Mme. St. Marie out. There she stands, and when madame has gone she pours out every cold, taunting fact she knows. M. O'Riordan is back! He has discovered the whereabouts of his wife! He will kill M. LaGarde… There, it is the humming of an auto in the drive. LaGarde, furious, rushes forward in the dim light. She fires.

"Then she goes out by the window, unseen as Villon and O'Riordan pass the corner of the house. *But she has missed her aim.* She has lodged the bullet in the dark panelling, where only a search with a glass will reveal it. LaGarde knows that he is trapped, unless he can be his calm, debonair self and insist that nobody was in the room. He locks the window, pulls down his mask, and attempting calmness, lights a cigarette when he sits down in a chair facing the door...

"You, M. O'Riordan, breaking open the door, face to face with LaGarde and seeing no one else in the room, conceive that he has shot her. You fired through the folds of your long cloak, and using a Maxim silencer on the pistol you had prepared for this event, you killed LaGarde in his chair."

VI

It seemed incredible—not these amazing statements of M. Bencolin, because they had about them the quiet clarity of truth, but that in so short a space of time Sylvie St. Marie should have undergone such a transformation. The falcon tossed its head, the body became stiff, the hardening lips suddenly grew rather horrible. You thought of no childish simplicity now. She shook back her red hair.

"You killed him!" she said.

O'Riordan shrugged; he tried a little laugh.

"That's it," he replied, blinking his eyes. "You've guessed it neatly. I was going to confess there, because I thought they would accuse you, but when I discovered you were out of the house... Now I suppose I'm arrested, eh, old top? Well..." He stood there, tall and dark, playing aimlessly with the empty sleeve. Then he said, "Oh, my God!" in such a voice that it gave away his self-control, and he shuddered.

There were no lamps at the shrine now. Vaguely M. Bencolin recalled that the Furies were supposed to have red hair. Sylvie, whose face was a weird thing between tears and hate, went to her husband and began tugging grotesquely at his sleeve. Her eyes were wide open in their stare.

"You killed François! You killed LaGarde! May God blast your soul!" she cried, striking at him. "I loved him! I never loved anybody else, do you hear that? I never loved anybody else…" Then she turned round, with the tears on her face. But she began to smile.

"Well, monsieur le gendarme," she added, triumphantly, "now that you have been so good as to tell me, will you go and report the matter to the authorities, or shall I?"

Bencolin had risen. He looked as though he could not believe what he had heard.

"Madame means," he muttered, "that she would betray her husband?"

"There is a telephone here," the woman answered. "Yes, there is a telephone here—by your arm, M. Bencolin! My husband! I knew LaGarde before I knew him. I loved LaGarde. Well, you simpering idiot, will you get me the police department, or whoever it is? You know the number."

"To hell with you!" O'Riordan suddenly shouted, and he laughed. "I'll call them myself. Here, give me the phone!"

Bencolin was angry too, but the little figure was clothed almost with dignity in it. "I have a commission to execute for madame," he said, and he bowed and took up the instrument. Then he stood looking at them over it with eyes that had become glittery.

"We shall give them the information, yes," he went on. "Yes, and because I was mistaken in madame, we shall give them other information too, which I suppressed because I thought you loved the man who will be guillotined for you. We shall tell them, madame, who was the accomplice of LaGarde in the employ of another government—who was the spy who, because she was married to a French official, could obtain the information LaGarde wanted. We shall tell them whose name besides LaGarde's is written on that identification card"—he gave a number into the telephone—"and finally, we shall tell them where that damning identification card may be found. I should have been fool enough to have concealed all this for the sake of a man who loved France only less than he loved you. Take part of your information or all of mine—but in the name of God, let there be an equal falsehood or an equal truth!... Madame," said M. Bencolin, extending the telephone, "here is your party."

The telephone buzzed and tinkled with a tiny voice. Bencolin was still holding it out to the motionless woman when O'Riordan burst out laughing.

"Right again!" he cried. "I knew it all when I came back, but I was going to be treacherous enough to conceal it because of... Sylvie. I had discovered where the piece of paper was that contained the names, and when I saw that self-rolled cigarette in LaGarde's hand after the murder, I even squashed it out to preserve it intact... But how did you know all this?"

"A man of such fastidious tastes, smoking a rolled cigarette when he had on him a full case of manufactured ones?" queried Bencolin. "What does it suggest, especially as we have the police hunting for a missing paper which they will swear is nowhere about the house? Does it not at least require an examination? Then, when one finds Mme. St. Marie's name on the cigarette paper also, it will explain that her husband knew, because for no reason at all he attempted to put it out—that in itself would first have drawn my attention to the cigarette. In LaGarde's haste he took out of his case the one cigarette he had always intended to save. Why, how obvious it is! The murder in particular, as linked with it. Could LaGarde have been holding that newly lighted cigarette if he had been shot at the time we saw the shadow on the blind? He died instantly. Could he have been sitting *facing* the door, at right angles to the window, and be shot through the middle of the forehead by someone at the window? And above all, could there have been a bullet hole in the panelling if Mlle. Gratin's bullet had taken effect? No! Or consider this: LaGarde was wearing his mask down when he was murdered. Can one expect that during his tête-à-tête with Mme. St. Marie he wore it down? Or does one rather infer that he pulled it down after both women had gone? Only one person could have shot him, from his position, and that was a man in the doorway. Who alone had stood in the doorway before the murder? O'Riordan. Who alone wore a costume that would enable him to conceal, say, a silencer—"

"Put down the telephone, M. Bencolin," interrupted the woman. She looked at him defiantly. "You have won, I suppose. What do you intend to do?"

"Nothing, madame. Have there not been tragedies enough in this ghastly affair? And would not exposure interfere seriously with... madame's career?" the detective said. "Because of her husband, I shall not make these revelations, but I shall be watching her henceforth. And monsieur? Look out the window: you see the Arc de Triomphe? Once I saw him ride under that..." Shamblingly, apologetically, Bencolin gathered up his hat and stick. "You flatter me, madame, you flatter a poor simpering idiot of a gendarme. I have lost."

VII

M. le Comte de Villon was exultant when Bencolin came to call on him that night. They sat as they had sat two evenings before, in the big lighted office; but now Villon regarded his companion mockingly.

"I have often wondered, my friend, where you get your reputation," Villon observed. "I understand now. Monsieur has been reading too much fiction. He loves to puzzle, he loves to hint. And yet without phenomenal luck, he can do nothing." He smiled in his expansive fashion. "Did not monsieur assure me that Mlle. Gratin was innocent?"

"I fear so," Bencolin admitted, and he sighed.

"Yet we have her confession. You see," went on Villon airily, "it is all very simple at bottom. Now that we have it explained, I could not swear that the window was locked on the inside. I do not doubt that I was merely mistaken about the window. You know, of course, that I suspected Mlle. Gratin from the first. I have given my explanation to my own superiors, and they agree. Ah, it is splendid!"

"M. le Comte is to be congratulated," murmured Bencolin.

"It is nothing. Again, my friend, you failed signally to locate the paper. *I* have done that! Stop, monsieur; let me explain. Is it not odd that the great Bencolin should have been beaten by a woman?" asked Villon merrily. "This afternoon Mme. Sylvie St. Marie came to me. She explained why she had been in the room that night. She had been aiding her husband, trying to find the paper herself! From him she stole the paper, and as LaGarde sought to take it from her, she destroyed it before she could read it. It is a pity that we do not know who employed LaGarde, but at least the paper is done away with. *Madame St. Marie told me to search no further for it.* Ah, there is a woman, Bencolin! I admit that I was mistaken in her."

Bencolin smiled very faintly.

"And all your brave mysterious talk," continued Villon, "was a rather amusing fraud. Bencolin, Bencolin, will you never learn that the true brain scoffs at theories? And monsieur had the temerity to suggest to me some weird tale of a Maxim silencer!"

"Yes," returned Bencolin, smiling again, "I fear I had the temerity to suggest that also… Parbleu!" he added, searching in his pockets. "I have no cigars! Well, here are some vile cigarettes. I have been forced to adopt LaGarde's method of rolling them myself. Will M. le Comte honour me by accepting one?"

"In your honour, Bencolin—thank you. It gives me great pleasure to smoke this way, as LaGarde smoked, and smile at you as he must have smiled could he have known the strange theories you would build up..." Whimsically Villon took the cigarette. "You are a bad manufacturer, my friend. This has a wilted appearance. You must have tried several times before you rolled it correctly."

They both lighted their cigarettes. Villon kept talking, pointing out one fact after another. He was in high spirits when Bencolin finally rose to go.

"Well, good-bye, my friend," said Villon, nodding his big head. "Perhaps we shall have need of your romancing another time." He flipped his cigarette out the window.

"Did madame by chance tell you where the paper was hidden?" Bencolin asked, his hand on the knob, his old top hat askew.

"Alas, no! Except that he carried it with him. I did not pry into these secrets of hers," replied Villon, winking. "And yet I confess it irritates me that I did not find it. Apparently the whole thing was right under my nose the whole time!"

"M. le Comte," said Bencolin, making a flourishing salute with his stick, "speaks more truly than he knows!"

ALSO BY JOHN DICKSON CARR

In the smoke-wreathed gloom of a Parisian salon, Inspector Bencolin has summoned his allies to discuss a peculiar case. A would-be murderer, imprisoned for his attempt to kill his wife, has escaped and is known to have visited a plastic surgeon. The fugitive's whereabouts are uncertain, though with his former wife poised to marry again, Bencolin predicts his return.

Sure enough, the Inspector's worst suspicions are realised when the beheaded body of the new suitor is discovered in a locked room of the salon, from which it appears nobody could have escaped unseen. The challenge set, Bencolin sets off into the Parisian night to unravel the dumbfounding mystery and track down the sadistic killer.

This new edition of Carr's first mystery novel also includes the rare Inspector Bencolin short story 'The Shadow of the Goat'.

London. 22nd December. Chief Inspector Brett Nightingale and Sergeant Beddoes have been called to a gloomy flat off Islington High Street. An elderly woman lies dead on the bed, and her trunk has been looted. The woman is Princess Olga Karukhin – an émigré of Civil War Russia – and her trunk is missing its glittering treasure…

Out in the dizzying neon and festive chaos of the capital a colourful cast of suspects abound: the downtrodden grandson, a plutocratic jeweller, Bolsheviks with unfinished business? Beddoes and Nightingale have their work cut out in this tightly-paced, quirky and highly enjoyable jewel of the mystery genre.

A man is forbidden to uncover the secret of the tower in a fairy-tale castle by the Rhine. A headless corpse is found in a secret garden in Paris – belonging to the city's chief of police. And a drowned man is fished from the sea off the Italian Riviera, leaving the carabinieri to wonder why his socialite friends at the Villa Almirante are so unconcerned by his death.

These are three of the scenarios in this new collection of vintage crime stories. Detective stories from the golden age and beyond have used European settings – cosmopolitan cities, rural idylls and crumbling chateaux – to explore timeless themes of revenge, deception, murder and haunting.

Including lesser-known stories by Agatha Christie, Arthur Conan Doyle, G.K. Chesterton, J. Jefferson Farjeon and other classic writers, this collection reveals many hidden gems of British crime.

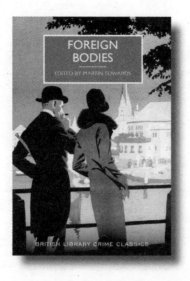

Today, translated crime fiction is in vogue – but this was not always the case. A century before Scandi noir, writers across Europe and beyond were publishing detective stories of high quality. Often these did not appear in English and they have been known only by a small number of experts. This is the first ever collection of classic crime in translation from the golden age of the genre in the 20th century. Many of these stories are exceptionally rare, and several have been translated for the first time to appear in this volume.

Featuring mysteries from Anton Chekhov, Maurice Leblanc, Koga Saburo, Sharadindu Bandyopadhyay and Maria Elvira Bermudez among many others.

BRITISH LIBRARY CRIME CLASSICS

ALSO AVAILABLE

Many of our titles are also available in eBook, large print and audio editions